Zem-Zem

Zem-Zem

a mystery

Jeanie duGal

Electric eBook Publishing

Zem-Zem: a mystery by Jeanie duGal
Copyright © 2003 Jeanie duGal

All rights reserved. No part of this book may be used or reproduced in any manner without prior written permission except in the case of brief quotations embodied in reviews.

Publisher's note: This book is a work of fiction. Names, characters, places and incidents are the product of the author's imagination or are used fictiously, and any resemblance to actual persons living or dead, events or locales is entirely coincidental.

Manufactured in Canada.

National Library of Canada Cataloguing in Publication Data

DuGal, Jeanie, 1949-
 Zem-Zem / Jeanie duGal.

ISBN 1-55352-083-1

 I. Title.
PS8557.U3213Z45 2003   C813'.6   C2003-911041-9

Electric eBook Publishing
PO Box 211
Powell River, B.C., Canada V8A 4Z6
http://www.electricebookpublishing.com

To My Mother

PROLOGUE

Lettie had been on worse jobs, like the one over on sixteenth, with blood trails all through the carpets and *messes* in every room. Took the cleaning team a whole day to set it right. But this one was a kitchen job with its own set of problems: table and chairs, cupboard doors, mouldings, an old place with a lot of built-in crannies.

And small, too, a single person house, probably a converted garage, the way it sat two steps and a holler from the split-level. They'd done the usual housecleaning in the rest of the place: living room, bedroom, washroom, shower, no tub. The victim kept a clean home, so the biggest problem was the fingerprint powder the police left everywhere.

As the last to leave, Lettie did a visual inspection of the rooms to be sure nothing had been left behind. One thing she could say about the job, after it was all done, nobody'd know there'd been a murder. The relatives could pack up without any telltale signs to remind them. She supposed even murdered drug dealers had relatives who cared.

And this murdered dealer had been a reader too, with a wall of books in the living room and more in the bedroom. Fancy TV and expensive stereo set up. Loads of tapes and CD's, had to be a drug dealer to afford all that. Hardly any room left in the tiny place for furniture.

They'd kept the TV tuned to the all-news channel as they worked and there was a press conference on now, some rich guy offering a reward for the killer of one of his employees—$250,000. Not bad. But she hadn't been a drug pusher. No one offered rewards for their killers.

Lettie turned off the TV and checked the bedroom. Out of curiosity she had a look through his closet and drawers, saw ordinary decent clothes, nothing flashy. She saw one green sweatshirt the exact colour of her teenage son's eyes. She stuffed it into the top of her overalls.

The heavy equipment had already been stowed away in the *Specialty Cleaning Service* van: the industrial wet-dry vac, the spotlights for catching the last drip or splatter. She stashed the sweatshirt in her tote bag, and then deposited the house keys in the mail slot of the split-level. She drove the van to the office, checked in with the boss and changed into her own clothes. Lettie stopped at Overwaitea on her way home. Chicken was on sale this week.

Nick was watching TV in the living room, throwing popcorn in the air, trying to catch it with his mouth. She told him she'd charge him a quarter for every kernel she had to pick up. She gave him the green sweatshirt. He asked if it was another one of her thrift shop buys. He hated that. He was also embarrassed by what she did for a living. But that was just too bad.

He said *Ah Mom*, but pulled it over his head. There was something stuck in the sleeve so he knew it was second hand. A photograph. She grabbed it. The sweatshirt fit perfectly and he went to look in the bathroom mirror.

It was an old picture, kids and some hippies. Might be something the police should know about? Might be a clue? It'd happened before on this kind of job. Something they'd missed. Other times when she'd found things she left them where they were and phoned the police. That was the *right* thing. She couldn't very well explain to Nick how she got the sweatshirt and why she had to put it back.

She could put it in a different shirtsleeve. But she didn't have the house keys anymore. It was only an old picture. Might not mean anything. He was killed over drugs. She started getting supper together, swearing she'd never take another souvenir again.

ONE

Charlie's favourite meal of the day was breakfast because cereal was her favourite food in the whole world. She loved the crunchy ones. She loved the soggy ones. She loved it with milk or even plain, right out of the box. Her brother Billy loved peanut butter sandwiches and her big sister Amy loved grilled cheese, but Charlie would be happy to eat breakfast all day long. She even had her special bowl. It was white with little ducks on the outside. And her special spoon too. It had a rose on the handle.

Except that now she couldn't eat anything at all.

Auntie Diane who came to look after them was trying to get Charlie to eat. And even though she thought breakfast belonged in the morning, she was putting Charlie's bowl in front of her and almost forcing her to take a spoonful. Amy lifted the corner of her sandwich, then pushed the plate away. Billy took a couple of bites of his peanut butter and jelly, a big gulp of milk, then pushed his away too.

Daddy was just sitting in the living room. Not doing anything. Just sitting there watching the turned off TV.

No one was eating. It was very quiet because no one was talking. Auntie Diane poured soup into a big mug and brought it out to Daddy. She said, "Jim, you have to eat something."

He took the mug, blew on it, and tasted it. He gulped it down and handed it back. Then he just sat there again.

Charlie came over and crawled in his lap. He put his hand on her cheek and looked at her for a minute. Then hugged her real hard and started to cry. She cried too. After a while they both stopped and she just sat on his lap. Then it was time for a bath and bed.

Auntie Diane was nice. Sometimes she was bossy, but nice-bossy. She'd been sitting in the kitchen when they came home from school, the day after Mommy didn't come home from work. Her eyes were all red and her face was all blotchy.

She said she had something to tell them. They all knew it was something bad.

She took Charlie on her lap and put her arms around Billy and Amy. She said the police had found Mommy. She took a deep breath and said that she was dead. A bad man had killed her. Billy said, "Mommy isn't coming home." And they all started to cry.

When Daddy came back from the police station he said they didn't find the man yet but they were looking for him. He was very tired. He took a liquor bottle from the cupboard and brought it into the living room. Auntie Diane gave him a glass.

They weren't allowed to turn on the TV or the radio because it would be on the news and scare them. After bedtime Charlie and Billy tiptoed to Emily's room and got under the covers with her. They whispered about it, trying to understand. Billy went back to his own bed but Charlie fell asleep holding onto her sister.

They were off school for a week and when they got back almost everyone was very nice. Some of the kids said things that hurt Charlie's feelings, but they were just stupid children. After school she went out to wait for Amy to pick her up. Charlie started to go to the front of the school when she walked past some of the grade five boys. They started to say things. Like, Did she see her mother's body and was it all bloody? She didn't want to cry, but she couldn't help it. Ryan walked over. He was the biggest grade seven, and the meanest boy in the school. He told the fives to shut up. He said her mother was killed by a serial killer and she was just a little kid so they'd better leave her alone or he'd beat them all up. He shook his fist and they all ran away. Then he came over to her and said if anyone bugged her again to tell him and he'd take care of them.

She saw Amy; they met Billy and all walked home together.

Auntie Diane was trying to get everyone to eat again. She had the table set and put down the sandwiches and filled Charlie's bowl with Cheerios and had the milk carton in her hand. Charlie was starving. She sat down and looked at the bowl of cereal and remembered what Ryan said. That her mother was murdered by a *cereal* killer. She put her hands over her head and shrieked. She ran shrieking up the stairs to Emily's room and fell down on the bed. She didn't stop shrieking. Auntie Diane ran after her. So did Amy. Even Daddy came up. Billy stood in the doorway. They rubbed her back and tried to pull her arms down. Auntie Diane shook her hard, yelling at her to stop. But Daddy put his hand on her shoulder and said, "Let her scream it out."

He got down on the bed and held her very tight until the shrieking stopped and she was hiccupping and sniffling.

Daddy was squashing her. She sat up. He asked her what made her get so upset. She told him what Ryan said, and seeing the Cheerios in the bowl. He said there was something she didn't learn in school yet. It was called a *homonym*. That was when two words sound the same but meant different things. Amy gave him a piece of paper and a pen. He wrote *cereal* and *serial*. He explained that the C word was what she ate in a bowl. The S word meant one thing after another. A serial killer is someone who murders one person after another. From the doorway Billy said, "He killed other people before."

Auntie Diane went down to the kitchen and took the Cheerios and the bowl away. Billy followed her down, not saying anything. When Daddy came down he was holding Charlie's hand. Amy was still in her room. He said he was going to dig in the garden, did Charlie want to help? He got their gum boots out of the closet. She looked at the table and said she didn't think she could eat *it* again. Daddy said she didn't have to, there were lots of other things to eat.

After they went outside Auntie Diane asked Billy to get a garbage bag. She put all the cereal boxes in it and tied it up. Billy took it out. He stuffed it down to the bottom of the can and was very very careful not to make any noise with the lid.

TWO

Rainie Castle has not left her apartment in nine months, not since the day of her husband's funeral. It was okay for the first few days with people coming and going, paying their respects, bringing food and sympathy. Saying things like: *He had so much to look forward to!* Reporters came for interviews, the TV news people too, but she sniffled, wiped her eyes and refused to see them. The police came with questions, each time shaking their heads when she asked if they found a suspect yet.

Leo's criminology instructor from his night school course turned up; his questions just as bad as the police, grilling her until she had nothing more to say, a hollow jar rattling with grief. He did a ten minute lecture on drive-by shootings and random violence in the urban environment. The detective agreed with him, filing it **UNSOLVED**.

She didn't remember the funeral very well; a hazy film shrouded the whole event. She remembered afterwards, sitting immobile on the couch, a box of tissues emptying beside her, wall to wall people drinking and talking.

What she was most clear about was waking up the next day to silence, laying dumbly for hours before rousing herself and shuffling to the coffee maker. No coffee. The visitors had consumed more than they brought. Out of habit she tidied the three room apartment before going out.

She felt light headed as her fingers traced the wallpaper pattern down the corridor to the elevator. The rumble of the motor echoed the pounding of her heart. The acceleration of the car raised the hair on her neck. Her palms broke out in sweat as she began the long walk through the marble lobby. She saw the entrance door. Her feet moved toward it. Heart beating faster, drumming in her ears, vision narrowing to a fuzzy edged crystal centre focus on the plate glass door, remembering Leo walking ahead of her and the gunfire blowing him back against the shattering glass.

She couldn't move any further. *They fixed the glass.* She shook so hard she almost fell as she turned and fled up the fire stairs, taking them two at a time to the third floor steel door, chanting, *they fixed the glass*, pulling on the door in panicked frustration, digging the keys from her purse, burning back down the corridor into the door slamming safety of her own home.

She dropped her coat and purse, and dived fully clothed into bed, shivering under the covers, squeezing her eyes shut, thinking how stupid to be afraid of a door, opening her eyes to the sight of his text books on the dresser, just the way he left them. She didn't have to be afraid of the door. They fixed it. But even thinking of it scared her and she pulled the covers over her head.

Those days were the worst, foraging what was left in the kitchen, running out of toilet paper, feeling cold and dizzy, everything looking different than it had before, shimmering with unreality. It was a neighbour who finally broke the spell, old Mrs. Rogers from next door, looking in on her. Rainie asked if she'd get a few things at the store, maybe check her mail.

Mrs. Rogers was glad to help; she was a widow too. She said, *it was hard* and *poor Rainie being so young.* Later on Rainie was able to hire Kari, one of the teenagers from the fifth floor, happy to earn some cash without babysitting a bunch of brats.

Each time Rainie thought about going out her heart pounded; she felt green, sweaty and weak. She stopped thinking about it.

She was surprised how easy it was never to leave the house. She worked, same as before, as a freelance typist and bookkeeper. Her clients dropped off the work and picked it up.

She ordered groceries on the Internet, sometimes pizza or wine by telephone. She surfed the web, sent for catalogues, used her credit card to call in orders for things she saw on TV. She joined clubs for books and music. When her clients paid by cheque it was easy to seal it in an envelope and have it mailed to the bank. Kari also picked up parcels from the post office, carried mail up from the lobby and took out the trash. When clients paid in cash she used that to pay Kari and the delivery people.

She stopped reading the newspaper. She stopped watching the news and most movies or dramas, because of the violence. She kept her narrow, neat trimness with daily TV aerobics and watched the talk shows when they did make-overs, experimenting with different make up techniques. She kept the ends of her shoulder length blonde hair trimmed and once in a while took the curling iron to it.

Sometimes friends dropped in, fewer and fewer as time went by. She didn't answer letters. She changed her phone to an unlisted number. Because she was ashamed of herself, she didn't tell anyone and sometimes played not-at-home, turning on the answering machine, turning off the lights, listening to the stormy winter wind hurling against the window panes.

Often she touched Leo's things, going through his papers and bureau drawers, burying her face in the smell of his sweaters still hanging on his side of the closet.

And sometimes, like now, late afternoon, work finished, arms folded along the open window, she leaned out from the old brick building, looking down at the back lane, smelling the new spring growth of trees budding green and fresh, hearing ball bouncing, bat swinging children shouting each other's names.

A blonde boy on a skateboard skimmed along the lane as she heard her apartment intercom buzz. She wasn't expecting anyone. She closed the window and sat with her head in her hands until the buzzing stopped.

THREE

After three years in cold storage, serving his debt to society, Mike Minchuck found himself at the airport in Calgary, Alberta, being hugged by a weeping granny, shaking hands with a grinning grandfather, neither of whom he remembered.

Granny thought they had to wait for his luggage but all he had were the clothes on his back and a paper grocery bag filled with letters and what few personal things he'd picked up inside. The suit he'd worn to court no longer fit well: too tight in the jacket, too loose in the waist.

Grandfather, a retired oil executive, was thin-haired and greying with a ruddy complexion and a couple of extra chins. He chauffeured the Mercedes. Granny cozied up beside Mike. A smartly dressed, compact woman, she smelled of hair spray, make up and sherry. She opened her calfskin purse and repaired her lipstick.

April in Calgary, at the edge of the prairies, winter trying for a dramatic wind-up; the Rocky Mountains barely visible on the horizon, under a gloomy sky. He remembered springtime in Vancouver, the city ringed by mountains close enough to touch, west coast sunshine sparkling on the water, daffodils in bloom.

Granny talked about the private investigator Grandfather hired to find him. How much it cost. How delighted she'd been when he surprised her with the news of Mike's visit. She didn't describe her reaction to finding him in the pen.

Grandfather, glancing across Granny's iron waves, said Mike resembled his father. Same clef chin, same dark curly hair. Granny *harrumphed.* She supposed Mike would want to meet the Minchucks. But he should know. *Bohunks*. They'll never get off the farm. Not like the Kubeks who were all professionals or business people. Or her own illustrious family, the Argatofs. She bad-mouthed the Minchucks as Grandfather exited the highway. Peter had seduced her darling daughter when she was only sixteen. Had to be forced to marry her. Harrumph, harrumph. Grandfather said nothing.

Mike knew his mom's side of the story. His own memories went as far back as the dim recollection of the train trip when he was three and she took him to British Columbia, to the other side of the mountains, far away from family hassles.

They arrived at a solid red brick two-story, patchy snow on the landscaped front yard. Mike held the car door open for Granny, the paper bag crackling under his arm. He started after her. Grandfather tapped his shoulder, "Just a minute, son," pulling him back of the car. "The family's inside waiting for you. Far as they know, you've been working in construction in Vancouver. Don't tell them any different. Understand?"

"If that's the way you want it."

"And keep your hands to yourself. I know you've been away from women for a long time. Leave the girls alone. Boys, too, for that matter. Understand?"

"Yes."

"And nothing goes missing. Not from purses or pockets or Granny's jewellery. Do I make myself clear?"

"Like crystal."

Grandfather nodded curtly and pushed Mike towards the front door. It opened on to an entire herd of strangers: Aunts, uncles, cousins, kids shouting "Welcome home, Mike!" The same words hung on a computer generated banner in the foyer. Someone had a video camera. Another a Nikon. All of the men and most of the women stood at least a head taller than Mike. All had excellent teeth. Female voices said how handsome he was, stage-whispered how he looked like his father. Mike was introduced all around and promptly forgot their names.

Granny, house proud, paraded him through the rooms. Two native women worked in the kitchen, Mary and her daughter Josie. Then it was up the stairs and into the guest room. She pulled the paper bag from under his arm and dropped it on the closet floor, closing the door as if closing off that part of his life. "Grandfather will loan you some clothes," she said, "until the airline can find your luggage." He nodded, understanding her remarks were for the benefit of the relatives poking their heads in the door.

He escaped to the washroom for some peace and quiet. But soon Grandfather bellowed up the stairs and Mike was escorted down to the basement rec room with the fully stocked wet bar.

"What'll it be?" Grandfather grinned. Mike accepted a cold beer. There was a pool table, dart board, sports trophies, moose antlers, gun rack with shotguns and hunting rifles. Through a door he saw a spick and span workshop, outline of each tool on the peg board.

The dining room table was formally set for eighteen, with Grandfather at one end, Mike at Granny's right at the other. The children had their own table set up at the side of the room. A woman opposite him, he guessed a cousin, took charge of the kids, admonishing, serving, keeping them in line. Grandfather carved the turkey.

The herd of strangers feasted, laughed, joked and peppered Mike with questions. He felt overwhelmed, but they were well meaning and he was prepared to be open. Until after dessert, after Mary and Josie cleared the table and people milled, refilled their glasses and a man about his own age, probably an old sandbox pal, elbowed him, leering, saying he'd take him downtown one night for some action, saying he'd find him a juicy squaw. Mike cringed, glancing around for the housekeepers. Someone said *it's snowing*. He looked out the double glazed window. Sure was: great big white flakes falling straight down.

The herd put on their coats, started up their cars and left. Granny and Grandfather settled down to some serious drinking in front of the TV. Mike slipped off to the rec room and put in a collect call to Kevin in Vancouver. No answer.

Mike stayed for a week, about five days too long. The day after he arrived he registered with the parole office, was given an appointment and had to hang around for that. He got along with his grandparents all right, but their way of life didn't interest him. He'd had enough boredom inside.

They listened to classical music, watched all the nature and news programs on TV, railed against abortion, welfare bums and immigrants, and continually told him how lucky he was to be home again and have a second chance at a decent life. They were under the mistaken belief that his parole was their doing, that he'd been released into their custody.

And they drank too. Granny after lunch, Grandfather with lunch, and both until bedtime.

Mary came every day to clean the house and cook supper. He went into the kitchen one afternoon to talk to her. Grandfather materialized, glaring from the doorway, and sent him off to buy milk. Mike wasn't about to jump her, and he'd been imprisoned for theft, not rape, but Grandfather wasn't taking any chances. He much preferred keeping one eye on Mike while the other scanned the job openings in the newspaper. He said a good carpenter could always find work. But Mike's truck and tools were back in Vancouver, and he didn't want to work in Alberta anyway.

Mike tried calling his friend Kevin each night but, he wasn't ever home. Probably with his girlfriend. Mike was happy for him, glad he finally found someone, but disappointed he wasn't there to say hello. He'd written, just before his release, about his unforeseen trip to Calgary. Maybe Kevin didn't expect to hear from him yet.

One chilly afternoon Granny took Mike up to her sewing room, a tiny refuge of porcelain, flower prints and dainty white furniture. She snagged a bottle of sherry and two glasses from beneath the flounced skirt of a corner table. Giggling, she poured and they toasted the day. A little early for Mike, but he went along with it.

Then it was ritual and ceremony, the sharing of the photographs. She brought out boxes and albums full. She spoke as if he knew all the faces, as if he cared.

He cared about his mother's pictures. Her sweet sixteen party, a few months later her wedding reception. His father, he saw the resemblance, strong and hardworking, but still just a kid. Mike and his dad on the farm tractor, wheat stretching in all directions. His other grandparents. His father's older brother.

Other pictures sent to Granny from British Columbia, were things he remembered. Mom in long skirt, hair held back with a beaded headband, arms filled with wildflowers.

Granny wiped her eyes, turned the pages and sipped her sherry. She said nothing until she came to the last picture. Mike, age twelve, in a tie-dyed shirt. He remembered that tee shirt. "She stopped writing to me. Do you think that's right? To stop writing to your own mother?"

Mike lifted his hands, noncommittal.

"Because she called me collect. She needed money. She said they'd taken you away. And she had to go to a hearing to get you back. She needed money to show them. And that her family was behind her because your father wouldn't send one red cent for you. I was going to send it to her. But your grandfather wouldn't allow it. He cut back my allowance and made me account for every penny he gave me. I had to save all my receipts." She sipped and sniffled and said, "It was all right, wasn't it? She got you back?"

"No. They said she was an unfit mother."

"But she loved you!"

"Evidently it wasn't enough. They didn't like hippies."

"At least someone showed good sense. The nights I stayed awake worrying. I lost so much sleep the doctor had to put me on pills to calm me down. But in the end my prayers were answered. She came home." She pointed across the narrow room to a blue and white ginger jar beneath the window. "There is your mother."

He didn't understand at first. "An urn?"

"Your mother's ashes."

He nodded, not knowing quite what to say. *Hi mum* didn't seem to cut it. He wondered if the jar was chosen to coordinate with the room or vice versa.

Granny refilled their glasses. She packed away the pictures. She talked about his foster parents, as if there was only one set, as if she knew them. How good it was he was able to learn *family values*. She didn't ask any questions and he didn't volunteer any truth. Much better not to allow nasty reality to intrude.

On a different day, after he'd been to the parole office, Grandfather surprised him with a stop at the Legion for sandwiches and beer, standing the chaps to a few rounds and swapping war stories. Grandfather hadn't actually seen combat but he had experienced London during the blitz. They drank to that. Mike thanked them for winning. They drank to that too.

Grandfather took him into a private room, a reading room with chairs and book shelves. The walls hung with black and white photographs of Allied leaders, generals and Canadian regiments. "What you young guys need is a good war," Grandfather said, "Smarten you up." He flopped down in a leather wing chair. "You'd see what's important. God, country, family. You ever been married Mike?"

"Not yet. Lived with a couple of women."

"Free and easy. No responsibilities. But you pay for it. No one's waiting for you, are they?"

"I had a girlfriend before I went in. She wrote for a while. Visited once. It petered out."

"Granny waited for me when I was overseas. Five years. I came back, finished my degree, got a good job and we were married. She was still a virgin on our wedding night."

"Were you?"

"Don't be silly."

Mike smiled and flipped through a copy of *Legion* magazine on the end table. "I'm going to Vancouver in a couple of days. I told the parole officer. I just have to wait for the papers. Need permission and all that."

"Stay here Mike. Stay with your own people."

"Maybe I'll visit at Christmas."

"You'll break your Granny's heart."

"They have this marvellous invention. It's called a telephone. I'll keep in touch."

"Why go back? There's nothing there for you."

"I have a job waiting. An old friend of mine manages an audio-video store. High-end market, salary plus commission."

"What about your carpentry?"

"I can go back to that if I want to."

"Sounds like you don't know what you want."

"Does it? One thing I don't want is hassles."

"Am I pressuring you? It's for your own good."

"I turned thirty a few months ago. You didn't want any part of me when I was a kid, no reason to start now. Thanks, but no thanks."

"That was because of your mother."

"My mother, yes. Surprised me that she came back here."

"She had cancer. No one to look after her."

"We lost track of each other. She moved around a lot. I tried to find her when I was going to trial. Heard she moved to Toronto. But the address I found, the letter came back unopened."

"Another one of her shack ups. Wouldn't stand by her when she was sick."

"I feel bad about that. She was really a wonderful woman. It's too bad you didn't hire a detective to find me then. I could've gotten compassionate leave. Seen her again before she died."

By the expression on Grandfather's face, by the way he wouldn't look at him, Mike guessed he did know where he was. He wondered if it was difficult for Grandfather to do what he thought was right, when he was basically a lying asshole and didn't know right from wrong. "I know why my mother couldn't wait to get out of your house. And why she left my father."

"She left your father because she was a tramp. One man couldn't satisfy her."

Mike took a deep breath and let it all spill out. "You beat her up regularly. Abuse is in the news every day now. Not like when she was young, when it was all kept in the family. In those days the only way she knew to get out was marriage. And at sixteen, the only way to get married was to get pregnant. She left her husband because they had an argument and he hit her. They lived with his parents on the farm and they backed him up. She was smart enough to see she'd gone from the frying pan into the fire. She packed me up and left. And no one ever smacked her around again." He waited but Grandfather didn't have anything to say.

"You rejected her when she desperately needed help. Then years later she came back. You said because she was sick. Maybe she missed her mother. It must've cost her a lot to come back. I'm sure you made certain she paid for every misdeed, real or imagined."

"Are you finished?"

"Just about. If you'd sent her money that time, supported her when we went to that Ministry hearing, our lives would have been completely different."

Grandfather folded his arms in silence. If he wasn't going to respond there was no point in continuing the monologue. Mike stood up, "Shall we go now?"

He couldn't believe it when Grandfather tried to bribe him into staying with the promise of a car, saying he wouldn't have to find work yet, he could do things around the house and be a companion to Granny. He even said, out of earshot of his wife, that he would understand if Mike stayed out late and was a *man* downtown.

Mike had already reserved a seat on the train. Granny didn't seem all that broken hearted. She said he'd enjoy the scenery. He didn't mention how much he was looking forward to a stop-over in Banff. All he had to do was register with the cop shop and stay out of trouble. He didn't want trouble, he wanted to party with a woman. He didn't have to check in with the parole office in Vancouver until the end of the week, lots of time to catch up on what he'd been missing.

He'd bought some clothes and a duffle bag. Granny came into the guest room as he was packing and handed him an antique blue glass mason jar.

"It's some of your mother," she said, "So you can have her with you always."

Very thoughtful of Granny. He kissed the jar, rolled it in a sweatshirt and tucked it into his bag. He kissed Granny too, and gave her a big hug.

Grandfather refused to drive him to the station. That wasn't enough of a reason to keep him in Calgary. Mike called a cab. He said good bye to Mary in the kitchen, slipping her an envelop for the extra work. The cab arrived and they went out with him. The snow had melted into the soggy lawn. Grandfather said spring was just around the corner. Mike hugged Granny again and promised to keep in touch. He shook hands with the old man.

Mike looked around the corner as the cab drove away. Another one of Grandfather's lies: He didn't see springtime at all.

FOUR

Charlie missed Mommy. *A lot.* She put her picture under her pillow every night when she went to sleep. It was the picture where Mommy was in the garden. She had on her pretty pink sweater. In back of her was the blue sky and all the flowers. Mommy smiled and smiled. Every night Charlie kissed the picture and said good night to Mommy. Some nights she dreamed about her. There was a bad dream where they carried Mommy's body into the gym at school. She was on a stretcher thing. Only her body. They couldn't fit the other parts on the stretcher. And then they lost them. In the dream Charlie kept looking for the other parts but she couldn't find them.

Before Auntie Diane went home she packed up Mommy's things. Everyone was very sad when she did that. Charlie hid Mommy's pretty pink sweater. The same pretty one from the picture. Auntie Diane did all of the laundry of Mommy's things but she didn't know about that sweater. There were a lot of Mommy's things all over the house. Some of them they didn't put away. Mommy's toothbrush was still in the bathroom.

Sometimes the police came to talk to Daddy. Or he came home from work and said they talked to him there. One time after supper Daddy didn't have any more to drink and went out to get some more. He didn't come back. They all got very scared that the bad man killed Daddy too. Charlie cried a lot and then went to sleep. In the middle of the night she got up to go pee and Daddy was asleep in his bed. He had all his clothes on and he was snoring loud. She felt so good to see him there. She put the covers over him.

The next morning she felt sick but there wasn't anyone to stay home with her. Daddy was sick too. But he had to go to work, and she had to go to school.

Banff was great but Vancouver was home. Mike landed in town with both feet running, getting his pick-up from storage, paying for insurance, checking in with the parole office, and calling his accountant. After he'd taken care of business he drove to Kevin's address.

He found the house easily enough—a little shack on the lane, wedged behind the big white split-level. He was happy to see a car angled up against the front. He skirted the blue Chevette, stomped up the three wooden steps and pounded on the door with the side of his fist, shouting, *Yeo! Kevin.*

A curtain on the window half of the door parted a crack. He saw straight honey amber hair. "Kevin at home, please?"

She moved and he saw the girl's face. High cheek bones, burnished bronze skin. Kevin told him blonde haired Indian from the north Island. Finnish on her father's side. She looked sixteen. She shook her head, "Who are you?"

"Mike Minchuck."

She opened the door. "I forgot he was expecting you. Come in."

There were several boxes on the floor, each half filled with kitchen paraphernalia and books. The window was open over the sink; an earth tone curtain moved gently with the breeze. She twisted a small engagement ring on her finger and looked down at her feet. "I'm sorry I have to be the one to tell you. He's gone."

He balanced on the threshold. "What do you mean *gone*?"

"Shot. Killed."

"No," he shook his head, "That's not funny." He pushed past her, shouting out, "Kevin. Bro. Quit messing around. Where are you man?"

"I'm sorry," she whispered behind him.

He turned to look at her and put it all together: the boxes on the floor, the tears in her eyes.

"When?"

"What day is it?"

"Friday."

"It'll be two weeks on Monday. I can't believe it's that long."

"That's the day I was released."

"It happened here, in the kitchen. The landlady had a janitor service come in to do the clean up. They haven't arrested anyone yet."

Mike leaned against the kitchen table to steady himself. "You're Wendy?"

"Yes."

"He wrote me about you. But he didn't say you were so young."

"I'm twenty-six. But without make-up or nice clothes." She plucked at her grey sweatshirt. "He called me that night to wish me sweet dreams. It must've been after that... Jehovah's Witnesses found him the next morning. They heard the radio playing... The curtain was open on the door and they looked in... I came home from work and saw it on the six o'clock news. Wheeling a stretcher out of this house... They said they were withholding the name pending notification of next of kin. I called them and said that if it was Kevin Woods he had no kin. Only me. I had to go down and ID him."

She sat in one of the ladder back kitchen chairs. "The cops found roaches in the ashtray. Traces of cocaine. And a set of scales. They think he was dealing, and it was a rip off."

He sat in a chair opposite. "What do you think?"

"I never saw scales. Never smelled pot. I'm not a user but I've seen enough substance abuse to be sensitive to it. I would've noticed if he was on something."

"And they said he didn't have to be a user to sell. And you don't live here. He could've kept the scales hidden."

"Exactly what they said." She slumped in the chair and sighed, "You missed the memorial service. He was cremated. I have the urn at my place."

"More ashes."

"What's that?"

"Sorry. My mother was cremated also."

"Yes, you just recently found out, didn't you? Kevin showed me that last letter you wrote from jail. It's too bad. How'd it go with your grandparents in Calgary?"

"Okay."

"Just okay?"

"A little on the weird side."

"Did you look up your father too?"

"No. Maybe another time."

"Kevin said you were like brothers."

"Wanted me to be best man at your wedding."

"Did he write to you often?"

"Only when there was something to say. The last letter I got from him was when he invited me to stay here."

"He told me he sent the parole board a letter offering you a job at the store."

"Yes and he said he hoped I wouldn't mind a drug and alcohol free house."

She gulped, "He wrote that?"

"Didn't want to screw things up with you."

"Do you have that letter?"

"Saved all the ones from prison."

"Give it to the cops. It'll prove he wasn't dealing."

"All it proves is that last month he didn't intend to. He had drug convictions ten years ago, but it's on computer and the cops won't look past that. His letter won't mean diddly unless they have another motive."

"Do you think he could've been dealing?"

"No. And he wasn't about to let anyone come in here with scales and weights or start smoking and tooting up."

"So you think it was a set up?"

"Had to be."

"That's what I told the cops but they didn't believe me. I don't know if they're working very hard at it. There was another murder the same day. Mother of three. Real estate agent. Much higher priority. There's a two hundred and fifty thousand dollar reward. Posters up all over town. Crime Stoppers on TV. It might be a serial killer. There was a similar case six months ago. They probably have a task force of fifty working on that and one guy with a file folder working on Kevin. He hated violence. And to end like that." She shook her head. "Made a big point of telling me you did burglary, not armed robbery."

"I hate guns."

"So do I." She blinked away tears. "How was it? Prison, I mean. Sorry," she grimaced, "Stupid question."

"That's okay. I read a lot. Lifted weights. Played baseball and chess. Met some good people. Met some bad ones. Mostly I was bored."

He turned away from her, propping his elbows on the table, dropping his head into his hands. He needed time to reorient himself. He'd had so many plans for when he got out, so many involving Kevin. "I can't believe it."

"I know. I thought he was *the one*. Takes a while to put the pieces back together. This is the first day I've been able to get it together enough to start packing his things."

"You shouldn't be doing this alone."

"My aunt offered to help. I don't know... Maybe I'm still in shock."

"Kinda hoping Kevin'll come back?"

"Yeah, I guess so. The rent's paid up until the end of the month. You can stay if you want. Haven't even gotten around to disconnecting the telephone."

"Sure. I'll wait for him."

"Might be a while."

"And I'll look after his things for you. You'll have time to decide what you want to keep."

"Thanks. I almost forgot. One of the detectives knew Kevin. Said the two of you always ran together. They'd taken almost everything of his on paper and he read your letter. Wanted to know if I'd heard from you. Ron Essery?"

"Oh yeah, Essery, sure. He was on foot patrol, Kevin and I were runaways, our first time around. Shortly after we were taken from the commune."

"Kevin told me about that. Zem-Zem. He was called Cedar and you were Moonbeam."

"Yeah, my nom de hippie. It was great until the end. They swooped in, a flying wedge of social workers and cops. We were clean, clothed, well fed. The ones of school age studied by correspondence. We were a happy, healthy pack of kids in an extended family. But hippies, by God, can't have that. They took all the ones without blood parents present. Kevin, me, and our little sister, Rainbow. Split us up."

He looked away, down into the nearest carton, picked up a tape: *Warming the Stone Child. Myths of Abandonment & the Unmothered Child.* "My mother tried to get me back, but his never even attempted. Did he talk about her at all?"

"Sometimes. But mostly he said it was communal living and he had many mothers. I did wonder about that tape though. He didn't show it to me, never saw it before today."

"Yeah, well, we each have to deal with our own personal history, but we don't have to make it the main topic of conversation. Gets pretty boring, know what I mean?"

"Sounds like something he would've said. But I've been thinking about it and I can't be sure he wasn't hiding something. He did have a hard time opening up. I thought it was, you know, because of all the foster homes. Kind of a fear of getting too close and having to move again. We talked about it. He wouldn't go to counselling but he did go down to Banyan Books and get all that self-help, healing the inner child stuff." She pointed to one of the boxes on the floor. "He joked that they still hadn't written the book he needed."

The corners of her mouth turned down, tears spilled from her eyes, "I don't know who killed him and I don't know why. Who could hate him that much?"

FIVE

After Wendy left, Mike turned the kitchen chair around and faced the door, listening for the sound of a key in the lock, watching for the first crack of light to appear, waiting for his mother and brother to walk through.

His mother was gone and Kevin was gone. They didn't say good bye.

The waiting was hard. His concentration broke. He wondered how many of his possessions were still around. When his court date had neared and he knew he'd be going away for a stretch, he'd packed his clothes and tools into the back of his canopied pick-up, and put it in storage. His girlfriend stayed in the apartment they'd shared, keeping his furniture, books, music collection, TV, stereo, a whole list of stuff. Until the day she called Kevin, said she was moving, and asked, probably out of guilt, if he wanted anything. She didn't tell Mike. He heard about it second hand.

From where he sat he could see two bookcases he'd built, the shorter one under the bedroom window, the tall one in the living room. There couldn't be room for much more in that small house. He motivated himself enough to get up and look. He recognized some of his books on the lower shelf in the bedroom. The top shelf was empty, packed into a box in the kitchen. More books in the living room, about half of his record collection on the bottom shelf, his tapes and CDs mixed in with Kevin's on a multi-tier rack in the corner. The sound system and TV in a wall unit, the couch and table were Kevin's, and filled the room.

He carried his clothes in from the truck. He wasn't sure what to do with the mason jar of his mother's ashes. He centred it on the kitchen table and put away Kevin's books and cooking pots. The house was so small there wasn't anywhere to stack the empty boxes. He broke them down and slid them underneath the bed.

He didn't know what else he could do. He sat in the kitchen for a while and watched the door. It didn't open; they didn't come in.

He thought he should make a ceremony for his dead mother and brother. He'd seen a package of incense in the living room. He lit a stick, stuck it in the earthenware burner and placed it beside his mother's ashes. He wasn't really sure how to go about making a ceremony. He chanted *OHM*. He cried a little. He tried to meditate.

He locked up and went for a walk. Still light, but the sun was starting to aim down towards the horizon. It was a neighbourhood of older homes with tidy gardens and mature horse chestnut trees lining the street. The cars were mostly Japanese imports with a few smaller Fords and Chevys. Working people living decent lives, raising their kids, making ends meet. He'd never steal from them. He did Big Doors, the ostentatious houses with pretentious cars.

After a few blocks he found Oak Street. He walked with his hands in his jeans pockets, looking in store windows, feeling guilty for enjoying the freedom to walk where he pleased, for being alive. He saw a Jewish bakery across the street and a few blocks up, a synagogue. He'd always wanted to go in one, see what the services were like. He continued walking until the stores petered out and it was all apartment blocks and houses. He crossed the street and started back. His stomach felt hunger and his mouth thirst, but his mind was too paralysed for food.

He approached a bus shelter, barely registering the advertising. REWARD caught his eye. The poster Wendy talked about, the woman killed the same day as Kevin. As he came closer the face looked familiar and reading the name Barbara Fleming, he did a double take and stopped in his tracks.

They'd known her. She was called Big Sister Dove on the commune because she was three or four years older.

He made it back to the house and got out Kevin's letters. Last summer he'd written that he'd seen her again. Then he met Wendy and hardly wrote of anything else.

Over the years Mike had kept in touch, off and on, with Barbara's mother, Marion, one of the founding mothers of Zem-Zem. She'd sent him a few letters and Christmas cards in jail. She'd written that she wanted to organize a reunion. Especially the children, to see how they all turned out. Mike didn't think it was such a hot idea, and not just because he was doing time. But she'd found Kevin's number in the phone book and told her daughter to give him a call. Now both were dead. Murdered on the same day.

Marion must be going nuts. He should call. He dug out her last note, the one decorated with dancing elves; she always drew a different design. She said she'd moved to a trailer near Courtenay. He tried the number, but it was out of service. She was like his mother, always moving.

He tried Directory Assistance. Nothing. He'd have to take the ferry to Vancouver Island, drive up to Courtenay, see if he could track her down. Too late to start now, it would take half a day just to get there. And the parole bullshit, too... He'd have to wait for his appointment on Monday. He felt crazy and jumpy and didn't know what to do so he went for a drive.

He drove east because if he went west he'd pass Big Doors and wanted to keep his distance. He took Broadway and turned up Kingsway, main commercial arteries that required him to concentrate on traffic, lights and pedestrians, only vaguely aware of the sky as it coloured with sunset.

When he saw the Pattullo Bridge up ahead he realized how far he'd driven, all the way to New Westminister, and turned down a side street, no place to go and all weekend to get there. Narrow streets, ancient commercial buildings, railroad tracks and warehouses, the elevated Skytrain line, new condo developments fronting the Fraser River.

He saw a hotel with a neon *licensed premises* sign. He parked the pick-up, checked to be sure the canopy was locked, and went into the bar. Almost blown away by industrial strength blues, party happy dancing crowd vibrating the floor and walls, braless women in skimpy tank tops. Booze, blues and the promise of illegal drugs. Good a place as any.

He spotted a woman leaning alone against the wall, with a bottle of beer in her hand and a tattoo on her shoulder. He wormed his way through the crowd.

Mike was sober enough by Monday morning to make it back to Kevin's house to change and get over to the parole office in time for his appointment. He was on time but the P.O. was busy. He had to sit around the waiting room with the other low lifes, nobody making eye contact, thumbing through outdated magazines and reading depressing AIDS posters on the walls. By the time he got in to see George Bell he had the story straight in his mind.

Yes, he'd settled in fine, he said. He'd be starting work at the end of the week. Late shift, until nine, and all weekends. They were open on Sundays too. So what he was thinking of doing was to go to Courtenay to see his foster mother. A couple of days. Then come back and get ready for his new job. He didn't say too much and didn't mention the murders. Honesty wouldn't help and he had a low opinion of social worker types. Bearded George Bell looked like he ran marathons, ate health foods and read literature for amusement. Not bad things in themselves, but Mike hated him anyway. He minded his manners, threw in a few polysyllabic words and watched his body language until he received the permission there was no reason not to give.

Mike enjoyed driving out to the ferry terminal at Horseshoe Bay. He didn't mind waiting in the line up. He didn't mind the water or the seagulls or the sunshine at all. The other passengers didn't bother him—the kids, the older couples in RVs. He'd hung in for three years and this was just fine.

He watched the ferry glide into the dock, heard the ramp clanking down. When it was his turn and he was waved aboard it was all the way he remembered, and he loved it. He stood in the cafeteria line for a bowl of his old favourite, clam chowder.

When he finished eating he went outside to the observation deck to sit in the sun and watch pretty tourist girls pointing at the tiny islands of rock and trees as the ferry rumbled from the mainland to Vancouver Island. When the announcement came on that they were nearing the terminal, he joined the crowd streaming down to the car decks. He heard a voice behind him say, "Look who the cat dragged in," and turned to see the grinning face of Gary Schmid, a guy he knew his first year inside. They'd played chess and shared books until Gary's parole. He'd been caught on a cultivation and trafficking charge. It wasn't the time to stop and talk, they were holding up the people stream.

They met again in the parking lot of a shopping centre at the top of the hill. There they could shake hands, hug and say how good each other looked. Gary was tall and thin, rock hard and rugged from working in the bush. His wife and kids got out of the car. Pretty Mandy, Mike remembered her picture. And Lance and Phil, eight year old twins. There was too much to say, standing in the parking lot, so Mike followed the Toyota out to their place.

It was a cramped frame house on a couple of acres with chickens, fruit trees and a German Shepard doing leaps to see them again after their overnight in Vancouver. Gary gave him the grand tour and showed him where he'd started framing in an addition before getting a call to work on a new tree planting contract. The lumber and plywood were stored under a tarp.

They got drunk that first night on homemade beer. Mandy put the kids to bed, then sat with the guys for a while before getting bored and going to sleep alone. They had a lot of catching up to do and a lot of things to be said that could only be understood by someone who'd done time. Mike told him about the murders and Gary had heard about Barbara because it was big news for a few nights at six o'clock. The conversation rambled and he offered to help with the addition, do some honest work for a couple of days. Mike slept on the couch.

He woke up the next morning after Gary had left to plant trees. Mike didn't feel hung over at all. Mandy said it was because they didn't put any weird shit in the beer and used pure spring water from their own well. Mike ate breakfast with the twins. Nice kids. After they left to catch the school bus and Mandy drove to her secretarial job, he went out to the truck and got his tools.

It felt good to have a hammer in his hands again, to feel the weight of the leather apron, to take off his shirt and feel the heat of the sun on his back.

SIX

Welfare Wednesday. Marion Peppard's day of liberation. She walked on Cliffe Avenue carrying a cloth shopping bag, switching its weight from shoulder to shoulder, her spongy new runners cushioning her sore feet from the hard sidewalk.

The late afternoon sun was surprisingly hot for a spring day. The ozone hole. They broke the sky. She ached from toes to teeth; a little sunburn wouldn't matter.

She stopped to use the rest room and sit on a bench at the bubbling fountain in the corner park beside the theatre. A long haired teen-age boy played a guitar. He wore jeans, tie-dyed tee shirt and a peace symbol on a leather thong around his neck. It brought her right back to the days when she used the name Happy. She *was* happy then. Earth Mother, sensuous lover, glistening auburn hair, lean, healthy body, joyous rebel holding the psychedelic keys to heaven.

The boy stopped playing. She struggled to her feet, hobbled over, handed him a twenty dollar bill and said, "Peace."

He grinned up in surprise. "Thanks!" He wore a button that read, *Tread lightly on the earth.*

She walked down the block to the library and returned two books, turning back to the sunshine with her bag conspicuously lighter. Another block took her past the shopping district and she ambled on with open senses, taking different streets, savouring everything—tulips, pansies, flowering crab-apples, camellias and rhododendrons, bright colours everywhere she looked. A hummingbird zipped up, hovering, investigating her red blouse and grey hair. It zipped away, to a feeder dangling in front of a kitchen window, becoming one of half a dozen hummers taking turns sipping the sugary syrup. A cat sat on a railing twenty feet away, twitching its tail. She saw another cat in a window a few houses up the street, sitting statue-like, a black cat with a large red bow at its neck.

She caught glimpses of the Puntledge River between houses and laboured uphill for a better view. Narrow, its banks edged with lush alders, the river rushed towards the estuary. She continued her circle tour. A tiny white poodle barked and ran back and forth in its fenced yard as she passed. She saw crows and starlings. A small plane droned overhead. Cars roared, trucks rumbled and lawnmowers buzzed. She ran her fingers along the rough bark of a fir tree and across the weathered smoothness of a telephone pole.

Back in the shopping district she passed the Sally Ann thrift stop. Busy today, this Welfare Wednesday, almost a monthly holiday. The bars would be jumping tonight. The drug dealers bustling with baggies and slips of folded paper. Later, the emergency room would treat the casualties. Patrol cars already cruised the streets.

She walked a few blocks down and went into the Bar None Café. She took her time at the buffet, uncovering every hot pot, savouring the fragrance of every delicious offering. She filled her tray with a small bowl of miso soup with smoked tofu, a salad of kale and Swiss chard with sundried tomato dressing, a generous helping of a mushroom-phyllo dish and for desert, cappuccino sprinkled with chocolate on the foaming, steamed milk. Beautiful. Delectable. Perfect.

She was tired and wanted to go home. She did and she didn't. She had to carry the shopping bag in her hand, the shoulders and neck wouldn't take any weight at all. She walked up the street and into the art gallery. She admired the watercolours of Vancouver Island scenes, was touched by the raku pots and thrilled by the quilted wall hangings, but couldn't stay long because her legs throbbed badly from so much walking. She signed the guest book and wrote *excellent work*, and asked for a taxi to be called.

She'd never taken a cab back from downtown before. After her old beater car had died there was just the bus and the long, long walk. Only on this special day could she afford such an outrageous indulgence.

Marion rented a decaying trailer back of nowhere. The trailer shared a wooded parcel of land with an old seedy cabin, both sat at the edge of a curved, gravel drive between drainage ditches. Behind the cabin the land dropped off to a gully and narrow creek.

She'd spent the last few days cleaning and tidying and had finished up in the morning while she waited for the mail and her welfare cheque. It didn't take long. There was only a claustrophobic kitchen-living room and one tiny bedroom. She took four steps to cross the worn linoleum over the rotting floor and put her shopping bag on the pitted counter.

There wasn't room for a kitchen table or chairs. When she ate she took her meals on the sprung sofa. She leaned against the sink and looked out the window, watching a spider sit patiently on its web. She heard the roar of a motorcycle and turned away as the biker in the neighbouring cabin rode over the gravel, returning from work. Her whole trailer shook until he cut the engine.

She swallowed two aspirins, pulled off the new runners and stretched out on the lumpy sofa, staring up at the water-stained ceiling, waiting for the aches to subside. She dozed.

When she awoke the Divine had begun to dress the sky in brilliance. She had planned to take a walk about now, but wasn't up to it. She could no longer trust her legs. She watched from the window.

When it was too dark to see clearly she unpacked the shopping bag. First the tall beeswax candle and the brass holder. She lit the candle and took out the nightdress. White, Victorian style with long sleeves and lovely handmade lace. She put it on a hanger and hung it behind the bathroom door. She turned the tap on the tub. Water pressure was low. It would take a long time to fill.

She had bought a package of fine rice paper, beige, bordered with sepia bamboo. She sat on the sofa and wrote by the fragrant light of the beeswax candle.

Last Will And Testament

I am old, sick, poor and alone. I have nothing to look forward to but more of the same. My only child, my daughter, has recently been murdered. My remaining family wants nothing to do with me.

For these reasons I choose to end my life now while I am still able to do so.

I regret the distress finding my remains will cause the person who does find me. As a small recompense I bequeath to that person all my worldly goods and chattels, including the cash enclosed in this envelope. It is not much, but what is left from my welfare cheque. I spent the rest enjoying a very pleasant day, my last day on earth.

She wrote *Peace*, signed, *Marion Lucille Dekker Peppard*, and dated it. She tucked it in the envelope. On the outside she wrote: *For*

Whomever Finds Me, and underlined it. She placed it on the kitchen counter.

She carried the beeswax candle into the bathroom. She undressed and lowered herself into the tub. It wasn't quite full. The water dribbling out was no longer hot. The propane tank must be empty. She didn't have to worry about such mundane matters any longer.

In her lovely lace trimmed nightdress, Marion padded barefoot in the bedroom, making the final preparations. The candle on the night table. The three vials of pills. The vodka, glass, and bottle of freshly squeezed organic orange juice. She put all the wrappings and receipts back in the shopping bag and hung it on the door knob. She took her box of memories and climbed into bed.

Through all the moves, all the years, good and bad, she'd kept a box of memories. It was a sturdy banker's box that she'd covered inside and out with green velvet. In it she kept pictures, little souvenirs and keepsakes, unmatched earrings, beads, peace buttons, the heart-shaped pin cushion made from her wedding gown. A lock of her daughter's baby hair.

She drank down a handful of pills with a good mouthful of juice. She waited a minute to be sure they stayed down. She mixed more juice with the vodka. She sipped it as she looked at the pictures. Zem-Zem. The best years of her life. The children would never have a reunion now. Her beautiful little dove, her daughter, dead. Rainbow's husband, dead. Cedar, dead. Moonbeam in jail. All she ever wanted was peace and love. How did it get so crazy?

She drank down more pills and refilled the glass with straight vodka. Tried not to think of her grandchildren. Or their father who hadn't even let her know. Drank down more pills and realized it was okay, she could cry now, she didn't have to hold it in any longer. It didn't matter now. Nothing mattered now.

Crying, clutching a baby picture of her daughter, tears running down her face as she finished the pills, she cried and closed her eyes and opened them and there was the full moon smiling in at her through the window.

SEVEN

Mike drove into Courtenay on Thursday morning. The first thing he did was rent a motel room; next he stopped at a travel info centre for a map and directions to Marion's last address. It wasn't in town, but five miles out, down some rural side road.

It took some doing to find the place; he saw her old car first, sitting right where it must have died, and not recently either, judging by the scattering of twigs and leaf mould. That was a surprise, but even worse was the shock at seeing where she had been living: a dinky one bedroom travel trailer too ripe for a junk yard. He knocked, but got no response. The next door cabin was in even worse shape; the shiny Harley Sportster in front was worth about ten times as much as the shack. He knocked there and a long haired, bearded guy in a tee shirt opened up. "Sorry to bother you," Mike said, "But I'm looking for the lady who lived next door. Marion? You happen to know where she moved to?"

"Hasn't moved anywhere, far as I know. Seen her yesterday afternoon through her window." He came outside, down the wooden steps.

"Her phone's not in service, that's why I thought she moved."

The guy walked around the trailer with him. "Maybe she didn't pay the bill. She's on welfare."

"Maybe." Mike knocked on the door again and called her name.

"You her son?"

"Foster son. Friend."

"Hope she's okay."

"Yeah." Mike stood on his toes and stretched to look in the window. "Jeez, pretty shabby. What she doing in a place like this?" He walked to the back of the trailer but the window there was too high up. Mike knocked on the loose siding, "Marion? You in there? Happy? You okay?" He looked around for something to stand on. The guy found him a five gallon bucket.

He climbed up, looked in and said *shit*, denting the wall, slamming his fist against the side.

"What is it?"

Mike jumped down. He leaned against the trailer and closed his eyes. "Looks like suicide. There's pill bottles and liquor. Better call the cops."

The guy had a look first. "Jesus. What'd she do that for? Didn't know she was hurtin' so bad. Wish I'd known I'd of done something. She was a nice lady. Always a smile. What'd she do that for?"

Mike groaned, "Oh *man*. Her daughter was off'd in Vancouver a few weeks ago. Fuckin' *shit*. How'd she end up here? Didn't her family look after her? They've got fuckin' bags of money." He kicked the side of the trailer.

The guy, his name was Ralph, brought him into his cabin. Ralph called the Mounties, gave Mike a beer and let him roll a cigarette from his can of Export. Mike *had* quit five years ago, but he needed a hit of nicotine fast.

The cops came, stood on the bucket, looked in, pried open the door. One, O'Brien, went in while the other, Ashford, stayed outside and asked Mike questions. O'Brien came out and said it looked like she did it the night before. He mumbled something about rigor. He held an envelope addressed *To Whomever Finds Me*. O'Brien read it, Ashford read it; Mike read it and almost puked. He said, "I wanted you, Marion, but I didn't get here in time." Ashford counted the money. He said that if it was the change left from her welfare cheque, she would've spent over two hundred dollars. He noticed a tag on the electric meter and said the hydro had been shut off.

O'Brien knew what she meant about her daughter being murdered. They decided it was related to the Crime of the Month as they waited for the coroner.

The area was pretty secluded, but they started to draw a crowd anyway. A woman came out of nowhere. An old man came from a house across the road, wanting to know what happened. The coroner came. He said there'd be an autopsy. The cops asked where Mike would be; he told them his room number at the motel.

There was a lot of waiting. They let him stay with her for a little while but then asked him to wait outside because it was so cramped. Mike leaned against the outside of the trailer, as close to Marion as he could get, just on the other side of the wall from her bed and body. People came and went. He could feel the vibration of their movement through the wall. He tried to be *present* but didn't want to be. He was aware as she was placed into a body bag. Everyone was polite and respectful. There was no black humour. They took Marion away.

Mike bummed another smoke from Ralph but his hands shook so much it came out looking like a raggedy assed joint with a lump in the middle. The biker said he had some shake. They went back to his cabin and smoked up. The shake was okay, He got a decent buzz, but not enough to go astral planing to a better reality.

EIGHT

Mike's motel room had a queen size bed, direct dial phone, cable TV, and enough guilt to last a lifetime. Because he knew, *knew* that if he had come straight to Courtenay, instead of hammering around with Gary's addition, Marion would still be alive.

He thought he'd dry-cleaned his karma in jail, been released with a fresh slate. But here he was, wandered off The Path again while his family dropped like flies. He had a lot to make up for.

If she'd even said that she was on welfare.... He hadn't thought about it. She always got by. But if she had he would've instructed his accountant to send her money. Because it was there, collecting interest, not doing anybody any good all the time he was inside. She could've gone to welfare about the hydro and telephone bills. They had a crisis grant they never told people about. She didn't have to live like that. Or die like that.

The Mounties got back to him in the evening. Constable O'Brien had been at the trailer. He introduced a new one, Detective Ferrier, in suit and tie, from Vancouver. They waltzed in without asking permission. O'Brien smiled, "Well. Moonbeam."

Cops loved the name. He hadn't voluntarily used it since he got yanked from the commune, but it was there on his file, *Also Known As*, and he'd never live it down.

"You didn't tell us everything, Moonbeam."

"I don't know everything,"

"You didn't tell us who you are."

"It's not like I'm some great celebrity."

"Sure you are."

"I was in shock." The cop bullshit made him itchy. He asked about Marion.

Ferrier sighed, "It's a shame. Our elderly are our most valuable resource, but she wasn't even that old. Only fifty-nine. Where'd you know her from?"

"She looked after me sometimes when I was a kid. A second mother. She wrote to me in the Pen but she didn't say how she was living. Guess she figured I couldn't do anything about it. Why worry me."

Ferrier nodded. "Her son-in-law has been contacted."

"That's one thing you guys are good for. Breaking bad news to total strangers."

"You never met James Fleming?"

"No. I only knew her daughter from when I was a kid. We kinda moved in different circles."

"But Mrs. Peppard spoke about her?"

"From time to time. The highlights. When she graduated from university, got married. Marion told me about her grandchildren."

"What do you know about the death of Barbara Fleming?"

"Nothing."

Ferrier crossed the room and sat in one of the two chairs beside the window. He put his notebook on the table. Authoritative. Deep Voice. And Mike was in a place he hoped he'd never be again, face to face with a cop, giving an account of his movements, where and when.

Mike sunk down on the edge of the bed and talked about Calgary and Banff and Vancouver—seeing the reward poster for the killer. He wanted to talk about seeing Marion, one quick look and he *knew*. But Ferrier was a member of the task force investigating Barbara's death, and, like Kevin's girlfriend said, it had priority.

Mike was having a lot of trouble fitting another corpse into his mind. His mother. Kevin. Marion. He couldn't grasp it, couldn't fit it in place. And he'd *seen* her. He answered the Mountie's questions, riding it out. He didn't talk about Kevin; he was Essery's case, Vancouver police, Ferrier wouldn't make the connection. Nothing about Zem-Zem. Very careful. No key words like *commune* or *hippies*.

Ferrier moved ahead. "I came along when Mrs. Peppard was notified of her daughter's death. After the funeral."

"Barbara's husband didn't make the effort to contact her?"

"No. But Barbara's father lives in Australia. He was notified and arrived in time for the funeral."

"Poor Marion."

"She didn't take it well. What do you know about James Fleming?"

"Not much. He's some kind of engineer, isn't he? That's about all I know. He had money. Barbara was in real estate. Why didn't they send her support?"

Ferrier shook his head. "Thought you might know."

"Marion never said a word about it."

"She moved to that trailer in January. Applied for Social Assistance under her maiden name. What do you know about that?"

"I knew she moved. That was in the last letter she sent. She didn't say anything about the name."

The cops fell silent, presumably to give him time to remember something. "Marion's funeral," Mike said at last, "Is James Fleming going to handle the arrangements? Because if he's not, I'll be happy to. Not *happy* but I'll take the responsibility."

"Maybe you should discuss it with him." Ferrier said.

"Yeah."

"He should be home by now. You could give him a call-"

"I'll have a hard time being polite. Maybe if I keep in mind that he just lost his wife."

"Just be natural," Ferrier said. "Maybe you'd care to record your conversation." He took a micro recorder and telephone pick-up from his inside jacket pocket. Mike smiled and looked away. It wasn't hard to believe this shit. He was a parolee with as many options as a Popsicle. Freeze, melt or be eaten alive. He slid over to the phone.

Ferrier hooked it up and gave it a test run. He wrote out the number. Mike punched it in. A little girl answered. He asked for her father. She put the phone down and called, *Daddy. It's for you.*

Mike heard a tentative, "Hello?"

"This is Mike Minchuck. We've never met but I was a friend of Marion's. I was the one who found her."

"Oh."

"I'm sorry about Barbara."

"Yeah. Thanks."

"I understand the police notified you. You heard how Marion died?"

"Haven't stopped thinking about it. Never liked the woman, was afraid she'd come in here with all her hippie flags flying. But I should've realized. Her daughter..."

"Why didn't you like her?"

"Not to speak ill of the dead but God she was crazy. Too much LSD."

"She could've used some support. I saw way she was living."

"How was she living?"

"Squalid poverty. She used her welfare cheque to pay for the pills and liquor she used to kill herself."

"Ridiculous. She was so squirrelly she probably had her mattress stuffed with cash."

"Why do you say that?"

"She was loaded. She gave us the down payment on our first house as a wedding present."

"When was this?"

"Twelve years ago."

"That's when she won the lottery. She bought me a used truck and a set of tools."

After a pause James Fleming said, "I didn't know that. She said she had money put away. Barbara's father paid for the wedding. She said she wanted to do something to help us get started. How much did she win?"

"A little over twenty thousand."

"And she spent it all on other people? Didn't save any for herself?"

"She was like that."

"That's hard to believe."

"Doesn't matter now. The reason I'm calling... I'm not a relative, just a friend, but I'm willing to look after the final arrangements. Is that all right with you? Or would you prefer to come over to the Island and deal with it yourself?"

"No, I've missed quite a bit of work lately. You can, if you feel the call." There was a hesitation. "Cremation is cheapest."

"I suppose it is. But don't worry about it, I'll take care of the bill. Have you told your children?"

"No. They've had enough death as it is."

"Must be hard."

"You wouldn't believe it."

Mike hung up after the good byes. Ferrier leaped in to replay the tape. Mike went to the washroom while they listened. When he came out Ferrier asked what he thought.

"If what he's saying is true, there was a whole other side to

Marion I never saw. She wasn't crazy. She was different, I'll grant you that. Came out of the beat generation. Black turtlenecks, coffeehouses, jazz. Loved the sixties. Too much acid? How much is too much? She used it as a spiritual tool, not recreation."

"Maybe her daughter was embarrassed by her," O'Brien said. "She was marrying an engineer. Hoping for an up-scale lifestyle. Once the fiction was established it would be hard to admit to lying."

"I'm surprised he didn't ask about a will," Ferrier said. "He'd expect Barbara to be the beneficiary. And that the assets would be passed to him or his children. When he stops to think about it I'm willing to bet he'll think Moonbeam here is running a con on him. I fully expect his lawyer to make contact."

"Sure." O'Brien answered. "And he'll discover there is a will, leaving everything to the one who found her. But don't worry about it Moonbeam, that will isn't legal. If it doesn't have the signature of two witnesses, it doesn't count at all...."

Mike shook his head, "She's always been non-material. There was her old car, but it looked like it hadn't been driven in a while. I guess it'd had the biscuit. No, I don't expect there's anything. Have you found any hidden assets in the trailer?"

"No," Ferrier said, "In fact, she'd cleaned the place out since I was there earlier. According to the neighbours she'd put out a pile of garbage bags for collection. And yesterday the Salvation Army truck made a pick up. There wasn't even a frying pan left. The refrigerator had been unplugged and washed out. She saved only enough for personal and immediate use. And one box of photographs."

They kept talking, but Mike could only nod dumbly. He rubbed his face and sighed. He wished they'd leave so he could smoke the joint Ralph gave him.

"You said when she wrote to you in jail she never said how she was living. Did she say she was on welfare?" O'Brien asked.

"No."

"Did she make herself out to be rich?"

"No. Maybe a book she'd read. Or hiking. She put a good face on things. Pride I guess."

"It's a tragedy," Ferrier said, "Not quite old enough to be eligible for a pension or senior discount. Failing health. Alienated from the family."

The cops stood. Finally. They gave Mike their cards. Ferrier wanted to know if and when anything happened with James Fleming. Or his lawyer.

"You obviously suspect him of killing Barbara."

"The investigation is on-going."

"You've ruled out a serial killer?"

"That was strictly media speculation. It was a poor copy. We haven't released any details. That way we have a base to check against any tips that come in."

Mike read Ferrier's card. "Why is this an RCMP case? Why not Vancouver homicide?"

"Her body was found near UBC. In Pacific Spirit Park. Our jurisdiction."

As soon as they left he went into the washroom, turned on the ceiling fan to exhaust the smell and smoked up.

NINE

Charlie hated school. She didn't used to but now she did. She wished she could skip without getting caught. The secretary called home if you didn't come and if no one was there, or if they said you already went, everyone got crazy and called the police and went looking for you. Then you got grounded or suspended or had to write a million lines.

They were doing Mother's Day stuff now. Pasting messy paper on stupid glass jars and folding ugly paper flowers that never came out nice. Charlie wouldn't do it because she didn't have a mother.

All the other kids had mothers. Sean lived with his father but he *had* a mother and went to stay with her in the summer. Ms. Lundel said she could do it for her grandmother or auntie and Charlie said that was *stupid*. It was called Mother's Day, not anything else.

Charlie felt scared inside talking like that. All the kids looked at her and Ms. Lundel told her to go to the office. Then Mr. Roth, the vice-principle, made her go to see Mrs. Carten, the counselor, again. Then she had to tell about her feelings and about Mommy. She didn't want to talk about Mommy. She knew Mommy was dead and that she was never coming home again. Every time Charlie said something Mrs. Carten wrote it down on her paper. Charlie tried to read it but it was upside down and in handwriting and she didn't know that yet. She stopped talking and wouldn't say anything.

Mrs. Carten tried to give her a hug but they told her about touching and Charlie said NO real loud and pushed her away. Mrs. Carten looked all scared and said she was trying to be nice. Charlie wanted to say a bad word but didn't.

The house was always messy when they came home from school except for Thursdays when Beverly came. She used to come before, too. Daddy said maybe she should come everyday but she said she couldn't because she worked for other people.

There was never anything good to eat except when Daddy brought home McDonalds or called for pizza. Charlie helped Daddy go shopping for groceries but then they ate up all the good stuff and everything went bad in the fridge and it smelled funny. Daddy said it was a science experiment and told them about mould. But they had to throw out lots of food.

The police came again and every time they talked to Daddy he got upset. He would drink and sometimes cry or yell. One night he did both. Charlie and her brother and sister didn't like that - It scared them. If the bottle was empty Daddy would go out and not come back for a long time. One time Billy put water in the bottle when he saw it was almost empty so he wouldn't go out but Daddy could tell and yelled *who did it?* until Billy told. Then Daddy cried again.

She didn't tell about it at school to Mrs. Carten because Daddy said they shouldn't talk about private things. And because Mrs. Carten wouldn't understand. Charlie asked her one time if she had a mother and she said yes, I'm very lucky. And she was old! Older than Daddy.

Mike hung around Courtenay for a couple of days until Marion's body was released to the funeral home. Constable O'Brien was pretty decent over the whole thing. He supposed cops had their uses. When Mike heard what she'd done on her last day he checked out the art gallery she visited. He saw the raku display and knew she loved it. He called up the potter, explained the situation, and was invited to the studio. The one he picked had a dark umber background with iridescent blues and reds. He dropped it off at the funeral home to be filled with her ashes. He gave Kevin's address in Vancouver for the courier.

The ferry crossing seemed long and tedious. He sat inside, at a window, staring out at the water with Marion's green velvet box on his lap. He didn't have the courage to open it. They told him she'd been looking at the pictures as she died.

Back to the city. He checked in at the parole office, then drove to Kevin's little house on the lane, changed into a jacket, shirt and tie. He thought it was about time he showed up at that job he was supposed to be starting. Quality Systems on Broadway. For the serious, and seriously rich, only. The new manager, electronically literate, moved forward to assist in selection. "Hi," Mike said, smiling, being casual about it.

Thirty seconds later he was back out on the street. Friend of that murdered drug dealer? No way.

Mike's feelings weren't hurt for himself, but they were for Kevin. Cleaned up his act. Hadn't dealt in five or six years. Found a good women. Got a good job. Started work on the negative shit in the past. But he would only be remembered as a murdered drug dealer.

He drove back to the house. He changed into normal clothes: jeans and tee shirt. He sat at the kitchen table, moved his mother's ashes aside, and made room for Marion's green velvet box.

He found loose pictures in photo finishing envelopes, an album of Barbara and her children, a wedding album, a smaller, pocket size album of Zem-Zem and a floral covered address book. The remainder of the contents, the leavings and snippets of her world were precious because Marion cared enough to save them when she'd emptied her life of everything else. He opened the Zem-Zem album, smiling, seeing old friends, seeing his mother and Marion again.

Until he saw one particular picture and the smile died on his lips. He recognized one of the key events shaping his life. Occurring only a couple of days before they were taken from the commune, both events overlapped in chilling memory.

Almost everyone had left the commune that day to go into the city. For some it was welfare day, for others money-from-home day. And there was some protest, anti-Vietnam War or anti-War Measures Act or anti-something. For whatever reason only a few had stayed behind. There were animals to look after and chores to do.

The four kids, Barbara, Kevin, Mike and Rainbow, with Rainbow's mother, Lotus, went for a walk on the power line road up back of the farm. Raven joined the group. Raven, a Day-Glo tribal freak in fringed leather vest and bell bottoms. They were having a great time, grooving on nature when Snake came up. Snake because of the tattoo on his forearm. He was drunk. And jealous over Lotus.

Mike and his mother had lived on the commune for five years. There'd been lots of acid and mushroom tripping, lots of homegrown pot and homemade wine. But no anger. Peace and love were taken as seriously as organic food. They had no TV, they never went to the movies; it was the first violence he'd ever seen.

Lotus tried to calm him down. She grabbed his arms. He shoved her away. He started throwing punches. Raven was no match. He fell, got up, blood pouring from his nose, grabbed a loose branch and started swinging. Snake ducked and came up with a right. Raven fell back against a rock. They heard the crack as his neck broke.

Snake took Lotus away after that. He made very serious threats. Said if she ever tried to turn him in, he'd come back and kill all the kids. Told the kids, especially Rainbow, that if they ever told, he'd kill her mother.

Mike didn't know about the others, but he and Kevin never told. Even when they were grown men, they brought it up only once or twice and only when alone together and supremely stoned.

But now two witnesses were dead, Kevin and Barbara. Was it only two? What happened to Rainbow? The address book went back eight years; Marion had his last two addresses before prison. The pages weren't crowded with names. He went through and saw Rainie (Rainbow) and Leo Castle. How many Rainbows could she have known?

He reached behind him for the telephone and called her number. Out of service. With a knot in the pit of his stomach he tried Directory Assistance. Like an instant replay, the operator said she had no listing.

He bolted for his truck. He wasn't going to waste any time. Not stop off to get drunk and get laid, not stop off to work on someone's domestic project. Do it *now*.

The address had a name, Sandpiper Apartments, built to last, in brick and marble. The door was locked. He tried bell number one, *manager*. No answer. He walked around to the back of the building.

An old timer in jeans, work shirt and Canucks cap swept the willow-shaded benches between the parking lot and the back door.

"Excuse me," Mike said, "Are you the manager?"

"Yes." The man stopped sweeping and looked up. "But there's no vacancies."

"It's not about that. I'm looking for some friends. Last address I have is here. Rainie and Leo Castle."

The manager lifted his cap and scratched his grey head, eyeing Mike, "Guess you didn't hear about Leo."

Mike went cold. "What happened?"

"Last fall. Drive by shooting. Happened right out front. Terrible thing. Missed her. But he was dead before the ambulance came. Hit a couple of other people but he was the only one who died. Hadn't seen anything like it since the war. Probably one of them youth gangs. Good case for bringing back the death penalty. If they ever catch them."

"I have to see her. Can you give me her forwarding address please?"

"Well, don't know if Mrs. Castle would want me giving out her information to a stranger."

"It's vital I get in touch with her. More than ever, now that you've told me about Leo."

"I could call her, see what she says. What's your name?"

"Mike Minchuck."

The manager nodded and started inside.

"Wait." Mike smiled. "She might not remember it. Tell her it's Moonbeam from Zem-Zem. I got this address from Marion."

"Moonbeam from Zem-Zem? Like one of them hippie things?"

"Our mothers were the hippies. We were just kids."

"All right," he said, sounding dubious. He left Mike standing alone.

TEN

Rainie had the last of her work cleared away by one o'clock. The afternoon sun cast a patch of white light on Leo's armchair. She curled up to read a book in its warmth. She'd lately discovered historical romance and ordered a whole slew of titles from the book club.

When the phone rang she put the book face down on the arm of the chair and got up to answer it. Mr. Marshall said there was a man downstairs looking for her.

She listened to who it was and her first reaction was to tell him to go away. But she remembered Moonbeam. Remembered the fun times playing with him. There was another boy too. They were both much older but they let her tag along. She told Mr. Marshall to send him up.

There had been a tree house. She was scared to climb the ladder. She'd always been scared but they didn't make fun of her. Moonbeam carried her piggy-back. He was strong. The other boy waited at the top and helped her up. They had food there and sleeping bags and a telescope. She was even more frightened to climb down the ladder. But Moonbeam carried her again. They helped her and taught her to do it herself until she could scramble up and down like a nimble monkey.

She knew she'd be embarrassed to tell him she couldn't go out. But maybe he could help her. The way he did with the tree house ladder.

The door bell rang and she looked through the peep hole. She didn't remember what he looked like but she opened the door. He was shorter than Leo, but more muscular. He had a dimple in his chin and curly hair. He said, "Hello, little sister. It's good to find you after so many years. I always wondered what happened to you."

He gave her a hug. It was the first time she'd been touched by a man since Leo. He said he was sorry to hear about her husband.

She thanked him and asked if he'd like something. There was some coffee made fairly recently. He followed her into the kitchen. She poured out two big mugs and they sat at the table.

"How's Marion?"

"I'm afraid I have some bad news."

She felt sick to her stomach as he described what happened. "I should've written to her. But after Leo died I stopped everything."

"We both have our regrets."

"How did you hear about Leo?"

"Just now, from the manager. I wanted to see you because of what happened to Barbara and Kevin. Maybe you knew something. But now, hearing about your husband too. Three out of four of us have been touched."

"What are you talking about? Who are Barbara and Kevin?"

"Don't you know? You're as bad as I am. Marion's daughter, Barbara Fleming. Big Sister Dove on the commune. And my friend Kevin Woods. Cedar."

"Cedar? Was that the other boy who played with us?"

"Yes."

"What about them?" But she already guessed. "Someone told."

"Yes, I think that's what must've happened." After a pause he said, "The manager was discreet about you still living here. Have you changed your phone number?"

"Yes. It's unlisted." Her hands were shaking. He explained what he knew of Barbara and Kevin's deaths. He asked her about Leo.

"I didn't see anything. There's always traffic on the street; I wasn't paying attention. But he must've because he grabbed me and pushed me down..."

He put his hand over hers. "Go on."

"He fell. The glass broke." Her voice quivered, "He fell against me and knocked me down." She whispered, "He saved me."

Mike squeezed her hand. His warmth felt good. "Where were you going?"

"Out to dinner."

"Any special occasion?"

"Saturday night. We always ate out on Saturday night. Then we went to the movies or to a club."

"Where would you eat?"

"Different places."

"What did Leo do?"

"He was a shipper-receiver in a warehouse. Only started there a few months before he died. But he'd applied to the RCMP. He was taking criminology at night. His last two courses and then he'd have his degree."

"Did they come after you again?"

"No."

"I'm not sorry of course, but it doesn't fit with my theory. To know two people who were killed in separate events seems an unlikely coincidence. But a third attempt, with all of them sharing an ugly secret, seems remote. But it's a dangerous world. There are drive-by shootings and lunatics on the loose and maybe Kevin made one last bad luck deal to earn some extra scratch to pay for the perfect honeymoon."

Rainie said, *But*, and turned away.

"But what?"

"They may not realize I still live here." She bit her lip. "I don't go out."

"Not at all?"

"No. I work at home. I'm a bookkeeper. And I have everything delivered. You thought I moved too." She kept her face averted. "But what about you? You're okay."

"Oh, well I've been out of town," he smiled, "Didn't Marion tell you?"

"No. Mostly about herself. And Barbara."

"I've been in jail for three years. Robbery and conspiracy to defraud. I got out a few weeks ago. First I heard my mother had died. Then Kevin. Then Barbara. Next it was Marion and now I hear about your husband."

"Your mother too? Did she know what happened?"

"No. She died of cancer. Two and a half years ago, but no one tried to find me." He thought of Barbara's husband not attempting to find Marion. There were patterns here, circles of dysfunction. "How did you meet Marion again?"

"We never met. We wrote letters. Leo saw a classified she put in the paper. Looking for anyone who'd been in the commune Zem-Zem."

"She wrote me in jail that she wanted to get a reunion together."

"I never told him what happened. But you know, people meet and fall in love and they want to know everything about each other. I said I was in foster homes and didn't know where my mother was." She turned to look at him. "I never saw her again. Do you think she's dead too?"

"I don't know."

"Leo and I were together four years and sometimes I said different things. I talked about the hippies. And that my mother abandoned me. Went off with a man. He had a tattoo of a snake on his arm and he was missing part of his pinkie finger. I asked him one time what happened to his finger and he stuck it in my face and flexed his arm and said the snake ate it. Scared me so much I started to cry. He laughed. He was cruel. I told Leo about that. But I never, ever told what happened. He saw the ad and recognized the name Zem-Zem and wanted me to write. I only remembered the name because of the social workers. Rainbow from Zem-Zem. They thought it was cute."

"Same way the cops think Moonbeam is cute."

"Is that your real name?"

"No, Michael. So you wrote to Marion?"

"She had her real name and then Happy. I remembered Happy. Leo thought she might have some information about my mother. Human Resources could never find her. They said she used a false name to get welfare. They thought I was Rainbow Smith, but never did find a record of my birth."

"Maybe you don't exist," he smiled.

"I try not to."

"Did Happy know anything about your mother?"

"Not her last name. Her first was Lois. She used Lotus because it was close. She came from a wealthy family in California. Her birthday was on Halloween. They had a double party."

"I remember that."

"We came early in the spring. They took me away just before my mother's second birthday party there."

"October twenty-ninth, I remember the date."

"That makes it a year and a half. I was very young but I remember because the people were so kind."

"Great place to grow up. Until the end, of course. And then the social workers took us."

"I hate social workers."

"So do I. They took you in one car, Kevin and me in another. Don't think I'll ever forget the look on your face."

"I thought they knew. And that he'd see me with them and think I was the one who told."

"They didn't know."

"No. They never said anything."

"It's all related in my mind. One humongous, horrendous episode. What happened with Snake, then being taken by the gestapo."

"It *is* related. My mother turned us in. I found out a long time afterwards. She called Human Resources. She said she was abandoning me. Wanted them to take me. Told a lot of lies about how we were being abused. Named you and your friend and Dove. Barbara. She meant to protect us, I think."

"So he wouldn't come back and kill us?"

"Yes."

He concentrated on his black coffee. Little Rainbow had grown into a delicate, slim, pale beauty. With blue eyes dilated by fright and every muscle stiff with tension. After a time he said, "Some of those foster parents weren't screened very well."

"The ones I had were okay. Maybe it was different for you because you were older. And a boy. I never got into trouble."

"I made it a point to. Before they separated us Kevin and I whispered and made plans to run away as soon as we could. We'd leave notes for each other in secret places. Where we were staying. Phone numbers. We both asked about you but they wouldn't tell us anything. We'd get caught and sent back. Or moved to another home. Later on there were group homes. We both did time in juvie. As it works out, the first cop to ever bust us on the street is now a detective. Ron Essery. He's working on Kevin's case."

"I've met Detective Essery. He worked on Leo's case."

"Now there's a cosmic coincidence."

"Are you going to talk to him?"

"I don't know. If I do I'll have to *tell*. I never have before. And I know Kevin didn't either. Do you remember it? You were only six. Or did you suppress all memory of the traumatic event?" He stumbled over the word *traumatic*.

"I remember. I remember very well. Did you finish school?"

"No. They tried putting me in a classroom but I wouldn't have any of it. The straight kids didn't know anything. Some polyester jerk of a teacher. I'd been on correspondence on the commune and said I wanted to go back on. But I wasn't allowed. Didn't get back to it until I was in prison. I wrote the equivalency exam. I have my grade twelve now."

"Congratulations."

"Thanks. It felt good. I'd always read, of course. I was no dummy. But it felt good to get the certificate. What about you?"

"I finished grade twelve the ordinary way. Then I took two years of business. Worked part time, too."

"I went into carpentry."

"I married Leo. What about jail? How did that happen?"

"Thievery was my avocation. My way of getting back at the world. Homes, offices, but always the high end, never stole from poor people."

"Like Robin Hood?"

"I'm sure I fancied myself as part of the myth from time to time. I put my carpentry pay cheques into the bank. Rent, truck payments, everything on paper came from the legal money. But I always had cash in my pocket."

"And you got caught."

"I made the mistake of getting mixed up with the wrong crowd."

"Mafia?"

"No. White collars. Insurance. Call it arranged theft. Go away for the weekend, come back, act surprised, call the police, make a claim. There was an adjuster who was my contact. He'd call me up, tell me what to do. His ex-girlfriend blew the whistle. Just didn't treat her right I guess. The cops bugged his phones. They heard him call me.

"They let me go through with it, nabbed me on the way out. Break and enter, thief over, possession of stolen goods, conspiracy to defraud, whatever else the Crown Prosecutor could think up. He was really disappointed I wasn't carrying a gun. He could've tacked on another couple of years. I did three and I'm on parole now. I got a longer sentence than warranted because they made me out to be the mastermind. The adjuster got a hundred thousand dollar fine and a year. Of which he probably served four months in minimum security. He lost his house and his promising career in the insurance industry."

"Would you do it again?"

"No. But the thing was, the ex-girlfriend didn't know everything. There were a few twists that went a lot deeper. It wasn't just a simple case of insurance fraud. The adjuster and I were both approached to keep our mouths shut."

"You were bribed?"

"The immortal words were, and I quote, 'Get out of jail with a nice nest egg or die, asshole'"

"I could never handle anything like that. I'd be too scared."

"Like they say, don't do the crime if you can't do the time. But at least I know where to get you a good deal on tenant's insurance."

"I think I'll pass."

"Good decision. Think we've caught up enough for the time being, Rainbow?"

"For now, Moonbeam."

"Because we have to talk about it."

"I know."

"We never forgot that day. What the four of us witnessed. Last year Marion puts her ad in the paper. You make contact by mail. Kevin and Barbara meet again. I only know about one meeting, I don't know what was said or anything. Then last fall Leo is killed. Maybe aiming at you too?"

"Maybe."

"But no one comes after you again. Then a few weeks ago Barbara and Kevin are killed on the same day. What did Leo do? Did he talk to them? What's the missing connection?"

"He never said he'd spoken to them. But... let me tell you about Leo. One time I was looking in a magazine and they had a spread about a helicopter picnic. Way up on top of a mountain. Wicker basket, gourmet food, the works. I showed it to him, said wouldn't that be nice? I forgot about it. On my next birthday he said he had a surprise. There was a limousine waiting downstairs, a vintage Rolls Royce. Took us to the heliport on the waterfront. The wicker basket was waiting on board. He never said a word to me, but he'd been saving up all that time."

"Must've been nice."

"Wonderful. But he was like that. He'd remember something you said. An offhand remark, just a picture you saw in a magazine once. And for something serious—I did say I'd like to find my mother. And he did say he'd look for her."

"You think somehow—"

"Marion had a name for Snake. She's seen it on an envelope when she picked up the mail from the post office. She remembered because, well, the name was Richard Nixon. Like the American president. She wasn't sure if it was his real name or not. Maybe Leo tracked him down. Went to see him. Wanting to know about my mother."

"Would he know how to do that? Learned something from his courses?"

"Maybe. And we have Internet. There are bulletin boards, data banks. I never paid much attention. He'd spend hours at the computer. Maybe he thought he'd find her and surprise me. Like the way he did with the helicopter picnic."

"Not knowing what he was getting himself into. Could you do that now? Go online?"

"I wouldn't know where to start. Took me a long time just to learn the programs I need for work. And I had Leo helping me. It's sounding more and more like you should go to the police."

"Yeah. But I hate them worse than social workers."

"I wouldn't want anything to happen to you."

"I'm not too keen on that myself. There's a reward for Barbara's killer. Quarter of a million. Going to the cops, opening Pandora's box, might get something out of it besides verbal abuse. I'll split it with you."

"Won't bring Leo back."

"Or Kevin or Barbara. Or Marion."

"Who put up the reward?"

"Good question. I don't know. That's something I can do before I go to Detective Essery. Research. At least find the relevant newspaper articles. Might be stuff I'm missing that's common knowledge."

"The library keeps clipping files."

"That's what I'll do then."

"Please be careful."

"I will. It's just between you and me. I'll come back tomorrow, let you know what I found out."

"Call first. I never open the door unless I'm expecting someone."

"That's good. Better give me your number then." He followed her to the work station in the living room. She wrote down her number, he wrote down his. "I'm staying in Kevin's house."

"You think that's safe?"

"Probably not, but I haven't been there much. I'll find another place soon. Have to look for a job too."

"What about your nest egg?"

"That's stashed away. For my retirement. Or an emergency. Which ever comes first. I still have money in the bank from before I went to jail. I'm okay for a while. It's just for the P.O., the parole officer. I should *appear* to be looking. Go on an interview or two. Send out some resumes."

Before he left she brought out two pictures in silver frames from the bedroom. Her husband looked like a pretty ordinary guy with a moustache and black, wavy hair.

"That's my Leo," she said, smiling, "Isn't he handsome?" To be polite he had to agree. The other picture of her mother, he'd seen in Marion's Zem-Zem album. She'd sent Rainbow a copy. He looked from the picture to Rainie's face.

"You look almost exactly alike."

"That's what Leo said. She must've been about my age when this was taken."

It wasn't just the high cheek bones and blue eyes, but the hair too. Rainie's was shoulder length, Lotus' longer, but both straight and blonde with a centre part. "She's very pretty," he said, "So are you little sister. It's good to see you again, all grown up. Even under the circumstances."

Rainie stayed up late that night, holding Leo's picture, thinking about their picnic. The helicopter set them down on a plateau, higher than the trees. It flew off, leaving them alone with the immensity of nature. The plateau was rocky but flat. They walked hand in hand to the edge. There was so much to see; it was so beautiful and silent, they couldn't speak.

The sky was clear blue from one end of the earth to the other. All around and below were mountains and they could see lakes and rivulets and the tops of trees. To the east were higher mountains, glaciers sparkling in the sun. Leo said, "Happy birthday." They made love.

The wicker basket held everything, white table cloth, real silver, crystal and bone china, champagne, food more delicious than anything she had ever tasted.

ELEVEN

Mike didn't know it'd bother him to sleep in Kevin's bed until he stripped down to his shorts and climbed in. The bed was comfortable enough, a cotton futon on a wooden platform, lots of warm blankets, down and feather pillows, but his brother's spirit still haunted the sheets.

He felt too weird and wired to sleep. He got up, dressed again, and roamed the small rooms. It wasn't really dark. Even with the curtains closed the neighbours' backyard lights filtered through. It didn't matter where he stepped, Kevin's spirit haunted the entire house.

He sat in the kitchen, maybe on the exact place where Kevin died. He tried to be still and *know*. Not much came through but the beating of his own heart.

He couldn't stay. He got in his truck and drove. He checked into the nearest hotel.

It was the kind of room that would run to two bills downtown; the northern view itself worth the extra hundred. Funny, the things he'd forgotten. City lights, he remembered that, like other cities, but Vancouver's uniqueness glittered in the blazing dome of Science World, sparkling with an internal rhythm, flashing white-hot. The skyline. The bridge traffic. City Hall, brightly lit clocks on two sides, the Canadian flag hanging limply, the city spilling up, like water in a bowl, from Burrard Inlet up the side of the mountain. The string of lights on Grouse Mountain floated on the darkness like a constellation of satellites.

He'd never been up there. He didn't have the kind of childhood with outings and day trips or showing out-of-town relatives the sights. High rises surrounded the hotel, some apartments with lights on, but he couldn't see in very well.

Kevin didn't haunt the hotel room but he still couldn't sleep. He dozed off and on. When he got up at three, hoping to be buoyed by the lights, he felt an eerie chill instead. The dome had been turned off, leaving nothing but a black hole on the edge of False Creek.

He was up and out early. Kevin's place didn't feel so weird in the daylight. From the neighbouring backyard came the sounds of splashing, swooping and chirping. He looked out the kitchen window and saw the little feathered guys partying in a birdbath made from an inverted washing machine agitator. A hummingbird feeder hung from a tree. Two seed feeders stood on a tall pole. There were so many birds, moving so quickly, that he couldn't keep count. A nice sight to start the day.

He made coffee but there wasn't anything in the house to eat. He did push-ups and sit-ups, thought it was about time he found a gym and started a regular routine. Inside he'd worked out every day. He swept the floor and dusted the book cases and the tops of furniture.

He sat at the kitchen table with his second cup of coffee and studied the photographic evidence. Possibly the only evidence. Barbara, Rainbow, Kevin and Mike, sitting on a log, smiling up at the camera. Rainbow and Kevin holding frogs, beside Barbara, her boyfriend. At the edge of the picture, in the background, Snake, his tattoo and missing pinkie finger visible, standing with Raven.

He tuned the picture over.

September, 1970.

Richard Nixon! (Snake) Tony Perretti (Raven)

Duffy Dell (18) Dove (16) Rainbow (6) Cedar (12) Moonbeam (12)

He removed the picture from the album, replaced it with one of his mother shucking corn on the back porch of the main house. He hid it in a book, *The Meditating Frog*, on the bottom shelf of the bedroom bookcase.

He thought he might pick one of the pictures to carry in his wallet. A sunny Zem-Zem picture with all his friends laughing. If he could find one with Marion. A knock sounded at the door. Alarmed, he crept to the window—George Bell, his P.O.

He opened the door with a pleasant, "Good morning."

Bell walked swiftly to the living room, looked in, crossed the kitchen, checked the bedroom. "Whose truck is that outside?"

"Mine."

He came back to the kitchen, looked down at the pictures scattered over the table, pulled out a chair, slapped down his vinyl portfolio and sat.

"Come in. Have a seat. Make yourself at home."

"I don't like being lied to."

Mike knew that any hostility on his part, by word, action, gesture, or even expression, would be met with a geometric progression of bullshit. What he really wanted to do was take the P.O. by the scruff of the neck, smash his head against the wall and kick his ass out the door. Instead he moved mildly to the table and began collecting the pictures and putting them back in the box.

"You bought the truck on the Island?"

"No. In Vancouver."

"Paid for with what?"

"Regular monthly instalments from my pay cheque. I bought it seven years ago. Been in storage the last three, of course."

"You have the paperwork on that?"

"Should be in the back of the truck. Want me to get it?"

He didn't say, *That's okay, I believe you,* he nodded curtly. Mike brought back the registration and the accordion file, looked under T for truck and laid the proof in front of George Bell. He waited for another curt nod, replaced the papers, and sat at the table.

"You lied to me, Mike. You didn't tell me about your murdered friend. Or that the so-called foster mother you went to see was really the mother of Barbara Fleming."

"That wasn't a lie. It was an omission."

"Think you're smart, don't you Mike?"

"No, George. I know I'm very, very stupid. I should've gone right away to Courtenay as soon as possible instead of hanging around town a few more days. As it was, she committed suicide the day before I got there. Very, very sad." He lifted out a picture of Marion, "See, she was young and beautiful once. That wasn't how I found her."

Bell tipped the edge of the box and looked in. "These are hers?"

"Yes. The Mounties know I kept them. They interviewed me. It's all legal."

"You don't have a job."

"No. I went there but they don't want me."

"Did you really expect them to?"

"I thought they might be short handed."

"The police will be coming around to question you."

"I wish I knew something. I'd like to be of help."

"Planning any more trips?"

"No. I'll get the newspapers. Look for jobs. Tomorrow morning I'll register with Canada Employment. And there's a guy I used to work for, home renovations. I'll call him up, see if he has anything."

"You're a journeyman carpenter?"

"That's right."

"Will you be applying for social assistance?"

"No."

"What will you be living on?"

"I have some savings."

"How much?"

"Enough to last until I find work."

"How much?"

There was no such thing as a personal question between P.O. and ex-con. He dug the last bank machine receipt from his wallet. He'd withdrawn two hundred and fifty, leaving a balance of a little more than forty-five hundred. He had other accounts, and an investment portfolio, but omitted to mention them. Why make the jerk jealous?

Bell didn't have anything else to hassle over. That didn't stop him. He delivered lecture Number Two. The one that began, *You seem an intelligent guy*. Mike tried to stay awake. Midway through he started listening for the rising inflection of a question mark. When it came he delivered response Number Seven, *I certainly did do a lot of thinking*, and the standard shit-eating Number Three.

George Bell hadn't read his file carefully enough because he launched into Number Five, *Victims of your crimes*, when it should've been Number Eight, *Fraud costs....* Mike waited politely until the end when it was his turn again. He reiterated Three and did a tap dance with responses Two and Four. He was ready with anything from Ten to Twenty, which were psycho-babble, but they weren't necessary.

Satisfied that Mike knew the rules of the game, Bell made a big show, clicking his pen, taking his time writing bureaucratic jargon on the pad inside the vinyl portfolio.

TWELVE

Mike presented himself at the periodicals desk of the main public library and said he was researching homicides in British Columbia. He was rewarded with clipping files for the last two years. He wasn't going to have much privacy, all the tables were crowded. He found a seat between a bag lady reading the *Province* and a Chinese girl taking notes from a book on the American Civil War.

Kevin and Barbara's murders weren't the most recent in the Lower Mainland. There'd been a stabbing in a sleaze bag hotel downtown and a shooting in a parking lot in Surrey. He didn't recognize the names, or any of the dozen other victims in the current year's clippings.

It took some getting used to, seeing Kevin and Barbara in cold newsprint. There wasn't much on Kevin. They mentioned where he worked and his previous police record, and that the cops suspected drug involvement. Kevin's girlfriend Wendy knew about the drug traces and scales being found, which was more than in the article.

Barbara rated more copy. There was a write up on her life and one on the well-attended funeral. No mention of her absent mother. Her husband and children looked numb and bereft. Her father looked distinguished: Professor of Political Science at the University of Auckland, Australia. They quoted him that it was a great tragedy and that he'd always thought of Canada as a safe place.

He found another familiar face and name in the next clipping; an answer to Rainie's question of who put up the reward: Duffy Dell, Barbara's boyfriend way back in Zem-Zem. He'd lost most of his hair.

Duffy Dell, president of Delta Realty. Barbara was one of their agents. No mention of their early relationship. Just that he cared about his people, cared about the violence in today's society. He was putting up the money from his own pocket in hopes someone who knew something would come forward.

In the last year's clippings Mike read about the other real estate woman who had been killed. She worked for a different company, not Delta, but, like Barbara, disappeared after her last appointment of the day, body dumped near UBC, car not recovered.

He read about Leo Castle. A witness saw two people wearing gorilla masks in a blue sedan, the passenger taking pot shots from the window. Three wounded, one dead.

He found no more familiar names. He took a photocopy of the article about Duffy Dell to show Rainie. He returned the files to the librarian with his thanks.

He stopped for a quick bite at a coffee shop before calling Rainie to let her know he was coming over. It wasn't far. He drove past his old apartment block on the way, looked up at the balcony. There were hanging planters there now, cascading flowers of red and blue. It made him think of his last girlfriend, wondered what she was up to. He wasn't moved enough to find out.

Rainie had done something to her hair and put on makeup. Mike could smell perfume too as they sat down on the sofa. He put Marion's Zem-Zem album on the coffee table.

"Do you remember Barbara's boyfriend?," he asked, "Duffy? Dove and Duffy?"

"I remember. I told you I remember everything. They used his truck."

"For what?"

"To move the body. They wrapped it in a tarp and put it in the back of the truck."

"I thought Snake buried it."

"He was going to, but it was too hard to dig."

"I never knew that."

"You went back down. But I stuck close to my mother and I saw."

"Duffy helped him?"

"Yes. It was in an orange tarp. And then they covered it over with other things. My mother said she had to go with him. That everything would be okay. I should be a good girl. I shouldn't tell.

She told me to go back to Big Sister Dove. Then she got in the front of the truck, in the middle. Snake got in the passenger side. He made a gun with his finger and shot at me. Then they drove away. I was left there standing all alone. That was the last time I ever saw my mother." She leaned against him and cried, just like she had when she was six years old. Mike hated this. He felt for her but didn't know what to do. He held her, stroking her hair, telling her it was all right. Even though it wasn't. She stopped crying and went to the washroom. He heard her blow her nose and run the water.

"You okay?" he asked when she came out. She sat on the sofa again, blue eyes bloodshot but make-up repaired. "Yes. Sorry I lost it there."

"I understand."

"I think you do, Mike. You might as well go on. I'll try to stay calm."

"Okay. I was in the tree house the next day when Duffy came back. He was alone. I watched him through the telescope. He found Dove. She went inside, came out with a backpack and they drove off. And neither one of them was there the day after—when the gestapo came."

"She was lucky."

"Right up until the end." He handed her the photograph. He watched her smile when she saw the kids, watched her eyes widen as she recognized Snake and Raven.

"It's them!" She turned it and read the names.

"Tony Perretti. Raven."

"This puts us all in the same place at the same time."

"And it has the names. This is something to bring to the police."

"Look at this." He showed her the photocopy he'd made in the library. "Duffy is in real estate now. He's the one who put up the quarter million reward for her killer."

She read the article. "He didn't know about Leo and Kevin."

"Just a couple of names in the news. If he even paid any attention. Have you ever been arrested?"

"No."

"The cops will listen to me. But they'll love you. Taking your statement, asking questions. Then they'll leave you all alone. Unprotected."

"Oh." Her cheeks flushed red. She put the article on the coffee table.

"Because the way things stand right now, we have no proof that Leo, Kevin and Barbara's deaths are related to each other. Or to Raven's death. At the very least we'll be adding to their caseload. Handing them an unsolved homicide from 1970. And along the way, implicating a rich hot shot."

"You don't want to go to the police? You want to investigate it yourself? Like Leo did? Get yourself killed like he did?"

"No. I want to move you out of here first. Stash you someplace safe. Then I'll go to the police."

"I can't." She felt it starting. Her stomach churned, hairs stood on the back of her neck, sweat trickled from under her arms.

"What do you mean, you can't?"

"Can't leave."

"Why not?"

"Scared. I get sick."

"A panic attack?"

"Is that what it's called?"

"You have agoraphobia?"

"It has a name?"

"It's a known condition."

"I thought I was crazy."

"No. When did it start?"

"When Leo was killed. I tried to go out once. I got as far as the door downstairs."

"It was triggered by the trauma. And you probably subconsciously associated it with Raven."

"I can't... "

"You have to."

"No. I..." She began to tremble. He put his arm around her again. "It's okay, Rainie. We'll get you drunk."

"I guess that'll help. But where can I go?"

"I'll find something. Furnished. An apartment hotel. Slightly better security than a motel."

"When?"

"Now. You have a Yellow Pages? I'll find a place and you go pack."

"But what about my clients? And there's a girl who runs errands for me."

"You can tell them you're going on holidays for a few days. And the manager too. Tell him to keep an eye on your apartment."

"How long?"

"Until this is settled."

"I don't know. I don't know if I can. I don't have anything more to drink."

"I'll pick you up and carry you out the door if I have to."

She looked at his face and knew he wasn't going to take no for an answer. She'd wanted him to help her, and now he was, and she didn't want it at all. "I could call up and have a bottle delivered. Is there time?"

"Yes, there's time for that."

"They're usually pretty fast." She got up unsteadily. He took the phone book from beside the desk. But she knew the delivery number by heart. "What should I order?"

"Whatever works best."

She ordered rum. He looked through the listings as she went to the bedroom to pack. She didn't know what to take. Things were moving too fast. Her hands were shaking. She had the suitcase from when they went to Hawaii. It still had the airline tag on the handle. Somehow she got it filled. Mike came into the room. "Found a place. Two bedrooms, living room and kitchen. All furnished. Pots, pans, everything."

"Two bedrooms?"

"I won't be able to stay at Kevin's any longer. The killer already has that address. Don't forget your bathroom stuff."

She liked the way he was so competent, knowing what to do, getting it done. He reminded her to call the manager. She did, and called Keri too, saying that she wouldn't be needing her to run errands for a while. He handled it when the delivery came. She said she had money but he told her not to worry about it. He made her a strong drink. There wasn't any mix, but there was ice. He gave her the glass and told her to take her medicine. He only had a short one.

She was afraid she'd get sick if she drank too fast. They sat in the living room and looked at Marion's pictures. The longer she stretched it out the longer it would be before she'd have to leave.

The pictures were interesting. Because she'd been moved around so much as a child there were images that lived in memory but without association, groundless, without relation to time or place. She did remember the big house, the duck pond and the tree house. But now she recognized people and things, like the mothers of the kids she played with and the smaller houses and the workshop.

She finished the drink. She felt better. She thought she'd have another to be sure. Mike didn't. He said he was driving. He told her to pack the bottle. She took the pictures of Leo and her mother too.

Mike turned on the answering machine. She didn't know how to access it by telephone because she'd never had to do that before. She stalled for time by looking for the manual.

THIRTEEN

The time came. She had to wipe the dust off her purse, she hadn't used it in so long. Mike carried her suitcase. They walked out of the apartment. She felt a little light headed from the rum. The closer they walked to the elevator the more panicky she felt. Her voice came out high and breathless, "Can we go by the stairs? I think it'll be better by the stairs."

They got through the fire door okay. He walked ahead. She gripped her purse tightly with one hand and held onto the banister with the other, leaving a trail of clammy sweat smears. She kept telling herself nothing was going to happen. She was a big girl. She could do it.

They got down to the bottom. She hesitated. "This is embarrassing."

"Hey, it's just your brother, Moonbeam." He moved so quickly she didn't have time to run. He opened the door, held it with his foot, took her arm and steered her through the lobby, singing *On the Road Again*, marching non-stop to the big glass entrance doors, leaning against the push bar and before she knew it they were out and walking on the sidewalk.

He loosened his grip. "Okay now?"

"Yes." She turned to look back at the entrance. She could see the pock marks left by the bullets in the brick.

His truck was parked half a block up. It felt odd to be at ground level again, to feel solid ground under her feet. He unlocked the passenger door for her, then opened the canopy and put the suitcase in the back.

He had to make one stop, at a bank machine. The nearest parking spot he could find was across the street. He told her to lock the doors. He had to stand in line, but he kept watch, smiling when he caught her eye.

When he came back to the truck she asked if he'd mind driving past English Bay. She'd like to see the water again. Her apartment faced nothing interesting and she'd missed a lot. It felt good to be out again.

It was the best kind of day to resurface in the world, with the sun dancing on the water, people tanning on the beach, jogging, bicycling, playing Frisbee, walking home from work swinging briefcases. Her eyes began to water.

He looked over and patted her arm, "Don't cry, Rainie. It's okay."

She giggled, "I know. I think it's from the glare. Haven't needed sunglasses in a long time."

The West Coast Inn stood ten stories high. Mike stated his business into the speaker of the underground garage. The gate was raised and he drove in. "This is good. I don't like parking on the street."

They took the stairs up to the lobby. She stood beside him as he registered. He used a false name and paid for a week in cash. He asked for a low floor but the best they could do was eight.

He cocked an eye at the elevator. "What do you think? It's a long walk up."

"I'm not sure."

The doors slid open and he took her arm and pulled her in. She clung to him during the short ride.

The apartment looked modern and clean. Bright prints on the wall, striped bedspreads, oak laminate furniture. The kitchen had a microwave and an electric drip coffee maker.

Rainie opened the drapes. "WOW."

He turned from his inspection of the washroom. They were high enough to see, not only English Bay, but beyond to the Island.

"I can see the mountains!" She bubbled, "And look at the glaciers! Sail boats! Everything! Where's that?" She pointed to the right.

"The North Shore mountains."

"This is fabulous!" She picked the front bedroom that shared the same view as the living room, put her clothes away and set up the photographs on the dresser.

He had to go to Kevin's house to get his stuff. She'd already remembered something she'd forgotten to pack—her book. He promised to bring her something to read.

Mike drove back to Kevin's house and packed up his clothes again. He had the blue mason jar of his mother's ashes now. And Marion's green velvet box. He'd also pretty much inherited Kevin's stuff. Except for whatever Wendy wanted to keep. That meant he'd gotten back his bookcases, tapes and records. He owned more worldly goods than he realized.

Marion had cleaned to the bone before she went. Like that picture of Ghandi's last effects; he tried to remember: eyeglasses, bowl, book and spinning wheel? She left few possessions, but she also carried the past.

He began feeling guilty about bailing out of Kevin's house. He sat in the kitchen chair and tried talking to the walls. The shouting silence made him feel worse.

He packed up a carton of books for Rainie. Kevin had been heavily into science-fiction. He put in some of the New Age magazines and self-healing books too. Sounded like she could use them. The only thing left to do was get groceries.

He found a supermarket with a million item selection. He had no idea what Rainie liked to eat. He picked all his favourites he'd craved inside. As he wheeled the buggy to the check-out he kept watch for Snake.

FOURTEEN

"We were a couple of tarnished angels," Mike told Detective Ron Essery. They sat in a red naugahyde booth in the rear of an east end greasy spoon. The Monday breakfast rush over, the waitress sighed into a corner with a cigarette and cup of coffee. They pretty much had the place to themselves.

"The tarnished part I know about, Moonbeam. But I'm not sure about angels."

Essery was in his early forties, in good shape but with a lot more grey in his hair since Mike had last seen him. He wore a Harris tweed jacket and a small patterned tie.

"So are cops. You guys do some good, but you also make snap judgements based on a person's appearance and a gloss of facts. And you have a vicious, brutal streak."

"Hey, Moonbeam. That's unfair. I'm a pussy cat."

"The same way a cougar is. Dragging small animals off into the bush. And the occasional young child."

Essery laughed and lit a cigarette. He tilted his head and blew smoke rings toward the ceiling. He tapped the burning tip into the ashtray and swiftly looked into Mike's eyes. "Who killed Kevin?"

"I have a suspicion. First, let me show you this." He handed him the last letter Kevin sent him in jail. Essery took out a pair of reading glasses. It was a short letter, only a page and a half on plain white paper. "See? Kevin was completely out of the drug business. He wouldn't lie to me."

Essery nodded, took off the glasses, folded them and placed them on the table. "Why was he killed?"

"Wait. The same day Kevin was killed, so was Barbara Fleming."

"There's a connection?"

"Yes. And last fall Leo Castle was killed. Your case?"

"Yes."

"Leo's wife, she calls herself Rainie now, but she was Rainbow back then, along with Barbara, Kevin and me. Rainbow, Big Sister Dove, Cedar and Moonbeam. We were kids together on a commune. Remember back when you first took Kevin and me in? We were runaways from foster homes?"

"I remember."

"We had been apprehended by the Ministry from that commune called Zem-Zem."

"You were being abused. Wasn't that why they put you in care?"

"No. There was no abuse whatsoever. But Rainie's mother called the Ministry and told them that. She named the four of us. They got Kevin, Rainie and me. Barbara wasn't there that day. When she did get back she was told to split so she wouldn't be grabbed. Eventually she went to live with her father."

"And why did Rainie's mother make the call?"

"To protect us. We had witnessed a homicide. On October 27, 1970." He brought out the photograph. "That's the killer and that's the victim." He told the secret. For the first time ever. And to a cop. *He was telling.* The physical reaction was immediate: sweat, trip hammering heart, queasy stomach. When he finished the story he drained his coffee cup because his mouth was so dry.

Essery put on his glasses to read the back of the picture. "Richard Nixon?"

"Don't know if that's his real name."

"And who's this? Duffy Dell? Is that the same one?" He turned over the picture.

"Yes. He was Barbara's boyfriend back then. He helped Snake dispose of the body." He described the situation and explained he hadn't seen that himself but Rainie had. "I moved her out of her apartment. Before I called you. I'm scared for her. She's agoraphobic. I don't know who's responsible for these latest killings, but it's a mind-boggling coincidence. I had to tell you."

Essery pushed his glasses to the tip of his nose and rubbed his chin. "That must be the angel part of you, Moonbeam."

"Don't call me that. My name is Mike."

"Okay. Mike."

Mike pulled out the letter where Kevin said he'd seen Barbara. He explained about Marion and her idea for a reunion. When he'd told everything he knew, he raised his cup in the direction of the waitress and she trundled over with the coffee pot.

Essery took his time thinking it over. He studied the picture, nodded to himself, smoked a cigarette, pulled out a notebook and began making notes. He asked questions. Mike answered.

"We'll need you to make a formal statement. And Mrs. Castle too."

"I know. But it has to be confidential. I can take care of myself, but Rainie is very vulnerable."

"That won't be a problem."

"Make sure of it."

"I will. When I picked you and Kevin up that first time, it was shortly after this happened?"

"A few months. We weren't bad kids. That came later. We had to learn to be bad."

"Tell me about the commune."

"It began as an idealistic, utopian community. Marion and her husband. Barbara was their only child. Three other couples and their kids. University types, intellectuals from back east. I think it was 1960, but I could be off a year or two either way. They bought land together, shared everything. More people joined. Then it was the Vietnam War and war objectors started coming. Hippies and rebels."

"When did you get there?"

"'65. The original members moved on. Marion was the only one who remained. I only vaguely remember her husband. I remember her crying when he left. There were always more people in the summer. But that last summer, 1970, even I could see it had changed. Transients, *bill* dodgers instead of draft dodgers. Parasites like Snake. For guys like him, sharing meant gimme. Zem-Zem continued for another couple of years after we were taken. But it was never the same. Police harassment. Social workers making periodic checks on the kids."

"Where'd the name come from?"

"They were great students of the eastern religions. One time they were teaching the kids about Zen. One of the tots couldn't pronounce it properly. Kept toddling around going Zem-Zem, Zem-Zem. The name stuck. That was before my mother and I got there, but I heard the story every time new people came up."

"How long did Duffy Dell live there?"

"I think it was only that summer. He didn't live there exactly. He came and went. He had a thing going with Barbara and it was only an hour or two from Vancouver. I didn't have much to do with him. And I don't think his name has come up since. Kevin never mentioned him. Marion wrote that her daughter was a real estate agent but didn't say Duffy was the head of the company."

"You weren't reading the business pages during your three year vacation. He's become a real mover and shaker in this town."

"This'll blow him out of the water."

"And you've never seen or heard of Snake, Richard Nixon, since then?"

"Not since that day."

"Who else are you in contact with from the commune?"

"There was only Marion and Kevin. Now there's only Rainie. I don't know who else Marion found. She didn't say in her letters. Maybe some of the names in her address book. She had Rainie in there. I didn't go through it very thoroughly after I got to C and found Castle."

"Do you have it with you?"

"Didn't know you'd want it."

"I'd like to have a look." Essery nodded and stroked his chin. He reread his notes, looked again at the photograph. "I have a problem here. Kevin is my case. And I worked on Leo Castle's. But Barbara belongs to the Horsemen. So would Tony Perretti from 1970."

"You have to share my information?"

He smiled, "Like you said about Snake. Share means gimme."

"And Barbara's high profile. Detective Ferrier came all the way to Courtenay to talk to me because her mother committed suicide."

"Bill Ferrier? He'll be all over you like fleas on a dog."

Mike told him about taping the call to James Fleming. "I was still in shock from finding Marion and he was asking about Barbara's husband. I had it in my mind. Barbara, Kevin, Snake, Zem-Zem. But I didn't really connect it all up yet. Not like this. I didn't say anything. But he won't believe me. He'll think I was withholding evidence. It'll be the same shit the Mounties have always given me. Thought we had an agreement to be confidential. Or doesn't that count?"

"It counts, Moon... Mike. It counts. And you've come forward now. Don't worry about it, okay?"

"At least you didn't say *trust me*. You have to run a check on Snake first anyway. For all I know he could've already been convicted of Raven's murder. Or been knifed to death in some bar-room brawl ten years ago."

"That still leaves Duffy Dell."

"Maybe I can help you. Maybe I should look him up. Tell him my suspicions, *warn* him. Hear what he has to say. Report back to you."

"Have you thought this out?"

"No. Came to me right now. I can keep Rainie out of it, say I was hiding in the bushes and saw him and Snake put the body in his truck."

"That's a dangerous game." He lit a cigarette and leaned back in the booth. But Mike could see he was interested. "You've been in prison, so whatever led up to it, you weren't involved. Willing to wear a wire?"

"No. But I'll tell you what he says."

"Because what I'm afraid of is that you'll pull a Rambo."

"I've never been violent. You know that."

"Three years in the Pen can change a man."

"That's the system you support, Essery."

"It isn't perfect."

"Neither am I. But if I was only after pay-back I wouldn't've come to you."

"True. But it sounds pretty dicey to me."

"What do I have to lose except my life?"

"You won't be so flippant when you're staring down the black hole of a barrel."

"Maybe it won't get that far."

"Maybe it will."

"How did Kevin die?"

"Quickly. Two .45 slugs to the chest. Silenced. Approximately between ten and midnight. No signs of forced entry."

"His girlfriend Wendy told me you found a roach, traces of coke and a set of electronic scales on the coffee table." Mike shook his head, "They weren't his. And how big were these scales? Meat locker size? Ones I've seen could be slipped under a jacket."

"Like that."

"So why didn't the shooter take them? Pretty valuable. If he was in deep enough to carry a gun, rip off drugs or money, why not walk out with the scales?"

"I thought of that. I put it down to the heat of the moment."

Mike handed over Kevin's letters. "And there's something else I just remembered. He was killed the same day I was released. You said between ten and midnight? I tried to call him from Calgary. Would've been about ten-fifteen, Vancouver time. He didn't answer and the machine wasn't on." He lit one of Essery's cigarettes. "Maybe if I'd called sooner...shit!"

"It wasn't your fault."

"I should've come straight back to Vancouver instead of meeting my grandparents. They were insistent and it sounded like a good idea. But it wasn't that great. Didn't change my life. Not like Kevin getting blown away changed my life."

"You can't think like that, you'll drive yourself crazy. It wasn't your fault. It was the shooter's fault. But you did the right thing in coming to me." He put the photograph and letters in the back of his notebook. "Keep it together. I'll go over the facts again in light of what you've told me. You're my C.I. now. That's Confidential Informant. And I take the confidential part seriously. I'll leave your name out of it but I'll have to talk it over with my boss. Because what looked like a drug homicide... And Castle, the drive-by that's driven us nuts... Looks to be far more complex. I'll call you. Same number you gave before?"

"Yes."

"And don't get any bright ideas and go off and do anything on your own. Don't contact Dell yet. It could be damn unhealthy."

"I hear you."

"You never heard me before."

"This time I have the example of my dead friends."

FIFTEEN

Rainie had never read any science fiction before. The first one she picked up from the box just seemed like a wild west cowboy story, only set in outer space. She read to page thirty but wasn't interested. Usually she finished a book she started, no matter how bad, but this time she had so many to choose from that she put it back and found another. Much better. Set on earth, in the near future, so that everything was recognizable. A lot of drugs. A lot of computers. Something called nano-technology. She hoped there wouldn't be any violence.

She loved to read. She could open a book, forget all her troubles and be somewhere else for a while. She wasn't sure about those other books in the box. The ones that had words like *healing* in the title. She could get to them later, after she'd read a novel or two. She was a fast reader. The one she'd started shouldn't take more than a day. Looked like there'd be lots of time. Nothing else to do but read or watch TV. She didn't know how long she'd be away. If it went longer than a week she'd be in big trouble with her clients.

She could look out the window, too, and watch the boats on the water. She tried to remember what it was like. One of her foster families had a boat and when the weather was nice like this they went out fishing. She caught a red snapper once. They had a couple of older kids. The father was a fire fighter. She liked them but the social worker moved her somewhere else. She never found out why.

Mike called. He said it went well with the detective. He knew she'd be wondering. He'd tell her about it later. He had some things to do but he'd be back in time to make supper.

She was glad he called. He seemed to be thoughtful and kind, and insisted they take turns making supper. She assumed she'd do all the housekeeping like she did for Leo, but he said he liked cooking and hadn't done it for three years. She couldn't imagine him breaking into people's houses. She went back to her book.

Mike's accountant had her office in one of those old time grimy brick buildings downtown with retail space on the ground level and a multitude of small offices above. He took the creaking elevator to the seventh floor. The door was unlocked but the secretary wasn't at her desk in the front room. He knocked at the inner office and stuck in his head. Constance gave a little yelp of surprise and ran around her desk. She gave him a kiss on the cheek and a big hug. "You're looking good. Jail must've agreed with you."

"Yeah, but I didn't agree with it."

Elise, her secretary, returned to the office and added to the general air of homecoming. They gave him coffee and cookies and chatted excitedly before Elise closed the inner door and went back to her desk.

Constance was at least six feet tall and rail thin, with waist length black hair plaited into a braid. She wore a rose coloured blouse and gold jewellery that brought out the glow in her complexion. She gestured with long, slim fingers as she gave him papers to sign and went over his financial statements.

The business over with, he leaned back in the chair and smiled, "Good to see you again, Constance."

"I'm really glad you made it okay. I worried about you. You know, you always hear things. And there are those terrible movies about prisons."

"I'm a lot tougher than you think."

She laughed softly, "I imagine you'd have to be."

The first time they met he was doing renovations on a house beside hers. She tripped out in a long multi-coloured skirt, hair blowing free in the wind, to inquire about a fence she wanted built around her garden. He fell in love on the spot. He just knew she couldn't be single. She wasn't. She shared her home with an equally beautiful and cultured woman. But when he discovered her talent as a discreet and creative accountant, they forged a relationship both meaningful and committed.

"I'd like you to do me a favour. Or not a favour, you can bill me for your time."

"What is it?"

"Run a background check." He pointed to the computer on her desk. "Two people. Finances. Personal stuff. As much as you can find out. In confidence."

"Everything I do is in confidence."

"Sorry."

She took a fresh sheet of paper and a pen, "Okay."

"First is Duffy Dell." She raised an eyebrow but didn't comment. He went on, "And Richard Nixon. Not the president. A man about ..." he had to stop and think, "forty, forty-five. Twenty years ago he was a slime ball. It's a long shot, don't know if that's his real name."

She nodded. "Is that it?"

"That's it."

She looked at her watch. "Come back tomorrow. And, you didn't get it from me."

He smiled. "I'm not planning a score."

"You still didn't get it from me."

She walked him out. As Elise smiled from her desk, Constance bent her head and kissed his forehead. "Be good. And if you can't be good, be careful."

Uncle Duffy came to visit them. Charlie knew him from Mommy's company Christmas parties and the summer picnic. He brought them presents. Charlie got Barbie's Magic Voyager. Billy got a remote control car. And Amy got a science set. He gave Daddy a bottle.

He took her toy out of the box and showed it to her. It looked like a van and could be a car and camper too. He put the batteries in Billy's remote control car and played with it. Then he read the instruction book and helped Amy start an experiment with chemicals. After he and Daddy went out on the deck, he said he'd help Daddy with the bottle.

Charlie played with Barbie and Ken in the camper for a while. Billy went zooming all over the downstairs with the car. Amy was quiet in the kitchen with the experiment. Then Charlie went out to the deck and listened to them talking. They knew she was there but didn't tell her to go away.

Daddy was telling him that it was hard on the kids but worse for Charlie because she was so young. He smiled at her. He said they called him from school and told about that. Uncle Duffy said they should go to a family counsellor. Charlie said she went to a counsellor at school and hated it. She didn't want to go to another one. He asked her why and she said it was yucky.

He said maybe that was because it was hard to talk about things that hurt. And because she was alone, but if they all went together as a family they could talk about it and find ways to make it easier. Then he gave Daddy a card and said he should call and make an appointment. He said the company would pay.

Daddy said the biggest problem was keeping up with the cleaning and everything. He said he thought about a housekeeper but he didn't know where to look for a good one. And good ones cost money. Daddy started talking about money. He talked about insurance and things she didn't understand. But then he said he was thinking of selling the house and moving to a less expensive place. Charlie got scared and said they couldn't move because then Mommy's ghost couldn't find them. She thought they would laugh, but they didn't.

Uncle Duffy told Charlie that she shouldn't worry because they weren't going to move. He told Daddy not to worry too. He said he'd take care of it until the insurance came and Daddy could pay him back. Charlie asked what insurance was. Daddy said that every year he and Mommy paid money so that if something happened to them the mortgage would be paid off and they'd get other money too. Charlie wanted to ask what a mortgage was but didn't.

Uncle Duffy said he could help about the housekeeper, too. He said he'd take care of it. They talked about other things and then Charlie got bored and went inside. Billy and Amy were fighting because Billy wanted to do an experiment and Amy wouldn't let him. The box said twelve and up and he was too young. Billy said she was only eleven so she was too young too. He made his remote control car bump her leg. She yelled and hit him. Daddy heard and came in.

SIXTEEN

Mike had the address of a job placement the P.O. had given him, but it wasn't like the old Canada Employment with the job openings on index cards pinned up on the board. This place was all computer terminals and Internet hook-ups. He was supposed to see a job counsellor, but something about the place hit him wrong. He turned and walked out the door.

Next on his *to do* list was finding a gym. No easy task since he couldn't even find a Yellow Pages. No phone booth was that well equipped. He found one by buying a coffee at a café and borrowing theirs. He wrote out a few addresses.

The first was too trendy for his taste. But the second wasn't bad. There were a couple of women but he didn't mind because they looked good in their brightly coloured skin tight leotards. He didn't have any work out clothes, but that didn't stop him. He could shower and change when he got back to the hotel. The four men on the equipment cast the odd glance in his direction, but both women paid him more attention. He tried to show off his arm curls but he could feel how much strength he'd lost since his last work out.

When he got back to the hotel he went immediately to the washroom and stood under the hot water for a good, long time. He felt okay when he dried off until he realized, to his alarm, that he'd neglected to bring fresh clothes in with him. The choice was walk out in front of Rainie with a towel draped around his privates or put on the stinkies again. He opted for the stinkies. He thought of her as his little sister but they hadn't had many years of childhood bonding.

He made it back to his bedroom, stripped, dressed, and reappeared fresh and sweet-smelling.

He made a salad, taking great pleasure in washing, patting dry and cutting the vegetables. He baked potatoes in the microwave and pan fried a couple of steaks. He made a dressing with olive oil and lemon, squeezing the juice through his fingers to catch the seeds. Cooking was a sensual pleasure. He'd missed it.

Rainie complimented him on his cooking. He said it was always better when he had an audience. He told her about his meeting with Essery but didn't say that he might be seeing Duffy. He didn't want to frighten her.

He made her laugh with his description of the bureaucrats. He sensed she hadn't laughed much since her husband died. He told her about the gym and she said she'd been doing exercises with the TV. They talked about books and she wanted to know about Kevin's self-help books, if they were any good.

"I haven't read them. But I don't think they'd hurt."

She chewed her steak thoughtfully. "Why did he buy them? Did he have problems?"

"Same as you and me."

She put her fork down. "You're not a wimp like I am. Was he?"

"I wouldn't call you a wimp."

"That's because you're polite. Don't you remember the tree house? How you had to carry me up the ladder on your back?"

"No, I don't remember that."

"I do. I remember everything. I was a really wimpy kid, but you were nice about it. You're still nice."

"Must be a character flaw."

"And I'm still a wimp." She forked up some of the baked potato. "You didn't answer the question. Was Kevin the nervous type?"

"No. But he'd gotten engaged to a nice lady. He wanted to put some work into coming to terms with the past."

"Did you meet her?"

"Yes. Her name's Wendy. It's very sad. I don't have to tell you how it is. I think she'll be okay, but it'll take time. You know."

"Yes. I do know. What did he have to come to terms with?"

"Like I said, same thing as you and me. Witnessing that murder. Being put in foster care. Losing our mothers. We can suppress it, make believe it doesn't matter any more, not think about it. But at some point we have to deal with it. And for you there's the added trauma of your husband's death. It ain't pretty, but you play the hand you're dealt and hope you win."

"But you don't hide."

"For a while maybe. Have to stick your head out of the sand at some point. Take a chance."

"And if you lose?"

"Losing isn't the worst thing in the world. When I went to jail I knew I'd played the odds for over ten years. My good luck ended."

"You're quite the philosopher."

"Not really. I've just learned to string the appropriate clichés together. See, when we were younger, Kevin tried to drown it out. Tried to stay stoned all the time. But drugs being illegal, and therefore expensive, he started selling to pay for his stash. Easy step, the money being so good, to sell for its own sake. Never worked that way with me."

"You didn't do drugs?",

"Sure I did. But it never became the focus of my life. Great for recreation, but for what I really enjoyed I preferred a clear head. Stealing. While Kevin was blasting his brain cells, I was out shoplifting. That's how it started. The five finger discount. Clothes, music, whatever you want. Then I graduated to break and enter. Now that was a real rush. Big Doors. That's what I called it. Those rich people's houses with the great big doors. I'd put one over on *them*. I always worked, so it wasn't just for the money. But now, only in the last few weeks, have I come to a glimmer of understanding of why."

"Why?"

"Subconsciously I was getting back at my rich asshole of a grandfather. He beat on my mother when she was a kid and when she really needed money, when she was trying to get me back, he refused to give it to her. It was one of those, you made your bed now lie in it things."

"Tough love."

"Yeah. I didn't even remember him, but my mother told me about it. And I was in the room when she phoned his office and he wouldn't take the call."

"I thought they took you away from her."

"They did, but that was one of the times I ran away from the foster home. She wasn't on the commune. She thought it would be better if she distanced herself. She rented an apartment in Vancouver. I stayed there a few days until they caught me."

"That sounds awful. What'd they do, drag you away from her?"

"Yeah. I was too old to hang on to her skirts, but she was crying and I was freaking out."

"You think the stealing was your reaction to all that?"

"Getting back at him. Or the symbol of him."

"What happened when you met him?"

"I sort of told him off. Don't know if it did any good. He's an old man. And all that stuff happened a long time ago. But it made me feel better."

"Does that mean you aren't going to steal again?"

"Probably not," he laughed.

"You haven't told me about Kevin's mother."

"Pretty off-the-wall lady. She got into heavy acid tripping. Always a new boyfriend. Then she got political and joined a group smuggling American army deserters across the border. After that she got religion. Some holy roller church. Speaking in tongues and all that. Then she met a man and they were going to hit the hippie trail and travel around the world. He got busted in Mexico and she took off. Indonesia. India. Australia for a while. Kevin would get picture post cards from exotic places once a year. Or less. Hadn't heard from her at all in the last ten years."

"Maybe something happened to her."

"Maybe."

"What about his father?"

"Denied paternity. Denied he'd ever slept with her. Denied everything."

"There are blood tests."

"They were never done. We all grew up without fathers. It was okay in Zem-Zem. There were men around. Role models and all that. And then the foster fathers. But maybe you had better luck than I did."

"Aren't you curious about your real father? Are you ever going to find him?"

"I've always known where he was. A few years back he had a lawyer locate my mother because he wanted to get remarried and had to divorce her first. He's still working the farm his grandparents homesteaded. I'm sure it's a great life. But it's not my life."

"I've always been curious. I don't know anything about my father at all. Not even his name. I registered with Parent Finders. But no one's looked for me."

"Don't sweat it. Why weren't you adopted? A pretty, blue-eyed blonde, good in school, didn't cause trouble. You should've been the first one off the shelf."

"The opposite of not causing trouble is called resistant and non-communicative. I didn't talk unless I had to. I didn't play with other kids. I kept to myself. I cried a lot. If I even heard the word *adoption* I'd throw a fit. I was waiting for my mother. I didn't want a new one."

"Did they put you in therapy?"

"They tried. They thought it was *abuse*. But if I was ever abused I don't remember it. I wouldn't cooperate. I'd throw a fit. That kept them busy, and then they'd leave me alone. I thought if I talked they'd find out the secret. So I talked as little as possible."

"You weren't stupid. That's a smart, workable plan."

"You understand, don't you?"

"I'm probably the only one who does."

Mike couldn't sleep that night, thinking about what he had done. He had second thoughts about going to the police, third thoughts, thoughts all the way down to pi squared. He lay in the dark, lifting his watch from the night table from time to time as the luminous hands crept around the dial.

At two-thirty he got up and moved his mother's ashes from the dresser to beside the bed. He thought about her, and how the murder of a hippie who called himself Raven had changed their lives. He counted the dead on his fingers and wondered what he should feel. The last time he looked before he fell asleep the watch said four AM.

SEVENTEEN

Mike settled into the client's chair as Constance slid papers across the desk. "Duffy Dell. I hope that's enough, Mike. You weren't specific. Any area you need more detail, let me know. Divorced in '83. No children. He lives in a five million dollar penthouse. I have a client on one of the lower floors. Security's as tight as the White House."

"Good. He should live long and prosper." He read through the papers and nodded. "Quite a few companies."

"On paper he's worth over three hundred million. The managing arm is Double Dee Enterprises. He's a real success story. Started out with one old house, fixed it up and flipped it. Bought two old houses. He never looked back. Now it's land development, residential real estate, hotels. Alternate technology, computer software. Retail—he has furniture and Uncle Duffy's Discount."

"I heard of that inside. A guy I talked to one time just met a really nice woman, very pretty, and sweet. He wanted to do something nice, on the off chance that when he got out—an old man, bald, arthritic—she'd still be single and remember him fondly."

"Is there a point to this, Mike?"

"He took her to Uncle Duffy's Discount. Because it was cheap. Most things, a dollar or two. Filled up a buggy with everything she needed. She'd been on the move for a long time, didn't have anything for the house. He bought kitchen stuff and stuff for the bathroom. A sewing kit and candle holders. Everything. He spent fifty dollars and they walked out with four big bags full, thanking Uncle Duffy all the way home. He's marketing himself, isn't he? Using his name that way?"

"He promotes himself as everyone's favourite uncle. Or his publicist does. Sees to it his name or picture is in the media at least once a week. Donates heavily to charity. Very progressive, his employees love him. Has a corporate green program. Speaks out on environmental issues and the plight of the Third World. But those cheap goods he sells in his discount chain, who do you think manufactures them? Underpaid, Third World people, working in sweatshop conditions with minimal or no safety regulations."

"You're saying he's a hypocrite."

"I'm saying don't believe his publicist. Uncle Duffy is in it for the buck. Read the second page and see his stock play. He's promoted everything from gold mines to solar powered cars. Last few years he's hyped biomedical and high tech issues. Start up companies. Highly speculative. Don't ask about track record, revenues or earnings, just dream of what might be. It's basically legal. Issuing false news releases and manipulating stock prices aren't, but he's never been investigated."

"Now he is. But not for stock fraud."

"That woman's murder?"

"It's a secret. But if I held any shares in his companies I'd be nervous."

"Thanks for the tip."

"You have something else for me? Richard Nixon?"

She shook her head. "I've discovered it's not an uncommon name. But none in B.C. in the age group you gave me. I checked between the ages thirty-five and fifty in case you were off a few years. Three in other parts of Canada. A priest, a surgeon, and a sculptor who emigrated from England eight years ago."

"Doesn't sound like him."

"Maybe the one you're looking for went down to the States or changed his name."

Essery called at dinner time the next day, "Hi. This is Ron. Like to get together with you. How about an hour? At the same place." Luckily Mike recognized his voice.

Essery was seated at the same booth they had before. Mike slipped in with a smile, "Next time we should meet where we can get a beer."

Essery shook his head, "I'm on the wagon."

"You have a drinking problem?"

He didn't answer, instead he said, "You and Mrs. Castle should move out of the West Coast Inn. It's owned by Dell Developments, which is owned by guess who."

Mike had seen the company on Constance's list but she hadn't listed all the holdings. "I used a false name. Haven't noticed any undo attention to my existence."

"What name?"

"John Murphy."

"Mean anything?"

"No."

Essery lit a cigarette. "My wife's been after me to give these up too but I'm not quite ready for Saint of the Year award."

"You probably won't live forever, anyway." He gave him the floral address book. "Here's Marion's book you wanted to see. I copied everyone down but I can't say that I recognized any of the names."

"That's okay. Thanks. You had the right name for Snake. Middle name Harold. one conviction, for impaired driving, in '72. We had prints of his nine fingers and a notation of the tattoo."

"Where is he?"

"Good question. Hasn't been heard from since '72. I'm checking with our friends to the south."

"What about Raven? Tony Perretti?"

"No record of his corpse turning up. His parents filed a missing persons report Boxing Day, 1970. They hadn't heard from him in three months. They didn't worry at first. He was nineteen and enjoying himself, but when he didn't call for Christmas, they knew something was wrong. He'd told them about the commune and the Horsemen asked questions but no one could say where he'd gone."

"All the ones who knew were dispersed."

"Tell me about him."

"About all I remember is his death."

"How long was he there?"

"I don't remember. There were a lot of people. They came. They went. It was a long time ago and I was only a kid."

"He wasn't a regular member?"

"No. Probably that summer. Like I said, mostly I only remember his death."

"What about his possessions? Were they left there? Or were they removed?"

Mike had to think about that. The waitress came around with the coffee pot. She filled a cup for him and topped up Essery's.

"He wasn't in the main house. I think he shared one of the smaller cabins. No, I don't remember. Maybe Rainie knows something. She said when they put the body in back of the truck it was wrapped in a tarp. They covered it with a blanket and other stuff. Maybe it was *his* other stuff. Are you going to take her statement soon? She wanted me to ask you."

"Not at the West Coast Inn. They know me. I investigated an Assault With there two months ago."

"Any connection to Duffy Dell?"

"None. This is an on-going investigation. I'm not your personal and private detective. There's a limit to what you'll get from me. Find another place and move out tonight. Understand? You hearing me?"

"I hear and I obey."

"Tonight."

"Yes, tonight. I hear you."

EIGHTEEN

Rainie found herself getting bored. She was accustomed to filling her days with work, clients, deliveries and chatting about school with Keri. Here she had nothing to do. The view was wonderful but she could only stare out the window for so long.

She decided to spend some time with Marion's pictures, and settled on the couch with the green velvet box on the coffee table. She thought about Marion having the courage to take her own life. Rainie had contemplated suicide, but was too chicken to carry through. And with her luck she'd probably botch it and wind up crippled or brain damaged.

She was interested in Barbara's wedding album. It was a large, expensive album with padded brocade covers. She'd had a large, expensive wedding. Rainie and Leo had a small one. She had no family. His people weren't wealthy. His parents took the bus down from Kamloops, with flowers from their garden packed in a camping cooler. His sister was living in Whitehorse at the time; she got a ride down with friends. His aunt and uncle and their kids took the ferry from Vancouver Island. They brought the wedding cake, fresh veggies and smoked salmon. They invited a few friends. It was a civil ceremony. Leo wore a new grey suit. Rainie sewed a pretty but simple white cotton dress. His father took the pictures. They went back to the apartment, ate salads, fish, Rainie's homemade bread and the wedding cake. They played tapes, danced, drank too much wine and had a great time. It was a wonderful wedding. She turned the thick, gilt-edged pages of Barbara's album and wondered if she'd ever stop dwelling in the past.

She found a small, yellow folder stuck in the page where the bride and groom were being showered with rose petals as they left the church. Printed on the cover in purple, *Snapack* and a shooting star. Inside a black and white photo, older style, with deckle edges, glued sideways. As she turned it around, several attached, fan-folded pictures dropped down. No people or animals. Just trees, bush, the ocean, a log cabin, interior shots of the single, large room. There were oil lamps and rustic, hand-hewn furniture covered by blankets. A wood heater, a Coleman stove on a long wooden counter, a burlap sack of potatoes on the floor.

She showed Mike the small, yellow folder when he came back and asked if he knew anything about it. He'd never seen it before. He'd bought some French pastries from a bakery downtown and went to the kitchen to put the kettle on for tea.

The pastries were rich and he put rum in the tea, more than enough for a healthy glow. He was being extra nice and she started to wonder if he had *plans* for the two of them. Until he told her they'd have to move again.

Rainie wished he'd told her before she'd eaten the pastries. She felt like losing them. She hoped that once he'd helped her out of her building it would all be okay, but it wasn't. She felt just as scared, sweaty and shaky as last time.

He made two trips. The first with their stuff, the second with her. He gripped her arm and marched her into the elevator, singing *On the Road Again*, calling it their theme song. He got her to sing too. Her voice came out thin and wobbly. They had to change elevators at the lobby floor. She was okay once they were belted into the truck seats.

It was dark when they drove up to the street. The new hotel was on the other side of town. He took Hastings. It must've been years since she was on that street. Hadn't changed much. He turned the radio on. A rap song was playing. He tapped out the rhythm on the steering wheel. She didn't like that kind of music but she didn't say anything.

The Royal Arms wasn't as new or as nice as the first hotel. For a view it had the roofs of houses and elevated Skytrain tracks. No microwave, no electric coffee maker. Aluminum percolator, toaster and ordinary stove. Worn carpets, mended bed spreads, TV chained to a shelf high on the wall. At least it was clean.

She unpacked, set up the pictures of Leo and her mother on the dresser and put her toothbrush and face cream in the washroom. All moved in. She wondered if she'd have to go through this often.

NINETEEN

Mike didn't go to the gym the next morning, he hung with Rainie, getting her settled in. She seemed okay but he hated to see the look of fear in her eyes and wanted to be sure.

He thought he should talk to Wendy, Kevin's girlfriend. She could marry, have eighteen kids, but he'd still think of her as Kevin's girlfriend. She worked at her aunt's florist shop. He didn't know the name, but the room had a Yellow Pages. He sat down and started calling. Never realized there were so many florists. "May I speak to Wendy, please?" He stopped counting after twenty. He hit the jackpot at Val's Floral Design when Wendy answered herself. She suggested they have lunch at her place, a five minute drive from the shop.

He said he'd pick her up in half an hour but he took an extra ten minutes to run into a gift shop to look for a container for Kevin's ashes. He found a small lidded bowl of black lacquer with iridescent goldfish. Made in Vietnam.

One wall of Val's Floral Design had a cutesy look, with baskets, balloons and stuffed animals. The other wall was done in romantic Victorian with white lace and roses. Wendy came down the middle calling his name.

She looked older and healthier. Green eyes clear, not bloodshot. She still wore her engagement ring. She brought him back to the workroom to introduce Aunt Val. She had to be from the robust Finnish side of the family. Blonde hair fading into silver. Green eyes the twin to Wendy's. She shook his hand sadly and said it was a tragic loss.

They both wore red and white striped aprons. Wendy untied hers, hung it on a peg beside the workbench and said she was going for lunch.

She'd decorated her boxy living room with wood, masses of potted greenery, feminine touches from the Victorian side of the flower shop and Native Indian prints. She put the kettle on for tea and opened the refrigerator.

"I'm not really hungry, Wendy."

"Neither am I." She closed the fridge. "Detective Essery came to talk to me again." They sat at the table in the dining area. "He showed me pictures of Barbara Fleming. And two men. Asked if I'd ever seen them. Or if Kevin ever mentioned them."

"Leo Castle and Richard Nixon. Alias Snake. Did you?"

"No. Never heard of them. Do you know what it's about?"

"Yeah. I'm the one put him onto that." He explained about finding Marion, about her pictures.

The kettle boiled and she got up to make the tea, listening, shaking her head. "Are you sure it was suicide?"

"The pill bottles they found all had her name on them. They didn't have the toxicology report back yet, but it looked like she'd saved up all the leftovers in the different meds. And she'd returned some books to the library that day. Books on pharmaceuticals. Like she was figuring what combination to use. The cop told me she'd booked an appointment with a doctor for that day. Welfare Day when she'd have some money. Told him some story and came away with another prescription. Then she went to the liquor store and bought a bottle of vodka. The time was on the receipt."

"That's just awful. Her planning it like that."

"I'm not sure. Her note said she had a pleasant day. Maybe it was like going on holidays. Planning is half the fun."

She brought the teapot to the table and carried over cups and a carton of milk. "It's still sad."

"No denying that."

"Do you take honey with your tea?"

"If you have it."

"Yes." She went to the cupboard. "Kevin always insisted." She brought a jar of fireweed honey to the table and sat down. "The detective asked me about Duffy Dell, too. What does this have to do with the pictures you found?"

"One special picture. From Zem-Zem. Kevin and me. Duffy Dell and Barbara Fleming. A little girl named Rainbow. She calls herself Rainie now. There was a drive-by shooting last fall. Missed her but killed her husband."

"I think I saw that on the news."

He told her about Snake and Raven in the background of the picture. He described Raven's death.

She nodded, "That's what it was, then. Not only losing his mother. Or the foster homes. How old was he?"

"We both were twelve."

"And he held it in and didn't tell me? Didn't he trust me?"

"Please don't take it wrong. I know he loved you and trusted you. Trust wasn't the issue. I'm sure he would've told you eventually."

"After how long? Five years? Ten? For our twenty-fifth wedding anniversary?"

He couldn't handle it. He crossed the living room and looked through the glass doors at the balcony. Two white resin chairs, a small round table, young plants in terra cotta pots. "We were kids. We saw this horrendous event. We were threatened not to tell and we took it seriously."

She came up beside him and touched his shoulder. "I'm sorry."

"Don't be offended. It's not rational to an outsider but there's an internal logic. We've all carried around this massive secret. Rainie never told her husband either."

"Do you feel better now that you told?"

"No. I'm scared shitless." He pointed to a red and black native print on the wall. "Is that a design of the Raven?"

"Yes. He bought it at Christmas when we went to Port McNeil to see my parents. He bought all the prints here. He said I neglected my heritage. It's the only thing we ever argued about." She walked to the dining table and poured out the tea. "He wanted me to be more Indian. The way he said it sounded racist. I have a dual heritage; no matter how I live it'll be wrong to someone. It took a while but I finally understood. *He* wanted to be an Indian. He identified with an oppressed people. He wanted to belong. Did he ever write to you about that?"

"Yes he did, but he never said anything negative about you. He said you knew some of the old stories and he liked that. He loved meeting your family, talking to the elders."

"Do you think I could read his letters sometime?"

"Sure. When I get them back from Essery." He looked up at the print. "I've read a couple of stories about Raven tricking the other animals. Is there anything about Raven and Snake?"

"Not that I know of."

He shrugged, "Just a thought."

"Do you really think he would've told me?"

"Maybe after he worked his way through those books and tapes on healing. After he'd talked to me about it. Because we were in it together. But I'm surprised he didn't say anything about Barbara. I know he did see her again, at least once." He smiled sadly. "We called her Big Sister Dove back on the commune."

"Did you say Dove?" She leaned forward, green eyes glistening. "I answered the phone at his place once. It was a woman who called herself Dove. I listened to him talking. I was curious. A woman, you know? It was shortly after we met. He said something like, it hasn't arrived yet. I'll call you when it does. He told me she was an old friend who wanted a deal on a new stereo system. Should I tell the detective?"

"Yes. Try to remember as much as you can."

They drank a cup of tea each. Wendy looked at her watch and said she had to get back to work.

"One more thing." Mike went to the hallway and got the bag with the black lacquer bowl. "I've brought this. I was hoping I could get some of Kevin's ashes."

She stared at him. "*Some* of them? That's grotesque."

"Is it? My grandmother gave me some of my mother's."

"You did say it was a little weird in Calgary."

"Yeah." He looked down at the covered bowl. "I thought ..."

"And I glued the lid on. I was afraid I'd knock it over and spill it. I haven't even thought about what I'll do with the ashes. But I know I'm not going to crack it open and start spooning it out."

"Yeah. Well ... He put the bowl on the kitchen counter. "Guess you can put candy in it. Or something."

"You're really disappointed, aren't you? We could share it." She brought it out from the bedroom. It was white, about two feet high, in a vaguely Grecian shape. "Take the urn for a while. You can be keeper of the flame." He cradled his brother in his arms and said thanks.

TWENTY

Mike returned to the Royal Arms. He heard voices in the kitchen, walked closer, took it all in: Essery and another cop at the table, a video camera on a tripod; Rainie's face red and swollen with crying.

"Assholes." He went to his bedroom and placed Kevin beside his mother on the dresser. Rainie ran to him and buried her sobbing face. He held her tightly and glared at Essery.

Both cops did an embarrassed foot shuffle. Essery said they were taking her statement. Rainie wailed. Mike got her out to the living room. He made drinks for both of them. He held her hand. With the other she gulped her drink. She asked for more.

It took a good half hour before she calmed down. Essery introduced Detective Luke Madison. Mike nodded curtly. The cops sat in the kitchen and eavesdropped until she could continue. She'd gotten as far as relating the killing but hadn't told about the body being moved yet.

Mike said he understood how she felt. It got to him too, telling the secret. He told her crying was a good safety valve, released the pressure.

When she was ready they moved back to the kitchen. She wanted Mike to sit with her but Essery said it was better if he stayed in his room. They were video taping so she'd only have to tell it once.

Mike went into exile and closed the door, pissed off at Essery for springing the statement without warning. And when she was alone. He opened the window wide and leaned out. He thought about living in one of those houses with a lawn to mow and a family to support. Maybe like what his old buddy Gary was doing out near Nanaimo with his wife and twin boys. Didn't sound too bad. Maybe he could marry Kevin's girlfriend after a decent grieving time and settle down. A good carpenter could always find work.

He went to the dresser and put a hand on his mother and brother. Maybe it would help, having them near, having something substantial to touch, a focal point for meditation. It made their deaths more real.

It took a good half hour before Essery knocked on his door. Rainie looked a lot better now that it was over. She had a couple of cheese sandwiches stacked on a plate and was working on building a couple more. Madison sat at the table with a mug of coffee. He was telling her about his trip to Mexico. Mike had been there once but probably had a lower-life experience than the cop. Maybe not. Maybe Madison was a dope fiend when he went on holidays. Mike poured a coffee and helped himself to a sandwich. He smiled at her and sat down. He didn't bother with small talk. The kitchen was too crowded with all of them; Essery leaned in the doorway.

They wanted her to go to her room while Mike gave his statement. Essery asked her as nicely as he knew how. She said she'd read. She went to the washroom first. Once she'd closed her door Mike became the star.

He'd already told it twice, once to Essery, then to Wendy. But this was official - lights, camera, action: scarier in a deeper way. He wished he had Rainie there for support. He didn't cry but sweat soaked his tee shirt and his heart beat like he was fourteen and running so he wouldn't be caught and sent back to the foster home.

When it was over Essery said he did good. Madison packed up the equipment and took it downstairs. Essery lit a smoke and wanted to know when Mike was planning to see Duffy Dell.

He wasn't sure. Maybe the next day. He'd take the evening to think about it, put it all in perspective. Essery was definite, saying Mike shouldn't do anything or see anyone without letting him know first. He slapped him on the back, and said they'd already lost Kevin, didn't want to lose him too.

He said good-bye to Rainie before he left. She looked okay when she came out of her room. She asked him how it went. He grinned, "Let's hit the bottle."

They sprawled at opposite ends of the sofa, big brother, little sister, drinking rum, eating cheese sandwiches and talking it out. They'd *told*. They'd carried it around for most of their lives and now The Secret wasn't a secret any longer.

He wasn't sure what to say about the future. He didn't want her to panic, or cry again. Her mind only expanded as far as the four walls. Going outside was a major undertaking. His mind roamed the street, where weird and nasty little fuckers pulled knives over bottles of cheap wine. He'd looked behind the Big Doors, seen expensive collections of pornography and stashes of exotic drugs, gone to prison to protect their greed.

But Rainie wanted a crystal ball. She wanted to be prepared. "Not like with Leo, when he did things without telling me, and left me crying without even knowing why."

He took a chance and told her all the fears he'd held back before. She didn't panic or cry or go crazy. She listened calmly and discussed it intelligently. It felt good to share with her. She understood. And, no matter what his grandparents said, she was the only real family he had.

TWENTY-ONE

Mike only had three hours sleep but he felt fully recharged, ready to go. He hung around until seven, but couldn't wait for Rainie to wake up. He left a note that he'd call later. He went to the gym for a work-out, had breakfast at a greasy spoon, lingered over coffee and read the *National Inquirer* from cover to cover. When he was sure Essery would be in his office, he phoned and said he'd thought about it and felt ready to meet Duffy. He didn't get an argument, just a shitload of warnings.

Mike presented himself at the indisputably Big Doors of Double Dee Enterprises. The receptionist, a commanding matriarch in a wheelchair, only wanted to know if he had an appointment. He didn't. She was sorry but Mr. Dell did not see anyone without an appointment. He asked to use her phone to make an appointment. She was sorry, but that was against company policy.

He smiled and turned on the charm. A door opened at the side of the reception area and a private pig in a dark suit rumbled to the desk. "Is there a problem, Mrs. Rico?"

She explained, turning it into more of a problem than it actually was. He must've been a cop at one time because he had that *I'm right and you're an asshole* tone of voice down pat, growling, "You will have to leave the premises immediately. Sir."

Mike left. He took the speed-of-light elevator down to street level. It was one of the newer office towers with security cameras but no pay phones in the lobby. He walked two blocks before he found one. He thought about how to make an approach. Just being himself hadn't worked with the receptionist. He had an idea. He went in search of another phone, indoors, away from the traffic noise.

He walked over to The Bay on Granville Street, took the escalator up a few floors and found a quiet phone beside the washrooms. He asked for Duffy's office. When the secretary answered Mike said, "Hello. Dr. Minchuck for Mr. Dell. Thank you."

"He's not available at the moment. May I take a message?"

"This is a medical matter. I'm sure he'll want to speak to me personally."

"Oh. You can try him at home."

"Very good then. Thank you."

The entrance to Duffy Dell's condominium did not have Big Doors. It had one steel door, a security camera and an intercom. He picked up the handset. There were no buttons to press. He was told to state his business.

"Duffy Dell, please. Tell him Moonbeam's here. Friend of Dove."

The voice thanked him, told him to wait. Minutes passed. He remained under the steady gaze of the camera. He'd learned patience waiting in prison but he wasn't inside any more. He wondered how long he was expected to hang around. Maybe it was an endurance test. He imagined himself a tree, putting down roots, sprouting leaves. Autumn chill, leaves falling. He was up to winter, and an insulating blanket of snow when the door buzzed open.

He entered Check Point Two. A bare air lock, camera ten feet up the wall. The outer door clicked shut behind him. He waited again, but only briefly. The inner door swung open automatically and he entered the lobby.

Very tasteful: Leather seating, chrome and glass table and lamps; piped in classical music. Concierge behind an oak counter. Uniformed security guard ready and waiting. "Would you step this way, please?"

Another door, a short corridor, a room marked *security*, a second guard and a thorough search. Mike had it figured out by then. Duffy had paid five million dollars to live in jail.

Having been approved at Check Point Three, he was escorted to the penthouse elevator and allowed to enter alone. He admired the polished aluminium interior during the short ride. The door slid open and he stepped into an atrium of trees and shrubs, growing nicely under a glass roof. He followed a path of glazed, green tiles through the garden, to the double bronze mother of all Big Doors. One side opened as he approached.

The doorman was at least twice Mike's size. Friendly enough, he said *Hi* and said Duffy was up on the terrace. Mike followed him past a marble foyer, up a curving staircase, through a solarium, and, finally, out to the terrace.

Duffy sat forty feet away, at a round table, under a canvas awning. In the newspaper photos he looked half bald but Mike could see the rest of his hair was long, tied back in a ponytail. Broad shoulders, solid chest, white silk buccaneer shirt tucked into jeans, barefoot. The doorman remained beside the sunroom. Mike crossed the terrace.

Duffy nodded, "Dr. Minchuck, I presume?"

"Strictly holistic. It's Mike Minchuck."

"Or Moonbeam."

"Been a long time since I used that one."

"Can't say I'm surprised to see you. Since I offered the reward everything's been crawling out of the woodwork."

Mike smiled pleasantly. He settled into a chair and enjoyed the view. The penthouse was so high he could almost see over the tops of the mountains on Vancouver Island, all the way to Japan. "You've done well for yourself, Duffy."

"Made my first million before I was twenty-five. Last I heard of you, you were in the hoosegow."

"I was a good boy. Learned my lesson. They let me out on parole."

Duffy lifted his glass and swirled the ice cubes. "What will you have?"

"Whatever you're having. Thanks."

Duffy motioned to the doorman. When he left the terrace Mike leaned in, "Do you know about Kevin?"

"Kevin who?"

"Kevin Woods. My buddy Cedar, from the commune."

"What about him?"

"He was murdered the same day as Barbara."

Duffy turned away. He didn't say anything. He sat stiffly, staring towards the North Shore mountains. A delicate Filipino woman glided in with a tray, placed a two-litre bottle of Diet 7-Up, a bucket of ice and a glass on the table. Duffy said, "Thank you, Merlee," and she glided away wordlessly. The doorman had taken up his post beside the solarium again. Duffy called to him, "Lenny, you don't have to stand in the sun. Go inside." When they were alone Duffy asked for details.

"He was blown away in his kitchen. Set up to look like a drug rip off, but Kevin'd been out of dealing for years. I wasn't here when it happened I got into Vancouver, I heard about him, then saw the posters about Barbara. I went to the library and read the clippings. Supposed to be a serial killer? I read through the last couple of years and found another related murder. Leo Castle, the husband of little Rainbow. Remember her? They were walking out of their apartment building and a car drives by going bang, bang, bang down the street. Injures three people. Misses her. Kills him. That wasn't any random drive by. The car started at their end of the block. The shooter emptied the clip to make it look random."

Duffy pulled a gold cigarette case from his pocket, extracted a joint, lit up with a gold lighter. He passed it to Mike. "Hope it's good enough. It's my daytime buzz."

"Whatyado? Keep the night time stuff in platinum?"

"Lifestyles of the nouveau riche."

They shared the joint and wet their dry throats with diet pop on ice. The dope was a hell of a lot better than the shake he'd shared with Ralph back in Courtenay. The smoke, the penthouse high in the sky, made death seem very far away.

"Are you semi-retired? Sick? Playing hooky from work today?"

"None of the above. I have an office here. I'm taking a lunch break."

A seagull flew past the terrace, almost close enough to touch. "I haven't told you about Barbara's mother yet."

He turned in surprise. "Was she killed too?"

"Suicide. I went out to see her in Courtenay. Got there a day too late. I still can't think about it without hurting. She was on welfare, living in a tiny rat trap trailer, her phone disconnected for no-payment, and her hydro cut off. Why didn't Barbara look after her?"

"I don't know about Barbara. She was funny about her mother. But why didn't Marion ask me? She was never shy about it before. She wrote to me before Christmas that she was broke and I sent her a thousand. Presents for the grandchildren and something for herself. But she wasn't in Courtenay, she was living in Nanaimo. I didn't hear from her after that."

"She moved in January. Downwardly mobile. Let the bills slide. Applied for welfare under her maiden name."

"What was she hiding from?"

"Thought you might know."

His face went grim and turned away. "I didn't hear anything."

"She only found out about Barbara when the cops came to interview her after the funeral. Her son-in-law didn't even try to find her. What did they have against her?"

"I went to see Barbara once when she was living with her father. They'd just returned from a year in Europe. He was teaching there. Zurich, I think. He'd bought one of those big old mansions in Shaughnessy and enrolled her for grade twelve in a private school. She was a completely different person. She didn't really want to see me. Just being polite. I only stayed about fifteen minutes, because it was so strained. When I knew her she was a sixteen-year-old flower child on a commune. A year and a half later, after Europe, she was sophisticated, worldly and arrogant. Hippies were passé. They went backwards while the world went ahead."

"Guess when her father left the commune, he brushed the dust off his feet and put on Gucci's."

"He definitely did a turn around, and turned Barbara against her mother. That's too bad. I always liked Happy."

"So did I. How'd it happen that Barbara worked for you?"

"We met again at a party about five years ago. Her husband was project manager on something a friend of mine was involved in. She'd matured enough to lose the arrogance. Her youngest child was a year old. She'd just gotten her broker's license and was ready to re-enter the work force. I suggested she come on board. From her point of view, I'd say, it was just a matter of networking. Because she knew the CEO from way back, she landed a slot in a good organization."

"And from your point of view?"

"Gave me great pleasure to know she was one of the little people, while I was head honcho. Seems childish, I know."

"Sounds like you still had residual feelings for her."

"No. I rarely saw her. Only when it was business related. She was wrapped up in that working mother bit, trying to be hundred percent perfect, a hundred percent of the time. Always looked tired because she was always on the run. I came into her office once and she was in a panic because she'd misplaced her day planner and was trying to remember her schedule for the rest of the week. The office manager had her appointments. She had day and evening showings. But that was only the half of it. She had a full plate outside of work. She kept muttering, it's Wednesday, that's groceries. She ferried the kids to and from lessons, sat on a couple of committees, did volunteer work and was taking some course."

"Did her husband set the same hectic pace?"

"Doubt it. He probably came home from work, put his feet up and waited for his appointment. Quality time comma Jim comma sex."

"But she didn't put *die* on her To-Do list. Barbara and Kevin. Leo Castle? Maybe Rainbow was the intended target. Only one way I know of that they'd be connected."

Duffy looked across the terrace to be certain Lenny wasn't listening in. "Why now?"

"I don't know. But I've come to warn you. If Snake's behind it, maybe he'll come after you too. Only other people would know are me and Rainbow's mother. And I've been out of circulation for three years. You know anything about the mother? Did she stay with him? I don't even remember her name."

"Lois Chase. He had her terrorized. Beat her up a few times. Took a year for her to get free. He thought he could trust her. Had her carry the money for a deal. Only out of his sight half an hour. Don't know if she planned to run. Maybe it was the realization that she was holding twenty k in cash."

"Where'd she go?"

"I don't know. Maybe back to California. What about Rainbow? You see her?"

"Can't find her."

"Where are you staying?"

"Nowhere. Everywhere. I use Kevin's answering machine for messages."

"Looking for work? I need a new set of bookshelves in my library. With glass doors. To protect the first editions."

"Don't be an asshole, Duffy. I don't need your money and I don't want you as my boss. No, Kevin was my brother. I have to see it through. Do you know where I can find Snake?"

"No. Wish I did."

"Know his real name?"

"Richard Nixon."

"No shit."

"Didn't like to be teased about it either."

"Can't say as I blame him." Mike paused. "Did you bury it?"

"No. Deep six."

"Ever hear of it washing up?"

"No. We weighed it down with rocks."

"Sounds like a gruesome scene."

"It was. But it's almost twenty years ago. Why kill the witnesses now? No one's talked. Extortion? I'm the one he'd go after and I haven't received any threats. Who else have you told?"

"No one. It's just between you and me. I've warned you. Seen your security. You'll be okay. I'll dig around. Maybe I'm wrong. Maybe Kevin really did start dealing again and it's like a one-in-a-billion coincidence with no connection to the past."

"What about the police?"

"You mean the Mounties who dragged me kicking and screaming from the commune? Or the Vancouver pigs who sent me up for three years?"

"What will you do if you find his killer?"

"Better for you not to ask." Mike stood up. He got an immediate head rush, almost lost his balance and grabbed the edge of the table, upsetting the pop.

Duffy righted the bottle and laughed, "Good shit, eh? You can talk and work, don't even think you're that stoned. A subtle high. Lasts for hours, too." He stood and stretched. "Yup. Needed something to smooth the edges the last few weeks. Been rough."

Mike walked to the railing and looked down at the toy size people and cars. Before vertigo attacked his brain he retreated to the table. "A word to the wise Duffy, you know? Take care."

"Thanks Dr. Moonbeam, for looking out for my health." He put his hands in his pockets and did a little terrace strut, "But you're the one needs to be careful. Out there all alone in the big, bad world. Is Kevin's number in the book?"

"Yes."

"I'll look it up if I hear anything." He led him to the sunroom. Lenny put down a copy of the *Financial Post* and got to his feet. "Show Dr. Moonbeam out, will you? And give him one of my cards. The number's unlisted, Doc. Don't spread it around."

When Mike got out to the street he couldn't remember where he parked his truck. Everything looked both familiar and strange at the same time. He crossed at the corner, made a left, walked down a couple of blocks and tried to orientate himself. Apartment buildings, rhododendrons, trees; one street looked like the next.

Duffy and his daytime smoke. He hated those rich guys. All alike. Take a guy like Ralph back there in Courtenay. Essery would call him a biker low life. Anything goes down within twenty miles, he'd be at his door in a flash. But he was cool. Righteous. Real kind to him after he found Marion. Gave him some shake to take away because he knew he'd need a buzz. That's the difference between him and a rich asshole like Duffy. Sitting on his billion dollar terrace with his gold cigarette case, rationing pin joints. He could afford to share. But no, nothing, nada.

Mike tried to think way back to when he was looking for a parking spot. He began to retrace his steps and remembered he hadn't crossed a street after he parked, he'd walked around the block. He felt a little optimistic until he noticed a man on the other side of the street, walking in his direction, watching him. It wasn't Lenny but he had the same size, style and intensity. The guy looked away quickly and continued walking.

Mike made it to the corner. He had to wait for a car to pass. He crossed. He turned down the block and, thankfully, saw his truck.

Paranoia took over. Should he get in and let the guy see what he drove and his license plate? Should he keep walking, find a bus, catch a cab? He didn't turn around but he could feel eyes heavy on the back of his head.

He approached the truck. Decision time. It was like it called to him, pulling the keys from his pocket, telling him it was safe, a haven, his haven, bought and paid for and - fuck you Duffy, you rich asshole.

He drove up to the corner and caught sight of the man again, nonchalantly tying the lace on his Nike. When he'd passed and looked in the rear view mirror, the man was out in the street, getting a good look at his license. So be it.

He drove across the Cambie Bridge and up the hill to the little house. He walked in and said, "Hiya, Bro," to Kevin's spirit floating in the air. He picked up the mail from the floor. He called Essery. Had to leave a message. Said he was safely out of the lion's den. He called Rainie. One good thing about agoraphobics, they were always in.

He thought he'd lie down for a few minutes. He'd been running around all day and hadn't slept much the night before. He didn't mind Kevin's bed. The futon felt pretty cozy. He curled up in the fetal position and closed his eyes.

TWENTY-TWO

Charlie had a new friend. She called her Nancy. It wasn't really her name but it sounded like it so she called her that. She was Chinese and came from Hong Kong. She was Charlie's age and had an older brother and sister like Charlie did. They moved into a big, giant new house on her block.

Charlie remembered when the old house was there. It was a lot smaller and it was torn down and the big one was built. Mommy sold the old house and made a lot of money but she didn't tell Nancy because she didn't know how to get her to understand. She didn't know English yet. Her mother and father knew English but she didn't tell them because she was shy.

She liked playing with Nancy. Her granny lived with her and took care of the kids when their parents were at work. She didn't know English either, but she was nice. She sang Chinese songs and made faces so Charlie would laugh. She gave them things to eat. The new house didn't have a nice yard, mostly just a place to sit, but Charlie had a swing set and big trees to climb and Nancy came to her house. She taught her to say different words. They played games like hippo and tumblers because they didn't have to talk. And because Nancy didn't know English she didn't ask questions about Mommy, and Charlie liked that.

Daddy said they had to clean out the extra room in the basement. He said Uncle Duffy found them a housekeeper and she'd live there. She was from the Philippines. He showed them on the globe. He said she knew English.

There were boxes and old clothes and all kinds of stuff in the basement room. At first Charlie felt like Christmas opening the boxes but then she found some of Mommy's things and felt sad.

Charlie started thinking about Nancy's granny living with her. She thought about her granny too. There was Daddy's mommy, but she couldn't come to live with them because she lived with Grandpa in a big house very, very far away. But she had another granny. Mommy's mommy. She didn't remember what she looked like but she always sent them nice stuff for Christmas and birthdays. Amy started sneezing from the dust in the basement room and couldn't help any more. Charlie asked her about Mommy's mommy. Amy said they saw her a long time ago when Charlie was a baby. She was nice. Amy and Billy said different things they remembered. She played with them and made a puppet theatre and stuff.

She went to Daddy and asked if Granny could come and live with them the way Nancy's did. He thought she meant his mommy but she said no, the other one. She could tell he didn't want to talk about her. Then he said Grandma was very, very sick. Amy asked if that was why she didn't come to the funeral and he said yes. Billy asked if she was going to die. Daddy said yes, very soon.

Charlie thought they should go to see her. Because after she was dead they couldn't any more. But Daddy said she was in a special hospital and they didn't allow children to visit.

Mike awoke from a nightmare of ringing telephones, of Rainie calling his name, of Essery giving him shit. He opened his eyes but couldn't figure out where he was. A blue wall? It wasn't his cell. It wasn't the hotel. He rolled over and understood. The clock-radio said a quarter to seven. He'd slept away the afternoon in Kevin's bed.

He went to the washroom, came out to the kitchen, saw the light blinking on the answering machine. He listened and discovered it wasn't a nightmare at all. He called and said Rainie should make a pot of coffee.

They were watching Much Music when he came in. Somehow that surprised him. He'd expect Essery to go for country music or show off how smart he was with *Jeopardy*. Mike poured a cup of coffee and sat in the wing chair.

Essery turned the sound down on the TV, "Where were you?"

"Asleep at Kevin's place. Duffy had some pot that knocked me out."

Rainie looked at Essery but he just smiled. "Did he confess?"

"No. You working the late shift now?"

"Pretty much around the clock on this one."

"Must be hard on your family."

"Yeah. But my wife understands. Ordinarily I don't tell her about my cases. This time I did. Because I'm starting to take it personal. I'm becoming obsessed."

"Why?"

"You probably don't realize this but the three of us came up together. I was new on the beat, you were new on the street. You were both smart kids, but the system failed you. I owe Kevin. Owe you too. Anyway," he waved his hand, "Before you tell me what Duffy said, what was your gut reaction? What sense did you have of the man?"

"Ultra cool. But not like hip, more like depressed and distant. He kept his face turned away most of the time. I couldn't see his eyes."

"Did that seem intentional?"

"Yes. As soon as I mentioned Kevin's name he told his bodyguard to go away. This was on the terrace of his penthouse. Said he works from an office at home. He didn't give me a tour but what I saw was like something from Architectural Digest. Claimed not to know about Kevin or Leo's deaths. I tell him, that's when he whips out this gold cigarette case filled with rolled joints. Seems he's been continually stoned since Barbara was killed."

"Out of guilt or grief?" Essery lit a cigarette and leaned forward.

"Grief certainly, but maybe both. He denied still caring for her, but I didn't believe it."

"What else didn't you believe?"

"He asked about motive. Why kill the witnesses now? Why would Snake come back after so long? I don't know…this is purely subjective …" He drank down his coffee and went to the kitchen for a refill.

From the kitchen doorway Mike said, "I had the feeling maybe he knew the motive but was asking me to see how much I knew. What confuses it is that we both know the secret about Raven. There was a lot left unsaid because it didn't have to be said. I did ask what they did with the body. He didn't hesitate in answering. Said they weighed it down with rocks and deep sixed it." He brought his coffee in and sat in the chair. "I asked about Rainie's mother." He smiled at her. "Lois Chase from California."

She looked startled and went pale. He came across the room, took her hand and kissed her forehead. He went back to his chair. "Stayed with Snake for a year. Didn't treat her right. Took off with twenty thousand in dope money."

"She did?"

"Yes. Maybe the good detective can check her out for you."

Essery nodded, "I'll do that."

Rainie folded her hands in her lap and turned her eyes toward the TV.

"And we were stoned so maybe I misread the signals. But he didn't seem surprised when I talked about Snake. I asked if he knew where he was and he said he wished he did. So I guess the gut feeling is that Duffy knows a lot more than he's letting on."

Essery brought out a notebook and led Mike through an exhaustive retelling of his conversation with Duffy Dell. When that was out of the way, Mike made a pan of scrambled eggs, Essery worked the toaster and Rainie asked how long it would take to find out about her mother. Essery's advice was to not even think about it.

TWENTY-THREE

Rainie read four science fiction novels and found them interesting but she still preferred historical romance. Out of desperation for a change of subject she looked through Kevin's other books on healing. One struck a responsive chord. It talked about affirmations of the positive. If she said she was stupid, or crazy or anything bad she had to say the exact opposite a hundred times. There was a part of the mind that listened to everything and if she said a negative she had to erase it until it absorbed the positive.

She said, in her head, *I am fearless*. She mouthed the words, then repeated them out loud. Mike wasn't there. He'd checked the messages on Kevin's machine and said he had to pick up Marion's ashes. The whole idea of keeping it in the house, along side his mother's and Kevin's ashes, was too icky for words. She repeated *I am fearless* but lost count. She started again, walking through the rooms, filling the loneliness, *IamfearlessIamfearlessIam*. When she got up to one hundred she felt she'd accomplished something.

Such a beautiful day outside. She felt a little jealous of Mike. He went out, came in, made no difference. It wasn't an *issue* the way it was for her. She was tired of it. Tired of being scared all the time. Tired of staying inside. Tired of the embarrassment, of being lead out like some senile old lady. She was only twenty-four. A twenty-four year old widow with no life.

IamfearlessIamfearlessIamfearlessIamfearlessIamfearless

The book had chapters on setting goals, long term and short term. It said to write them down. She used the lovely paper Marion had left. Special paper for her special goals.

I want to—be normal.

I want to—go and come, alone, unaided.

I want to—be happy.

I want to—she stopped. She knew what she wanted but she was afraid...

IamfearlessIamfearlessIamfearlessIamfearless
I want to—meet my mother again.
I want to—know who my father is.
I want to—meet my father.

That summed up her long term goals. She could write others down later. The book said goals weren't written in stone. They could change because life changed.

Short term goal. That was simple. Get the hell out. Next she was supposed to develop a plan to attain her goals. She sat with pen poised above the rice paper. Once she'd conquered her short term goal, the rest would fall into place. She looked at the door. She felt her heart speed up. The sweat started. She looked away. She put the pen down.

IamfearlessIamfearlessIamfearlessIamfearlessIamfearless.

What she thought she'd have to do was break it down into small bits. Win one step, then go on to the next. She didn't have to actually go out right away. She could just open the door and *look* out.

She needed to go to the washroom first. Then she was ready. Half of her was ready. The other half said hide under the covers. She reread her goals. The book said that was important. To keep them in mind. What if Detective Essery was able to locate her mother? She'd have to go out to meet her. Even talking on the phone, her mother would say, How are you Rainbow? And she'd have to say, *Just fine, only I can't leave the house.*

She held her goals in one hand and walked to the door, repeating her affirmation. She opened the door. She kept her hand on the knob. She looked out. Right. Left. Empty hallway. She closed the door.

She was shaky but she did it. She did it!

I am fearless!

She did it again.

And again.

She rewarded herself with the last of the rum and another trip to the washroom.

Mike drove to Kevin's house to check on the mail. There was a furniture store flier stuck halfway through the slot in the door and a pile of envelops that had made it all the way to the floor inside. He sorted them into junk and bills and found a third category, Detective Ferrier's card, with a note on the back for Mike to call.

Ferrier wanted to meet, offered to come to the house. Mike didn't want any cops meeting him at Kevin's. He suggested meeting on Wreck Beach, fairly close to the detachment. His suggestion was met with stern silence. He could've at least laughed; Essery would've. Wreck Beach was Vancouver's nude beach. They settled on fully clothed Spanish Banks.

Mike arrived first. He parked the truck and walked on the sand, listening to gentle waves lap against the shore. Two young mothers on a blanket kept eagle eyes on their pre-schoolers making mud pies at the water's edge. Three boys who should probably have been in school, fooled around with clumps of seaweed. An ancient man jogged slowly but determinedly down the beach. The water was still too cold for swimming but the sun warmed the air, making it comfortable for tee shirts and jeans. He parked his butt on a driftwood log within sight of his truck and waited.

He saw Ferrier before the cop saw him. Ferrier pulled off his tie and suit jacket and draped both carefully over the back of his car seat. He locked up and carried a briefcase down to the beach. Mike waved.

"Sorry it took so long," Ferrier said as he sat on the log, "Couple of last minute things I had to deal with. Beautiful day though, glad to get out of the office."

Mike smiled, nodded and agreed about the weather.

"Hope you've gotten yourself a good lawyer."

Mike braced for the worst. In his experience when cops started in with the L word it was usually followed by handcuffs.

"Mrs. Peppard's estate. Probate. Inheritance tax and so forth."

"You said the will wasn't legal."

"Might be there's an earlier will we haven't found yet. You were close to Mrs. Peppard. She would have remembered you."

"I have her memory box, that's all I need. Or do you think a box of photographs is heavily taxed?"

"There's more than snapshots. You might now be the proud owner of an entire island." He balanced the briefcase on his lap and took out a photocopy of a marine chart. "This is the best I could find. Too small to show up on most maps. Sea Spray Island. Approximately two miles long and one mile wide." He pointed with the tip of his pen. "About sixty miles west of Vancouver in the Strait of Georgia. Between Texada and Lasquesti Islands. Surrounded by even smaller islands."

"She never said anything about an island. Why didn't she live on it? Or sell it?"

"Good question. Her address as given is a by-the-month accommodation company on Broadway. Sea Spray was bought twelve years ago. For a million and a half. Taxes paid yearly."

"Who had it before?"

"An off-shore company. Abacus Holdings."

"Never heard of it. What does off-shore mean?"

"In this case it means registered in the Cayman Islands and forget tracing the principals."

"She was a front?"

"That's a good guess. Those lottery winnings she told you about? Bought you a truck and tools? Put the down payment on her daughter's first house? The lottery commission has no record of it."

Mike exhaled sharply, "Damn," and shook his head. "Who was she fronting for? Who paid her?"

"You have any ideas?"

He immediately thought of Duffy Dell but said no. "You saw the piece of shit she was living in. No hydro. No telephone. She killed herself because she thought it was the only option left. And all along there's someone playing big bucks with her name?"

"Angry?"

"Damn right, I'm angry."

"It's just luck you were the one to find her."

"Bad luck. Got there a day too late."

"Feel guilty?"

"Yeah."

"I can understand that. You cared about her. You'd known her since you were a kid. And you got there one day too late. Now you have a responsibility."

The two young mothers on the blanket called their children, waving tetra-packs of juice and small containers of yoghurt. The kids ran to them laughing, all arms and legs, shovels and pails.

"What do you want?" Mike asked.

"Barbara Fleming's killer. He is also indirectly responsible for Mrs. Peppard's death."

"What you're leading up to, is me going out there. Nosing around. See who and what turns up. You must really consider me disposable. I'm sure it hasn't escaped your notice that all those islands are prime growing territory. Warm and sheltered. The pot capital of Canada."

"Just what you always wanted, isn't it Moonbeam? Your own marijuana plantation?"

"Not one the Mounties know about." Mike smiled thinly as Ferrier laughed.

"We haven't found any indication of cultivation." He took a set of aerial photographs from his briefcase. "It's a unique spot. Protected, shallow anchorages. Fresh water. All the trees you would ever want to hug. There's a solid looking dock." He pointed, "And a boathouse. Above," he shifted a blow-up to the top of the pile, "is a sizable dwelling with a wrap around deck and solar panels on the roof. Three smaller dwellings, also with solar panels. Uphill, a wind turbine to generate power. A garden area planted with early vegetables. And a greenhouse too." He pulled out an even more detailed blow up. "Tomatoes, lettuce, salad foods and other plants just about ready to set out in the garden take up the whole interior. There's a fruit orchard. And other plantings, artichokes, kiwi and some vegetation no one could identify. There might be some cannabis camouflaged here and there, but none we could see, and not in any quantity." He pulled out two other pictures, "The remainder of the island appears to be in its natural state. According to the locals it's a fishing lodge, but whoever lives there full time keeps to themselves. There's frequent helicopter landings. Weekly. More often in the summer. We've checked the charter companies but came up empty."

Mike took the pictures on his lap. A lavish version of the Zem-Zem farm. He felt sick for Marion. There was something wrong in the pictures He couldn't put a finger on, something missing. "No people," he said when he understood, "Maybe they hid when they heard the chopper. Because there's a lot of work there, looking after the greenhouse and gardens. Too much for one person."

"Aren't you curious about who is using your island?"

"It's not my island. It goes to her grandchildren. And you're the one who's curious. Drop in and look around. Send a couple guys in undercover. Use a confiscated smuggler's boat. Out fishing for the day, thought they'd do some exploring."

"I'd really like to. But right now we don't have the manpower. You could do that. Rent a boat. Go exploring. Have a look around. Tell me who's there. I can pay your expenses. Give you some walking around money. Keep your P.O. off your back."

"I'm not saying yes. But I know I don't want your money." He shook his head, "This sounds like a really stupid idea."

"Think about it. And the money will be there if you do decide to accept it."

"Yeah, *money*, that makes all the difference."

The young mothers packed up their kids and headed up to the parking lot. The hooky playing kids had disappeared. In the distance he could see the old jogger working his way back. Mike asked the question that had been bothering him. "Did Barbara die quickly? Or did she suffer?"

"Quickly. She was shot at close range."

"Was she raped?"

"I can't answer that one for you, Mike. Sorry."

Ferrier gave him an overview shot of the island before he left. Mike returned to his truck. He put his hand on the courier box containing the raku vase of Marion's ashes. He slid out again and went to the pay phone at the edge of the parking lot. He called Essery and reported the meeting. He suggested he check to see if Duffy or any of his companies owned a helicopter.

TWENTY-FOUR

Charlie had a bath and was in her jammies in bed looking at a picture book. She started thinking about the Mommy's mommy granny. She decided to write a letter and draw a picture and send it to her in the hospital. She got out her crayons and started the picture first. But then she remembered she didn't know her name and how could she send a letter without a name. So she went downstairs to find Daddy and ask him.

A policeman came. It was a new one. He had a picture of a man and asked Daddy if he knew him. He didn't. He showed Amy and Billy but they didn't know him either. Charlie wanted to see too, and she knew him!

The policeman made her sit down and tell him everything. It was a long time ago, last year or something. Mommy took Charlie to Stanley Park. Amy and Billy didn't go; they wanted to play with their friends and Daddy was out of town on business. Then she remembered it was fall because she played with bunches of leaves that fell down from the trees.

Mommy said his name was Cedar Wood. Charlie thought that was a funny name. He called her Flower Child. He talked to Mommy and they looked at the animals in the zoo and bought popcorn and fed the peacocks and geese.

When they went to the cars, Cedar Wood took a big box from the back of his van and put it in the trunk of Mommy's car. She said it was a stereo for her office.

The policeman wanted to know about the van. If she remembered the colour, and if it was new or old. She said it looked like Megan's mother's van. Daddy said a burgundy Caravan.

The policeman wrote down what she said but it didn't make her mad like Mrs. Carten at school. It made her feel important. Billy asked if that was the man who killed Mommy and the policeman said no, but if he knew more about him it might help. He asked Charlie if she met him again and she remembered the other time. It was Christmas and she remembered because Mommy took her Christmas shopping at a mall. Cedar Wood was there. They went to a restaurant. There was a toy store on the other side and Mommy said she could look there when they talked. She saw things for presents and stuff she wanted too, but when she came back they were still talking. Cedar Wood bought her an ice cream.

Daddy went to the den and came out with a paper and said it was Mommy's credit card bill and it had the dates and stores and he gave that to the policeman.

He was a nice policeman. He had a funny last name but he said she could call him Detective Ron. He asked her about school and what she liked on TV. Then he asked her about Cedar Wood again and what they talked about. She didn't remember. Boring stuff and she didn't listen. He said it was important even if she only remembered one tiny bit of what they said. She tried hard to think. He said what made it boring and she thought it was real estate stuff like she heard Mommy talking on the telephone. He asked if Mommy had any papers but she didn't have her briefcase because they were going Christmas shopping. He said did they talk about an island and he said Sea Spray Island. Charlie said it was a pretty name. She didn't remember it from the talking. She felt bad because she couldn't remember.

He asked Daddy about the island but he didn't know it either. Detective Ron said she should think very hard about the times she saw Cedar Wood and if she remembered anything at all she should call him. He show her his card when he gave it to Daddy and she felt very grown up. Then he talked to Daddy alone.

Rainie and Ron Essery were on first name basis now, but Mike had known him for so long it seemed unnatural to call him by anything but Essery. Rainie looked happier, more rosy in the cheeks and sparkling in the eyes. He had a frightening thought that maybe she had a crush on Essery, but she didn't seem to be paying him any special attention. In fact, she seemed more self-absorbed, following the conversation but almost smiling at a private joke.

The aerial photograph of Sea Spray Island lay on the coffee table. Rainie and Essery sat on the couch. Mike took the brown tweed wing chair that was quickly becoming his favourite. Essery had already told him that Double Dee Enterprises owned a chopper, as well as a Lear jet. "Rainie, you said Leo took you on a helicopter picnic. Do you remember the company?"

She shook her head. "I didn't notice."

Essery lit a cigarette. Mike worked a few things out and asked Rainie for the name of Leo's employer. She told him, "Coastal United." He closed his eyes for a moment. He went to his bedroom and brought out the list Constance had made for him. He handed it to Essery, pointing to Coastal United. "Think back. Did he start the job before or after you heard from Marion?"

"After." Her eyes widened. "But how? I never told him about Duffy."

Essery was already writing it down. "Do you remember the date he started?"

"In February. I have the exact date at home. I don't understand this."

"Possibly he called Marion," Essery said, "Without telling you. She still had her telephone back then. Got a few names."

"When I was talking to Duffy," Mike said, "he offered me work. Maybe that's his style. You thought Leo might've gone looking for your mother. Maybe he asked Duffy."

Her face began to flush. "That thing about Kevin putting a stereo in Barbara's trunk? Leo bought a new one too. He said he got a good deal. It was during that same winter."

"Did you keep the receipt?" Essery asked, "Would you still have it?"

"I don't remember seeing it. But he kept all of those things, for the TV and the computer, kept it all in a box on the bedroom closet shelf. That's still there." She paused. "Do you want me to go back and get it?"

"I can do that for you. With your permission. Just give me the keys."

"Oh yes, thank you." She went for her purse, "And when you're there you can look through his other things. Now that you know more."

Mike looked at Essery. "They all knew each other."

"Take it slower, Mike. We don't have proof yet that Duffy hired Leo personally. Or that Leo bought the stereo from Kevin. But we do know Kevin and Barbara met three times last year. His, 'Guess who I met again' letter is dated June eighteenth. And twice more when she took her youngest daughter along. In Stanley Park. My estimate is late October. And at Metrotown Mall on December eleventh."

"What about this year?"

"I don't know. The Horsemen have her agenda book for this year."

Rainie returned with her key ring. "What about Kevin and Duffy? Did they ever meet?"

"No proof yet. I never saw an agenda."

"He kept one. I gave him my Filofax when I went to the pen."

"A thief with a Filofax!" Essery slapped his knee, laughing hard.

"It was a Christmas gift from my girlfriend."

"Maybe you could do an endorsement. In *my* busy schedule, day *and* night..."

Neither Rainie nor Mike shared his amusement. When he quit laughing Mike finished what he was saying. "He found it worked well for him. At the end of the year he wrote and asked where he could get a refill. Even this past year. He mentioned in a letter that he found a refill that fit the rings but was much cheaper."

Essery was serious again, writing on the yellow pad, "I never found it. Not in his home or in the store."

"Then the killer took it."

"Do you know if he saved back years?"

"He never mentioned it."

"Give me a description."

"Brown leather. My initials were engraved on the cover on a small brass plate. It had a phone index and dividers."

"Initials, M.M.?"

"Triple M. My middle name is Mathew."

"You still don't have a motive," Rainie said from her corner of the couch.

"No," Mike shook his head, "But when I was talking to Duffy he brought up the subject of extortion. Said he hadn't received any threats."

Essery stubbed out the cigarette that had burned down to the filter and lit a fresh one. "Maybe he brought it up because it was on his mind. Denied it out of guilt. When you interview a suspect you want him to talk. The more he talks the more he says."

"You think my Leo was a blackmailer?"

Mike came over and sat on the arm of the couch. He took her

hand, speaking gently; he didn't want to scare her. "We don't know anything for certain, Rainie. But you should prepare yourself, in case. It won't change what Leo was to you. What you were to each other."

"How nice." She pulled her hand away and reached for her coffee.

Mike was surprised she didn't want comfort. He went back to his chair.

Essery read the list of Duffy's holdings, "I don't see the store Kevin managed."

"No. Quality Systems is a chain with the head office in Toronto. And he got the job two years ago. Before Marion's classified about Zem-Zem. Now, what about Sea Spray Island? Ferrier is hot over me going to take a look. Seems to me that's police business, but he had all those excuses."

"It's true enough about being short handed. We are. There's a G-7 conference next week. And Prince Philip is coming to town for a speech. Everyone who can be spared goes on security detail. He wants a recon before he invests time and money."

"Sounds like sticking your hand in a deep, dark hole and hoping you don't get bit."

Rainie studied the photograph, "There are a lot of tiny islands and stuff on the way in. Do you know boating well enough to navigate through?"

"Maybe. I'd have to get the chart. It details the hazards."

"I've never been to Sea Spray," Essery said, "But I've fished in the area. Spectacular scenery. Eagles, seals, all that good stuff. And those little islands get hit by the winter storms. Carved the most unbelievable patterns and shapes on the rocks."

"Wait a minute. Mike, remember I showed you that little yellow folder that said *Snapack*? With the black and white pictures inside?"

"You think that's Sea Spray? Where's the folder?"

"I put it back where I found it. In Barbara's wedding album."

Mike brought it out and looked at the pictures again. "Could be. But, could be almost anywhere on the coast." He handed it to Essery. "You've been in the area."

The photos were small. Essery needed his glasses. Pushing them to the tip of his nose he compared one picture looking out to the water with the aerial shot. "Bet it is. Yeah, I'll bet it is." He laid them out on the coffee table. "Hard to see but I think in the distance there's those rock islets with dome shaped tops." He pointed to the aerial photo.

Mike leaned over the table and nodded. He lit one of Essery's cigarettes and went back to his chair. "In Marion's notes she said *all my worldly goods and chattels*. I thought she was being, you know, formal. But she meant it. About chattels." He took a couple of drags and put out the smoke. "But I don't know what it has to do with any of the deaths."

Essery folded his glasses and put them on top of the *Snapack*. "You won't like this, Mike. But I think it's time to share information."

"With the Mounties?"

"Yeah."

"Knew you'd have to eventually. Maybe you can work it as a joint investigation."

"That's a possibility."

"Because I'll only talk to you."

"Mike," Rainie asked, "You didn't tell that other detective you're talking to Ron?"

"No. I'm a *confidential* informant. Don't want it getting around I'm a snitch."

"But he's a policeman too."

Mike turned away shaking his head. "Essery can deal with him. I won't. I don't care if he names his snitch or if Ferrier figures it out. But from now on I won't even return his calls."

"I'll do my best, Mike." Essery said, folding his glasses and returning them to his jacket pocket. "One more thing. Remind me. Did you tell Duffy Dell about Marion's suicide note?"

"No. Just that I found her."

TWENTY-FIVE

Charlie thought about Cedar Wood and Mommy when she went to bed and when she woke up. She thought about them all the time at school. She didn't do her work. She looked out the window and thought. Ms. Lundel didn't say anything. If Charlie wasn't cheeky and behaved, it was okay.

At recess she went outside, but didn't play. It wasn't fun, it was boring. She had important things to think about. She came back in and sat at her desk. She was all alone in the classroom and she liked that. It was quiet. She took Detective Ron's card from her pencil case and looked at it and felt bad because she couldn't remember what Mommy said to Cedar Wood. She started to cry.

Ms. Lundel came in and sat on her desk and patted her head and said it was okay, but it wasn't. Charlie was just a stupid baby who didn't listen when the grown ups talked, and now they'd never find Mommy's killer and it was all her fault.

The next morning Mike felt like going swimming, must've been all the talk of water. Rainie suggested the Aquatic Centre on Sunset Beach. That's where she and Leo used to go.

Rainie felt uncomfortable doing aerobics when he was around. As soon as he left she turned on the TV but it was the wrong time for her show. She switched to Much Music and did twenty minutes of sweaty dancing with the videos.

After her shower she called her answering machine. She had two messages from clients. She wasn't doing right by them. She'd made a commitment and they were understandably anxious over what was happening. She got out her list of goals and wrote down a medium term one. To go to her apartment and get her work and the computer.

The day before she'd gone all the way out to the hall. She walked up and down, leaving the door wide open. Her goals of the day were, first, to go out and close the door. Second, to walk to the elevator.

In preparation she read another chapter in her self-help book. She realized *self-help* was exactly right. She felt good doing this on her own.

When she was ready she went to the door. This was easy now, she'd conquered it the day before. She held her key in her hand. She went out to the empty hallway. She closed the door behind her. She walked in one direction, wheeled around and walked back. To get to the elevator she'd have to turn a corner and walk down another hallway. She didn't go that far. She returned to her door and opened it. She went inside. She was sweating, her heart beat quickly, but she'd done it and was glad.

She practiced it a couple more times. The second time she heard a door opening down the hall. Without thinking she rushed back to her apartment and hurried inside. She counted that as a setback. She put her ear to the door and listened until the footsteps disappeared.

She needed the washroom before she could try again. She did it six times in all. On the last practice she went to the corner of the hallway and peeked around. It looked just like the other hallway. She couldn't see the elevator itself because it was set into the wall: halfway down, she remembered. But she didn't feel ready.

Mike enjoyed his swim but hated the chlorine. He showered it off and dressed in street clothes. The weather was changing, cooler and cloudy, looked like rain. His hair was still damp and he felt a chill as a wind blew in off the water.

He drove to the post office, bought stamps and mailed off Kevin's telephone and hydro payments. That made him think of Marion again. He needed a drink. He couldn't park in front of the post office for very long. He found a pay lot a couple of blocks away and left the truck there.

He felt the first few drops of wind-blown rain and put his collar up, buttoned his jean jacket halfway and stuck his hands in his pockets. He stopped in a pub for a pint of pain killer.

One pint wouldn't be enough, he knew that. But he sipped it slowly and watched the people. Old men, pensioners, shuffling in to join their friends and pass the time. Native Indians, young and old. He thought of conversations he'd had with a couple of guys inside, activists put away on trumped up charges. They called themselves *niggers of the north* and put the oppression of the First Nations into historical perspective. He'd never find them in a sleaze hole like this. He'd never find Wendy here either. Maybe he'd talk to her about it sometime. He drained his glass and went out in search of a decent place where he wouldn't have to think.

Wrong part of town. The welfare poor, the panhandlers, dealers and rip-offs, nibbling away at the edges of renovated Gastown with the touristy restaurants and gift shops. Brought to mind the Gastown riots.

He'd just recently been moved to his second foster home when Kevin saw the posters announcing the rally. They thought they might see their mothers and give them their phone numbers.

He didn't remember the point of the demonstration. What he remembered was the cops going into a brutal frenzy. He saw a cop on horseback drive two hippies into a doorway, pinning them, beating them with his club.

They never did find their mothers. There was too much screaming, bottle throwing and hysteria. They ran away. The next day his foster parents saw it on the news and talked about the drug crazed hippies: *take-a-bath, cut-your-hair, get-a-job*. And they talked about the noble police who only did what was necessary. They didn't know he was there; he saw. He wondered what Essery was doing then. Probably right in there, swinging his club with the rest of them.

He asked him about it that night. Essery returned Rainie's keys and said she could rest easy. The stereo wasn't hot.

"No one said it was hot." She shook her head, "The question was, did he buy it from Kevin?"

"Yes, he did."

She looked stricken. That's when Mike changed the subject and asked about the Gastown Riots.

"Yeah. I was there. Got hit in the shoulder with a flying bottle."

"What a shame."

"I know it must break your heart. What made you think of that?"

"I was walking in Gastown today."

Rainie asked what they were talking about. Essery gave her his version. "There was a mass gathering of about two thousand in

Maple Tree Square. Against the drug laws, because we'd had an undercover operation and made a lot of arrests. The crowd turned ugly. There were some Yippie agitators there, provoking violence. They wanted a confrontation, and we gave it to them."

"With horses," Mike said, "And clubs."

"You were there?"

"Yeah."

"Get hurt?"

"No."

"We got into quite a bit of shit over that. We're better prepared for crowd control now."

"Live and learn."

"Don't hate me, Mike. I was just a young piglet then. I'm older and wiser now."

"I can see you're older."

"But the wiser part I have to prove?" He laughed. "I have something else. Rainie, did you ever speak to Marion on the phone?"

"No."

"There was a sixty-three minute call made from your home to her number. Shortly after you received her letter. That's when she was still living in Nanaimo."

"Leo must've called her, but he never told me."

"You're a bookkeeper, didn't you do your own household accounts? Didn't you check over bills that came in? Check for errors?"

"Yes. But he has an aunt in Nanaimo. Had an aunt. I probably just saw the name of the town and didn't verify the phone number. He didn't tell me." She looked at Mike, "Why didn't he tell me?"

Mike didn't know. He shrugged his shoulders and shook his head. "But we aren't just jumping to conclusions now. This establishes a link. From her he would've heard about Kevin, Barbara and Duffy."

"Are you sure Marion didn't know about Raven and Snake?"

"No, I can't be sure. I only know that you and I didn't tell her."

"But maybe Barbara did?"

"Maybe. But knowing Marion, she would've asked me about it and she never did. They weren't close. Marion had her facade of living well. And Barbara, I don't know what was in her head. For her to tell her mother this major trauma would require a real heart-to-heart talk. Far as I can see, they never had one."

"I went out to the Coastal United warehouse today," Essery said. "Talked to Leo's co-workers again. Well liked, but they didn't know much about him. Just that he was married. He didn't talk about his criminology courses, or applying to the RCMP. They didn't think there was anything special in how he was hired. There was an opening, he was experienced, been working someplace else. He said Coastal United paid better. Then I reread Leo's personnel file. There's a notation. R-E-F H-0. Referred from Head Office."

"Mike?" Rainie's voice quavered. "Didn't you buy some wine today?"

"Yeah, I'll get it." He stood up and headed for the fridge. "And I bought a six-pack of buzzless brew for Essery. Point five alcohol content for the wagoneer."

"Thanks, Moonbeam. You'll make a fine host when you grow up." Essery leaned towards Rainie. "We're getting closer, piece by piece," he said softly, "There'll be an end to it. I promise you."

TWENTY-SIX

Rainie waited anxiously for Mike to leave so she could practice walking to the elevator. She hadn't told him about it yet. It seemed easier to keep it to herself, plug away at her own pace and not talk about it. But it was Sunday and he seemed content to lounge around and watch sports on TV.

He hadn't shaved. His curly hair could do with a trim. Even the stupid dimple in his chin was beginning to bother her. She didn't want a roommate. What was he supposed to be, her bodyguard? She'd done just fine on her own.

The day dragged on. She went to her room and closed the door. She looked through the healing books again. She started another science fiction novel. When she came out to make a late lunch he was still playing couch potato. Chair potato. He'd staked out the only living room chair as his own territory, watching drag racing.

He'd made coffee; the percolator was still hot. At least he was good for something. She made a cheese sandwich and brought it back to her room. When she came out to use the washroom he was still there, eyes straight ahead at the tube. His whiskers looked fuzzier. He'd turned the station from the drag racing to a home renovation show.

She felt bloated and tense with a dull ache in her belly. She knew what that meant. She didn't have to check the calendar. And how was she going to get napkins? Ask *him* to bring them back? The grocery that made deliveries for her was over in the West End near her apartment. And she was on the other side of town.

She didn't know where she was. Not the address or the exact location of the hotel. They took Hastings. Burnaby, wasn't it? There wasn't any hotel stationery in the room. It wasn't that kind of place. She should know where she was. She could ask the clerk, ask for the mailing address with the postal code, so she wouldn't sound like a complete dummy. If Mike ever left.

It wasn't until five o'clock that he put on his jean jacket and said he was going out. He'd pick up some take-out on the way back.

As soon as he closed the door she began repeating her affirmations. She no longer felt apprehensive about going out to the hall. She felt excited, looking forward to her next victory.

She picked up her keys and walked out. She didn't even feel the need to go to the washroom first. Down the hall, around the corner and right up to the elevator. She touched it, like touching first base, turned around and walked back. Nothing to it.

The next time she not only touched the elevator but pressed the down button. She waited. It was the most natural thing in the world to wait for an elevator. The doors opened and she entered. She pressed the lobby button. The doors closed. She felt uneasy but not panicked; she could deal with it. The doors slid open. She could see the entrance and the counter. The clerk wasn't there. She was glad no one would see her. The doors closed automatically and she rode back up to her floor.

She went to her bedroom and reread her goals. Meeting her father was a well defined goal, but it might never happen and she would need napkins in a day or two. Reality.

She'd either have to go out and get them herself or ask *him*. She didn't know if he'd be embarrassed to buy them, but she'd definitely be embarrassed to ask. There were shops on the same block as the hotel; she remembered from when they came in. Fear or embarrassment, she'd have to decide which was stronger.

She thought of an intermediate step she could try before going out on her own. The laundry room on the lobby floor. She could run a load through. She'd been doing her wash by hand ever since Leo was killed and she'd been wondering about it too because she was running out of underwear. She didn't want to drape the bathroom with them. And she'd certainly need fresh ones soon. She gathered her dirty clothes into a pillow case, took her wallet, and went out to the elevator.

The clerk sat at the counter when she came out. He looked up and smiled. She smiled back. She followed the signs to the laundry room. It had a creepy and lonely feel, no windows, harsh fluorescent tubes hung from the ceiling. Clothes tumbled in one drier. She repeated her affirmations as she counted out the change for the washer and a box of detergent from the dispenser.

She gave it half an hour, came back down to switch the clothes to the drier. It surprised her that she felt okay. The other drier had stopped but the clothes were still there. On the way out she passed an old man coming for his laundry. He said they were in for a real storm that night. Rainie hadn't noticed. She should start. Her world was opening up again and she'd need to know what to wear.

TWENTY-SEVEN

The storm howled all night and all the next day. Mountain creeks, already swollen by the spring thaw, washed out roads, carving new channels to salt water. Fallen trees pulled down power lines, smashed parked cars and blocked city streets. Wind-driven plastic bags, disposable diapers and junk food wrappers caught on fences and bushes.

With the power out, Rainie stayed in her room with the door closed. Mike sat in the kitchen with a box of Stoned Wheat Thins and a block of cheese, reading Kevin's new age magazines.

When he got bored he went to his bedroom to rearrange his family grouping. He had the three containers on the dresser. Kevin's white, vaguely Grecian, the tallest. Marion's beautiful raku vase shorter but wider. His mother's blue mason jar smallest of all. He put one on each side and his mother in the middle. He switched them around. He clustered them together. From a strictly decorative point of view they just didn't match. Marion's, the only one he'd chosen himself, definitely stood out. Maybe if he put something underneath, a nice piece of fabric, an Indian print or a tapestry. Or he could build a box to tote them around in. A *cedar* box, and carve the top and sides to represent their lives.

In the afternoon, when the power came back on, he made coffee and heated some canned soup. Rainie came out and they watched a couple of talk shows, but only after she checked the *TV Guide* to be sure the subject matter wouldn't offend her delicate sensibilities.

She faded into her room while he watched the six o'clock news but came out for *Wheel of Fortune* and *Jeopardy*. He wanted to watch *Cops* but she wouldn't go for it and they sat through a couple of mindless sit-coms instead. During every commercial he went to the window to check on the storm.

The wind died down during the eleven o'clock news, leaving

the rain to bucket straight down. Mike wondered how Kevin's little house had held up and decided to drive over for a look. He knocked on her door, she was still awake, and told her where he was going.

He drove slowly through a slick maze of branches and garbage, plugged storm sewers and rushes of water glistening with a light sheen of oil.

Tree limbs as thick as his arm blocked the lane fronting Kevin's house. He ran through the downpour and unlocked the door. It was like walking into a refrigerator. Flashing electronic lights from each room cut the darkness. Power had gone out and been restored there also. He switched on the overheads and picked up the mail from the floor. Rain drummed on the roof. He turned on the kitchen baseboard heater.

He couldn't believe the bedroom. A limb had smashed through the window, its sodden tip balanced on the foot of the bed. Shards of glass everywhere, even on the clock-radio on the night table in the farthest corner. Books, carpet, furniture, bedding, the whole kit and caboodle soaking wet. He tried to lift and push the limb out but it was at an angle and wouldn't budge. He had to go back into the rain to pull it clear.

The landlady's house was dark, no car parked in the lane. He didn't see anything lying around he could use to board the window up. He went back in, shivering and dripping from head to foot. He found a pack of garbage bags in the kitchen but had to go out to his truck for a hammer and nails. He tacked up several as a temporary measure.

He decided to have a hot shower and change into dry clothes before starting on the major clean up. He felt better afterwards. It didn't bother him that he wore Kevin's clothes and Kevin's gum boots. The tree limb he'd pulled outside was from a cedar tree and it all seemed to fit in a cosmic sense.

He cleaned off the furniture, stripped the bed, picked up the larger pieces of glass, bark and cedar needles. In the morning he could rent an industrial vac and do the rug. He reset the clock-radio, answering machine, TV, stereo and microwave. He pulled Kevin's toque over his ears. On the way back to his truck he dragged the tree limbs off to the side of the lane.

The rain continued all night. By morning the wind returned. Not as strong as the day before, but certainly not a day for boating to Sea Spray Island. He rented the vacuum and drove back to

Kevin's. The garbage bags had blown in. He rang the landlady's bell to tell her about the window but she still wasn't home.

Kevin's door wasn't locked. Muddy footprints crisscrossed the floor. The answering machine was gone. So was the microwave. And the TV, stereo, and clock-radio. A crime of opportunity. Mike knew exactly how it was. Some asshole saw the window was gone and helped himself. Had to be someone close by, maybe living right on the lane, because the house wasn't visible to the street. Most reprobates didn't go looking to score on dark and stormy nights. He should probably report it, or at least tell Essery.

The phone was gone too. He went outside, wondering how far it was to a pay phone. He thought he saw someone moving in the basement suite of the house on the other side of the lane. He walked across.

A pale, bony kid with lank blonde hair and reeking of weed answered the door. Mike politely asked if he could use the phone. The kid let him in, pointing to the telephone on the kitchen table. He went back to frying a huge steak on the stove. Grease sputtered and splattered.

Mike was careful not to turn his back on the kid as he punched in the number and asked for Ron Essery. While he waited he looked around at the mess. Stacks of dirty dishes, piles of clothes, a garbage can overflowing with instant noodle wrappers and generic macaroni and cheese boxes. There were a couple of birthday cards on top of the refrigerator, a phone bill, and the brown envelope Social Services used to mail out the welfare cheques.

Essery was taking his own sweet time getting to the phone. The kid flipped his steak over. On the counter beside the stove Mike noticed an unopened bottle of rye and a fresh case of beer doing a poor job of concealing a baggie of weed.

When Essery got on the line, Mike cheerfully said, "Hey, Ron. The storm smashed in a window of the little house. Come on over and help me out."

"You're the carpenter."

"I need a hand."

"You sound odd."

"That's right."

"You have something?"

"You said it."

"I'll be right over."

The kid ran hot water over a dirty plate. He shook it and slapped on the steak. Mike thanked him for the use of the phone and headed back.

Essery laughed and asked how it felt to get a taste of his own medicine when Mike told him about the rip-off. He ignored the bullshit and told him about the kid. "You'd call him low-life scum."

"Yeah? What would you call him, Mike?"

"Low-life scum. If he's on welfare, payday is ten days away. Where'd he get the money for all the goodies this time of the month?"

"I can't run him in just because he's eating steak."

"But I saw the dope. A quarter ounce maybe. You can get a search warrant based on the information of your reliable informant."

Essery nodded. He had a look around for anything else missing, stepping carefully to avoid smearing the footprints. He knew the inventory better than Mike did. He'd seen right away that books and clothes were missing from the bedroom.

Mike told him he'd taken the books to Rainie and changed into dry clothes the day before. That still left one green sweatshirt from the bureau drawer unaccounted for.

TWENTY-EIGHT

Mike returned to the Royal Arms bursting to tell Rainie. He walked in calling her name. The door to her room was closed. He knocked. He knocked louder and opened it a crack. She wasn't there.

She wasn't there. The agoraphobic wasn't home. He went nuts thinking the worst. He called down to the front desk. The clerk said she'd just gone out. He asked who with, trying to get a description. She went out alone. He worried, he wondered, he paced between window and door.

Ten minutes later he heard her key in the lock. She came in, rain splotched, with a big smile on her face and a plastic shopping bag in her hand.

"Where the hell were you?"

"Went to the grocery down the block," she held the bag up, "Milk and oatmeal cookies. I've had a victory, Mike. I went out all by myself. My first solo."

"Just like that?"

"I've been practicing the last few days. Aren't you happy for me?"

"Thrilled. Scared me to death you weren't here when I got back." He had to smile because she obviously didn't care. "Why didn't you tell me about it?"

She shrugged and brought the bag to the kitchen. "It's chilly out. And wet." She wore a blouse over a tee shirt. "I need a jacket. I have a good one at home. That's going to be my next goal. Going back there. I have to get my computer anyway."

"Today?"

"No. But it's the next thing I'm working towards."

"Alone? I can give you a lift if you like."

"I don't know. I have to think about that." She slipped off to her room with whatever else she had in the bag.

They talked over her victory as they sat at the kitchen table dunking cookies in milk. "It's practice," she said. "I take it bit by bit and work through it. Those books helped a lot and I guess the time is right."

"I'm just glad you're safe."

"Thanks."

His cookie dropped in the milk. He fished it out with a spoon. "It might be the right time for you psychologically, but in other ways it's not a great idea to go out alone."

"I didn't go far."

"That's not the point. It's a matter of unreasonable fear versus self-preservation. Once this is over you'll be free to do whatever you want. Right now I don't think you should go anywhere. Stay here where you're safe."

"You go out."

"We're different."

"Why? Because you're a man?"

"Little sister, I'm tough. I just did three years inside. Don't go back to your apartment. I wouldn't even want to drive you. We don't know if it's being watched."

She nodded slowly and finished her milk. "I said it was my next goal. I didn't say I have a timetable."

He could see she was getting nervous again. To take her mind off it he told her about the rip-off from Kevin's house and the dirty stoned kid across the lane. Maybe it wasn't the best idea because she went a little pale; her blue eyes got that scared rabbit look and she scurried back to her room. She closed the door.

Now he had no one to talk to. He tried watching TV but couldn't sit still. He thought of something he could do but felt funny about telling her he was going out again. He debated just leaving without telling her or writing a note, but decided that was rude. He knocked on her door. "Rainie?"

"Yes."

"I'm going to see my accountant. See if she has anything new on Duffy. Will you be okay?"

"I'll be fine. Good-bye."

He hesitated, "Because someone has to stay here in case Essery calls."

"Don't worry. I'll stay here. Safe and sound."

The rain continued to pour, no let up in sight. Mike didn't mind, it matched his mood, grey and sloppy. He parked under

Pacific Centre and walked through the rain to Constance's office, feeling shitty in a way he couldn't describe. Something to do with Rainie, the way she changed so quickly from happy to scared. Or maybe it was the rip-off and the kid and letting Essery take care of it legally.

Elise was doing a hundred and twenty on the keyboard as he walked in. "Hello, Mike. She's in but we're busy and can't stop to talk." She took some papers from a bottom desk drawer. "Here's that Dell information. She said to tell you no charge. She got interested. Interlocking directorships, I think. There's probably more but she doesn't have the time now for research." She waved him away and went back to the keyboard.

So much for always counting on a friendly smile. He folded the papers in quarters and buttoned them into his jean jacket pocket. "Tell her thanks." Elise nodded but she only had eyes for the monitor.

He still felt guilty for leaving Rainie alone. But he didn't want to go back to the hotel where he had nothing to do but pace the floor and wait for Essery. He wandered around Pacific Centre for a while, looking in store windows, wondering if he should buy her something. He'd daydreamed inside about finding a woman when he got out but didn't expect a neurotic little sister. He stopped at a bookstore. Maybe one of those historical romances she liked.

He found a whole rack of the genre but the covers looked so ridiculously lurid he felt embarrassed standing there. And he didn't want to pick one she'd already read. He decided to call. Maybe she could tell him an author or something.

Rainie said she had enough to read but Ron wanted him and he should call the office right away.

Essery asked where he was, exactly where he was parked, and said to go down to the garage and wait in his truck. He'd get there as soon as he could.

Mike drummed on the steering wheel and debated buying a pack of cigarettes. He played a U2 tape and knew it was time to buy some new music. Something produced in the last three years.

He could've walked to the cop shop on Hastings and Main, walked there and back and stopped for a coffee by the time Essery pulled up beside him.

He slid into the passenger seat. "Had to take a break. I need you to make an ID and sign a statement." He opened an evidence bag and handed Mike a brown leather binder with the initials M-M-M on a small brass plate.

"You found it in the kid's place?" He turned the pages, seeing Kevin's handwriting, feeling sick. He saw his own writing on the O-P divider, a number for pizza delivery. "I'm sure it's mine. Did he do Kevin?"

"I wish I could beat the shit out of him to get him to talk. Not talk, confess. He's done a lot of talking. Lies so much he contradicts himself every other sentence."

"What's his name?"

"Raymond Kaslo. Twenty years old. Another one the system failed. Did he talk to you at all?"

"No. Pointed to the phone. Grunted when I said good-bye."

"He's off centre. My theory is his brain was abducted by a UFO when he was a baby but they screwed up when they tried to return it. Wrong body in the wrong century. There's no way he'll ever fit in. You okay?"

"No. They put mine back in the right body. Let's get the statement over with."

TWENTY-NINE

Essery dragged in after midnight. "Saw your light on. Is Rainie asleep?"

"Yes."

"Good. I'd rather talk to you alone. You have anything to drink, Mike?"

"Thought you were on the wagon."

"Don't tell my wife."

"Rye or beer?"

"One of each." He collapsed on the couch, "Been a long day. Haven't been home yet."

Mike brought out three fingers of rye and a bottle of beer. Essery reached out with both hands, "Thanks. You're a lifesaver." He shot back the rye and took a long swallow of beer. He sighed. "That hit the spot." He belched heartily. "Now I feel better." Mike laughed and brought out an ashtray, and a beer for himself.

Essery snapped his lighter and lit a cigarette. "I have to thank you, Mike. I'm real proud of you. You passed along the information and didn't lose your head."

"What happened?"

"Kaslo confessed and recanted half a dozen homicides. Particularly adamant about Barbara Fleming. Went into great detail on how he'd raped her. Only thing was, she hadn't been raped. Went on and on. We'd ask questions about Kevin, he'd spin out stories. Always coming back to Barbara. Until we clued in that he thought if he confessed he'd get the quarter million reward. Right pissed off when we told him it's against the law to profit from murder."

"That's really interesting, but what about Kevin?"

"He confessed to that, too, but it didn't quite jibe with the facts."

"But he had the notebook."

"Yeah. He had to be there. It looks like a sociopath's quirk. Taking a souvenir. Said he swiped it from the kitchen table, stuck it under his shirt. Problem with that, I'll spare you the details, but it couldn't have been on the table."

"Splatter pattern of blood."

"Yeah. Said that when he had a chance to look at it closely he saw that the initials on the cover weren't Kevin's. He felt ripped off. That's why he stole the electronics when he saw the window gone."

"Traded goods for money; bought a steak. And symbolically consumed the flesh of his victim? Bullshit psycho-babble."

"We're going for DNA fingerprinting. See if he matches the dried saliva on the roaches left at the scene."

"What about motive? How many stories did he have for that?"

"A long list. His favourite was that he was paid a hundred thousand."

Mike lit a cigarette from Essery's pack. "I quit a long time ago."

"Believe me, I understand. You okay so far?"

"Yeah." Mike drank the beer and went for seconds, brought out the bottle of rye and another glass too. He had a quick double, shook his head and rolled the cold beer between his palms. "Whadya mean so far? There's more?"

"That was the bad news. Now comes the good." Essery still had his first beer going. He took a sip and a drag on his cigarette. "Kaslo gave us lots of names. We have to run them down. He has shit-for-brains but he still might light on the truth. About Leo Castle. He gave us the driver. He's in hospital. AIDS related cancer. Pretty bad shape. Nothing to lose in talking."

"Who is it?"

"I can't give you any names, Mike. Except for one. The shooter. *Rick*. He didn't know the last name. About five-ten. Early forties. Brown hair. Clean shaven. Tattoo of a snake on his right forearm. Missing the pinkie finger on the same hand."

"Snake."

"Rick. From Richard. As in Richard Nixon."

"Why don't I feel good about it?"

"Because it's your worst nightmare come true. Leo saw something when he was working in the warehouse he shouldn't have and started asking too many questions."

"What was Duffy moving? Drugs?"

"It wasn't Duffy. I'm sorry, but I really can't tell you much more. It's someone who hasn't come up before. But he's known to us. Wiggled out of some charges last year."

"You've been talking to the Mounties, haven't you? 1 knew this would happen. Total shut down."

"Don't take it wrong. I'll get the job done. We're getting closer. Have you heard from Duffy Dell recently?"

"Not since I went up to his penthouse."

"I think he skipped." Essery put his beer down and rubbed his eyes. "This is the most complex problem I've ever had. More loose ends then a ... I'm too beat to find a simile."

He went to the washroom and came out drying his hands on a towel. "Thanks, Mike. Can't tell you how helpful you've been."

"No matter who or what else you find, it all comes back to that day on the power line when I was twelve years old."

"You could be right. Watch your back and look after Rainie. I'm exhausted. I'm going home."

Rainie shivered in horror as she tip-toed back to bed and pulled the covers over her head. Snake killed Leo. *Snake*. The man who took her mother away. Bunching the blankets, hiding in the darkness, burying her head and her sobs. Her mother and her husband.

When she came up for air she heard the wind howling and Mike on the other side of the wall pacing in his room. He moved to the living room, back and forth, back and forth. She wiped her face, blew her nose and got dressed. She opened the door. Mike stopped pacing and turned to her.

"I heard everything."

They threw their arms around each other. She whispered *Snake*. He smelled of liquor and cigarette smoke. *Snake killed my husband!* She clung to him. *We're the only ones left.*

And we told, he whispered back.

THIRTY

Mike ate aspirins and Pepsi for breakfast, hoping to tame his rye and beer hangover to a dull roar. He had things to do. He called his accountant first.

"Hi, Constance. Thought you'd appreciate the latest news on Duffy Dell."

"I know something's going on. The market opened to heavy trading on two of his listings."

"He needs pocket money. He's skipped town."

"Glad you told me. But what's it about?"

"Don't think I can tell you yet. But it has to do with the police investigation. He's either skipped or doing a good job of staying out of touch."

"How was that information I compiled for you? Any help?"

"Great. Thanks." He didn't want to say he'd forgotten to look at it.

Mike bought a combination telephone-answering machine from a Radio Shack store and drove it over to Kevin's little house. He couldn't park beside the house because a Specialty Cleaning Service van filled the space. He parked the truck down the lane and walked back, looking towards the basement suite of Raymond Kaslo, UFO reject. Theft Over, Possession, Suspicion of Murder. He wouldn't be back home yet.

The storm-smashed bedroom window had been replaced. The kitchen floor was clean. A plump woman in blue overalls stood in the bedroom, vacuuming the rug. Mike shouted hello over the noise. She jumped a foot in the air.

"Sorry, didn't mean to scare you."

She turned off the vacuum. "Didn't hear you come in." She put a hand over her heart, "Whoa. A mile a minute. Are you a policeman?"

"No." He held up the answering machine box, "Brought a replacement." He read the embroidered name over her pocket. "Lettie. Don't think I ever met a Lettie before."

"It's short for Leticia. Ever meet one of those?"

"Can't say I have. I'm Mike. Bet you've met a few of those."

"One or two."

He unwrapped the machine on the kitchen table and began attaching the cords. "Guess you heard there was a rip-off."

"Yes. Can't leave a place alone for long."

"They probably won't recover anything but they caught the guy." Mike pointed out the window. "Lived over there in the basement."

Lettie looked out the window and shook her head. "He'd know there wasn't anyone home." She turned and watched Mike plug in the machine and test for a dial tone. "Are you living here? Didn't think anyone was. There's nothing new. I was one of the cleaning crew here before."

"After the murder?"

"Yes. Murders, suicides, wild parties. Storm damage. We get the worst messes."

"I don't envy you."

"It's a job."

"Good attitude. But he was my brother. Don't think I'd have the emotional equipment to handle it."

"Not many people do. It's better to get a service. Haven't seen in the paper about an arrest yet."

Mike wasn't sure if he should say anything, he shrugged his shoulders, but felt compelled to defend Kevin. "It wasn't over drugs, they're sure of that. It was set up to look that way but he hadn't been mixed up in that stuff for years."

"Really?"

"Yeah. They're still working on it. Guess I'd better let you get back to work. But would you hold off on the vacuum for a minute while I record a message? Then I'll get out of your way."

"Sure."

He couldn't think of anything clever to say and recorded the standard bullshit. He called *good-bye* and headed for the door. Lettie came out of the bedroom with a photograph. "I found this in back of the bed. Maybe you'd want it."

The picture. The four kids and Duffy, with Snake and Raven in the background. His headache came pounding back full force. The names and ages were written on the reverse but it wasn't Marion's or Kevin's handwriting. "In back of the bed?"

"We didn't move it last time. I had to now to get at the bits of glass."

He nodded. "That's me," he pointed, "And that's Kevin."

"You look the same age. Were you twins?"

"No. Just very close." He buttoned it into his jean jacket pocket. "Thanks."

Charlie and her brother and sister came straight home after school. Charlie always did but sometimes Amy and Billy went to the their friends or did other things. But this was the first day Merlee would be there when they came home and they wanted to see what it was like.

When Amy opened the door it smelled good from food cooking. Merlee came out of the kitchen and smiled and everything. She gave them milk and cookies. The cookies were still warm. They were yummy.

There was a chicken in the oven and soup on the stove. She was cutting up vegetables and let Charlie help. The house was shiny and clean. All the laundry was done and she'd even put it away in everyone's room.

When Daddy came home he said it smelled good too. When they had supper she put everyone's soup on the table and went back to the kitchen. She didn't eat with them. Charlie didn't know why. Daddy said that was how Merlee learned to do things.

The soup was good. It was just the juice with lots of noodles in it. When they were finished Merlee took all the bowls away and brought out the chicken and the other things.

Charlie ate and ate until she was stuffed. There was dessert, too. Merlee made a big giant chocolate cake.

When Daddy tucked Charlie in at bedtime he said things would be easier now that Merlee was there. Charlie said she still missed Mommy. He said he did too. Merlee wasn't there to take Mommy's place but to do all those things they had trouble with. Like cooking and cleaning. Daddy read a story but Charlie fell asleep before it was over.

THIRTY-ONE

Rainie stood at the window watching a bin diver collect pop cans from the dumpster behind the hotel. He wore a rain suit. The sun was shining but everything was still dripping wet. He put the cans in a homemade trailer attached to the back of his bicycle and pedaled away.

She wanted to be out there, too. Walking, tasting the fresh air, feeling the sun on her face. Not possible with *Snake* on the loose. She repeated her affirmations but no matter how many times she said the word *fearless* it wouldn't sink in. Even walking out to the hall seemed impossible now.

She might have to spend her entire existence staring out the window at other people's lives. Not only bin divers but the whole neighbourhood was out in the sun today. She counted five people in their yards tidying up after the storm. And two women hanging out the wash. She and Leo had planned to have a house someday. There'd be his six months training in Regina, then he'd receive his posting. Probably not in Vancouver. Maybe not even in B.C. It sounded exciting. Move to a new part of Canada, buy a house, be a Mountie wife, have little Mountie babies. She didn't know why she was thinking about something that would never happen.

She tried to read but the healing books were too damn positive and the science fiction left her cold. She couldn't eat yet, she'd had a drop too much rye trying to get to sleep and her stomach was still queasy. She wished Mike would come back. She turned on the music channel just to fill the silence.

A knock sounded at the door. She recognized it as Ron's but still felt a shiver of fear and checked through the peephole before opening up.

"Hi," she said, "I'll get the ashtray."

He laughed and sat on the couch. "How are you today?"

She brought the freshly washed ashtray from the kitchen and placed it on the coffee table. "I eavesdropped last night. Heard what you said."

"You okay?"

"What can I say?" She sat beside him. "You said it last night. Your worst nightmare come true."

"I know it's difficult."

"Yeah. I know you're going to ask me about Leo. He never told me anything." She sighed. "He never said a word about seeing anything in the warehouse. He never seemed worried or nervous."

He asked her a few questions but she had nothing to add. She asked him about Kaslo.

"The investigation's continuing. I'll tell you more later on."

"Later on I can read about it in the *Sun*."

"You're starting to sound like Mike. Been hanging around him too long." He laughed and lit a cigarette. "Where is he?"

"Went to buy a new answering machine for Kevin's house."

"I have a little something for you. I haven't located your mother yet. But I can tell you a few things about her. There was an FBI agent up here from L.A. a few years ago, working on a case. He owed me a few favours. I don't know what you were expecting..."

"I don't have any expectations."

"Then you won't be disappointed. He found a Lois Louise Chase, born Oct. 31, 1947, in Coalunga, California. That's about 170 miles north of L.A. Oil country."

"That goes along with what Marion wrote. More or less."

"She was the middle of three daughters. Smart girl. Graduated high school early. Matriculated at Stanford. But then she caught a dose of stupiditis. Dropped out after only a few months. Took off with another drop-out."

"My father?"

"Don't know for sure. Still haven't found a birth record. But the timing is right."

"Do you know anything about him?"

"His name was Daniel Andrew Morse. He worked in a book store. That's all I have. Want me to look further?"

"Yes. Please. When I registered with Parent Finders someone told me that it's often easier to find fathers than mothers. Because they don't change their names. Is there anything else about my mother?"

"Nothing until '73, when her parents were questioned. She'd been implicated in a smuggling conspiracy. But they claimed they hadn't heard from her in years."

"Claimed?"

"The investigating officer thought they were covering up. She has convictions for driving under the influence and other things."

"What other things?"

"Well Rainie, remember I said you shouldn't have any great expectations." He screwed his cigarette butt into the ashtray.

"It's either drugs, sex or money."

"Not money." He handed her a fax of her mother's mug shot. "She wasn't on the street. After Snake she set her sights higher. Married and divorced twice since then. One son from each relationship. They'd be 15 and 11 now."

"I never thought of that. That she'd have other children. What name does she use?"

"Winfield. Lois Winfield. Kept the last husband's name."

"But you don't know where she is?"

"No. Doesn't look like she'll be easy to find either. She's been living with a man named Jason Fulton for the last five years. If they're still together. Calls himself an investment counsellor. Leased a beautiful waterfront home down in Malibu, along with a yacht and two BMW's."

"Drugs?"

"So high up the ladder you'd get a nose bleed. Two years ago they were under surveillance. Wire tapped. The whole nine yards. Then one day they picked up the kids after school and disappeared."

"Disappeared?" she echoed. "Again?"

"I'm sorry Rainie."

"Not your fault she dumped me like an unwanted puppy and went on to continue breeding. Two boys from two different fathers? She kept *them*. What's that mean? Boys are better than girls?"

"I don't blame you for being angry."

"Well thank you very much. Is there a warrant out on her?"

"Yes, for both of them. Maybe she'll turn up. Then you can visit her in prison whenever you want."

"Great. Something to look forward to."

"Your grandparents are still alive. They appear to be stable. Albert and Margo Chase. I got the address and phone number for you."

"Do they know I exist?"

He looked around the room and back at Rainie. "There's no mention of you in what my FBI friend had. I don't know."

"I can just call up total strangers and say I'm Rainbow Smith - do you know who I am? What if she never told them?"

"But maybe she did. It's something to think about."

"I'm registered with Parent Finders and they never tried to look me up. And Marion wrote that her family was wealthy. What if they think it's some kind of trick just to get money from them?"

"You're not going to be asking for anything, are you? You only want to meet them. And don't you have pictures? Those ones from Marion's album?"

"Yes. And I do look like her. I guess I can get DNA blood testing."

"Think about it. Talk it over with Mike."

"He met his grandparents recently and he didn't like them."

"But that's Mike."

He walked in right on cue. "*All right*, you're here. I left a message at your office." He pulled a picture from his jacket pocket. "Look at what the cleaning lady found behind Kevin's bed."

He grimaced, "Behind the bed? Shit, I hate when I miss things."

"Kevin had the picture. He must've gotten it from Marion. He had the picture and he had it hidden and didn't write anything in a letter because he was waiting until I got out. But Snake killed him. Or paid Kaslo while he killed Barbara. Kevin and Barbara must've talked about *it*. He got the picture from her." He went to the washroom, shouting a monologue over the water sounds, came back to the living room, still talking, pacing the room, "And see I was right, it wasn't just a coincidence and this proves it, whatever else you found Kevin had the picture."

"Jesus, Mike. Settle down."

Mike sat on the chair for an instant, jumped up and paced in a wide circle, "He had the picture with Snake and Raven and Duffy and all of us."

Essery got up and stopped him with a hand on his shoulder. He looked in his eyes. "Shit, Moonbeam. Blow it up your nose why don't ya?"

"I ran into an old friend."

"Yeah, right. Sit down and shut up before I pull you in for possession."

"You've already done that."

"Don't let history repeat itself." He dragged him towards the chair and pushed him down. "Sit."

Rainie was grinning, nice to see it. Mike winked at her. Essery lit a cigarette and scratched his chin. "Check out the handwriting on the back," Mike said, "I don't know who it belongs to." Essery nodded.

THIRTY-TWO

Rainie had never tried coke but she'd smoked dope, once, in high school, just to say she'd done it. They turned the video station up to LOUD and partied. The coke went first, Mike hadn't bought much, but the half ounce of bud would last a few days. With careful rationing.

Whoever-it-was in the next room started hammering on the wall. They laughed and turned the volume down but the partying didn't end. They could talk without crying, and rip their hearts out, root and branch, without fear. Brother and sister, dancing, together or alone, two against the world, united by grief and past horror.

Until whoever-it-was *downstairs* started hammering. They collapsed on the couch in giggles, sweat-soaked, red-faced and panting. Mike wiped his forehead with the back of his hand.

"Think we worked it off?"

Rainie rolled her head against the back cushions and laughed. "I hope so. Any more of this and they'll kick us out."

Each lapsed into solitary thought. Mike made a pot of tea. Rainie turned off the television. It was time for silence. Time to spare, high time, lunar time, once upon a time, all in good time, pass the time, time after time, kill time. Kill. Mike went to his room first.

Felt way different with the door closed. Serious. Solemn. Reflective. With his family group of ashes on the dresser. Marion's brass candlestick. He'd forgotten to buy a candle again. The bed squeaked when he sat down.

He turned off the bedside lamp and settled back against the pillows. He thought of Marion the last time he saw her, Marion in her bed. He turned on the lamp, a magic talisman, protection against demons, ghosts and heartbreak.

Light carried its own weight of memory and each memory its own measure of pain. Kevin and his mom blew into the commune on a hot summer day, the old Van banging and rattling and churning great clouds of dust on the dirt road. One look: same age, same size, and they were off and playing hard, climbing trees, leaping into the swimming hole with Tarzan yells. And later, beside the crackling campfire, the light flickering red and orange as they whispered their seven year old histories. Falling asleep, sprawled one against the other, being carried to their bunks, inseparable for years until the Mounties came.

He may have dozed off. He may have dreamt answers but he didn't remember the questions. He understood the darkness on the other side of the window to mean night. And his brother and mothers on the dresser to mean time to chop wood and carry water. He brought out Marion's letters and reread them for the thousandth time.

One half of Rainie took comfort in knowing she was sleeping. Only dreaming. The other half fought panic with a sword of diamonds, a slashing rainbow of after-images. Leo dying in her arms, reaching the white light and turning back, standing there. *There.*

She sat up. He stood at the foot of the bed.

"Leo?"

He smiled. *His* smile, moustache, sad, so sad brown eyes. He raised his arm sending red hot sparks across the room and she stood in the yard at Zem-Zem, bare feet on the green grass. The mothers sat on a blanket, laughing, passing a joint around. Lotus. Happy. Shoshanna. Tiger Lily.

Leo said, "Happy Birthday. I found your mother for you."

She ran joyfully across the green grass to her mother's arms of solid rock, starburst, as dazed and voiceless as a dying raven.

Mike heard the heavy thud. Marion's letters scattered as he sprang off the bed and across the hall. "Rainie?" He shook the knob. "Rainie?." Weight on the other side. He could hear her groaning.

"Fuck," she said, "Fuck."

First time he ever heard her swear. "Are you okay? What happened?"

She groaned. She moaned. "I hit my head."

He got scared and started to worry that she'd broken something. Please God no, not her neck, and was wedged against the door paralysed, but then he heard her getting up.

She said, "Okay" and he opened the door. She was leaning, hanging on, the dresser. Deep burgundy blood dripped down her golden blonde hair. "I think I'm okay."

He got his arm around her waist and carried her back to the bed. He turned on the bedside lamp and looked at the side of her head. "Scared the shit out of me." He pulled up the top sheet and gently pressed it against the gash. "You hit the edge of the dresser on the way down."

"I'm bleeding!" It dripped onto her hands and on the bed. *Oh gross*, she wailed.

"It'll be fine. You're okay. It's just a cut. They always bleed like that from the head." He replaced the saturated sheeting with a fresh handful, getting a quick look at the wound. At least an inch long, hair stuck in it, he'd have to get her to the hospital. "It's okay, Rainie. You're okay. Does it hurt?"

"Yeah. And I think I bumped my head too." She reached up, gingerly touching the lump on her hairline, and grimaced. "Oh yeah. It hurts. Everything hurts."

"What happened?"

"I don't know but is pot usually that strong?"

He laughed, changing the sheet again, worrying about getting her out. "Actually, this is a little stronger than most. A psychedelic experience, as our mothers would say."

"I saw our mothers in Zem-Zem. Tiger Lily? Wasn't that your mother's name?"

"Yes."

"And Shoshanna was Kevin's mother. And Marion was Happy. And my mother was Lotus."

"You saw them?" He shifted so he could catch her eyes in the light and check her pupils. "Do you feel dizzy?"

"No. I'm okay. All our mothers were there. And I saw Leo too." She woke up or her mind cleared or something and she held back, not telling the whole dream or vision or whatever it was.

"You were sleep walking?"

"Sleep running."

"Away or to?"

"To. And just like real life my mother didn't want me."

"Yeah. She's starting to get violent. Feeling better?"

"Yes."

"I think you're going to need a stitch or two in that, Little Sister."

"Stitches? I've never had stitches."

"They'll just clean it and close it up so it heals right."

"I have to go the hospital? I dunno, Mike."

He didn't want the hassle either. Carry her into Emergency, no, he didn't beat her up, she backs him up but they think it's denial. "I'll get a towel. You can hold it on your head while I drive."

"Good thing I fell asleep in my clothes. I'm already dressed." She grabbed some sheet. Mike manoeuvred their hands so that she held it in place.

Mike raced to the bathroom, washed the blood off his hands, it *was* pretty gross, grabbed the freshest towels and raced back to Rainie.

"I'll need my wallet," she said, "It's in my purse. In the closet."

He did the few things that had to be done, checking for her medical card, getting his jacket, realizing she didn't have one to wear, draping his around her shoulders and standing her up. She was able to walk by herself. It wasn't as bad as he thought.

"Don't sing, Mike. Okay? My head hurts, I'm going to the emergency and I don't think I can handle your singing too."

"No singing. I promise."

They got to the door, he opened it, and there stood a bear-like man with a paw lifted to knock.

Mike stepped in quickly to shield Rainie. "Who are you?"

"Hotel security."

"Didn't know there was any."

"What's going on here?"

"I was sleep running," Rainie said, "I hit my head." He craned his neck to see, glancing suspiciously at Mike.

"I'm driving my sister to Emergency. Excuse me."

The bear said, *Oh sure*, and escorted them down the elevator, cleared the way through the empty lobby, throwing a few words at the night clerk as they passed, down the other elevator and over to Mike's truck. Rainie held the towel to her head. She felt so scared about that, going out was nothing.

Emergency was horrible. Fluorescent lights and unhappy people; she wasn't the only one with blood. Mike stayed with her the whole time. Only one high point. When they took her information and asked Mike's relationship, expecting boyfriend or husband, he said *brother*. And it was put in the computer, made official, *brother*.

They were sorry about her hair, but they had to trim it around the wound. And it was in front too, above the ear, but she didn't care right then. And they made her tell what happened, more than once, even though she drifted, so that she simplified the story and muttered about having a nightmare and running out of bed before she really woke up.

She didn't want to talk, she kept thinking about her mother, all the mothers. But when they were working on her head, with the big round light zeroing in, and the doctor and nurse, doing things to her, with the smells and the sounds, she said, "I don't like this."

Mike took her hand and laced their fingers together and said she should squeeze it if it hurt or she got scared. She thought she'd break it, she squeezed so hard, but she kept her eyes closed, kept hold of his hand, and thought about the mothers.

They decided to keep her for observation. Didn't think it was a concussion, but wanted to be sure. Mike remembered something from the news a few weeks ago. An old Indian guy, a drunk, fell and hit his head. They'd released him but he went into a coma afterwards. They were being more careful now. Probably would've been before that too, for a young and beautiful, blonde-haired, blue eyed, white woman.

She sat in a wheelchair, cold pack on her forehead, bandage over her right ear. A nurse stood behind, at the handgrips, ready to take her away. Without him.

"I'll be all right," Rainie said, "Don't worry. Go home and go to sleep. I'm sure they'll take good care of me."

The nurse agreed.

"All I want to do is lie down." She gave a little wave. "Night, Mike. Good bye. Good night. Thanks."

She was probably right, but he felt like a helpless idiot, watching the business-like way they disappeared around the corner, his blood-stained jacket folded over his arm.

THIRTY-THREE

It all seemed so wrong: the silent rooms, the blood on her bed, the loneliness. Mike took a long shower but couldn't relax enough for sleep. Three AM with nothing to do but think. Or chop wood, carry water. He gathered Marion's letters from the floor. He knew them by heart; he could find nothing between the lines, no clues or hints. Everything was fine, all blue skies.

He thought about Kevin's mother. Shoshanna, she was called on the commune. Funny, Rainie remembering that. They hadn't mentioned it before. Shoshanna: dead, stuck in some third world prison, happily married? Her real name was Sharon. Sharon Woods.

And Barbara's father. Marion's ex-husband. Did he know Marion was dead? Did he care? Mike had him listed in the copy he'd made of her address book. A professor in Auckland, Australia. He checked the long distance page in the telephone directory.

Eighteen hours ahead. Nine PM. He got an outside line, hit all the numbers and waited.

"Andrew Peppard?"

"Speaking."

"My name is Mike Minchuck. I'm calling from Vancouver."

"Yes?"

"I don't know if you'll remember me, but I was a child in Zem-Zem. I was called Moonbeam?"

"I know who you are. And it's the second time today I have heard your name. I spoke to Detective Ferrier of the RCMP. You will have to excuse me if I slur my words. I am trying to prolong the state of numbness for as long as possible."

Mike heard him drinking, lighting a cigarette, blowing smoke across the mouthpiece. "I'll wait if you need a refill, sir."

"Thank you, Moonbeam, but I am amply supplied with a jug of

red, right here at my desk. Suitably fortified for whatever tragic tidings, you, too, will bring."

"Sounds like you've already gotten it."

"Poor Marion. Why she didn't ask for help I'll never know. Did she think it was too soon? She called me before Christmas and I wired a thousand Canadian the next day. She didn't ask often, and I never complained when she did. Isolated. No one to turn to. Couldn't cope with Barbara's death. My son-in-law is a twit. As am I. I believed him when he said he couldn't find her. But he is consistent. He neglected to notify me of her suicide." He sighed. Classical music played in the background. "She was eternally child-like. Appropriate, perhaps, in a communal setting; not in the real world. I think she was happiest in the commune.

"Yes, I'm sure she was," he rambled, "She saved all the photographs and, I'm equally sure, dwelled on it far too much. Some years back she wrote to me with what I thought was a delusion. She had purchased an island. She would raise the flag of peace over a new utopia. The way we spoke years ago. I pitied her."

"It wasn't a delusion."

"No, the detective assured me it was not. Perhaps if I had not ridiculed her? There was her reunion? She put ads in the papers? I didn't take it seriously. It's as if her life stopped the day she left Zem-Zem. And I told her that. When she called, stoned I'm sure, all a twitter with elaborate plans." He stopped for a liquid break. "Perhaps if I had been kinder? Poor Marion, twittering about reuniting families because a man called her for information about his wife's mother. A fatuous little hippie who abandoned her."

"Leo Castle."

"Yes. He wanted to find the mother as a birthday gift for his wife. Marion gave him names of some of the commune dwellers and sent him an album with copies of her photographs."

"Did Barbara ever tell you about Snake killing Raven?"

"Not a word. I had no inkling. That too was a shock. I thought we had a close relationship. She telephoned me once a month, but she never spoke of Leo Castle. The detective was certain they met. She's dead. He's dead. And another witness too—Little Cedar. And so tonight I will drink myself into a stupor. Tomorrow I will be punished with a hangover. And all the time knowing it won't make one whit of difference."

"It's a bitch all right."

"That it is. And in this time of regret and self-reproach, I find myself filled with contrition. I owe you an apology, Moonbeam. It is, indeed, the only thing I remember about you. A small event, you may not even remember. An accident, but I shouted at you at the top of my voice."

"When I dropped the cake in your typewriter?"

"You do remember. I offer my most humble apologies and the hope that the in-ci-dent did not scar you for life."

"Thanks but it's too late. It was all down hill after that. Turned me into a career criminal with a permanent twitch and a phobia about typewriters."

"I'm sorry. Truly I am."

"I'm joking. Don't worry about it. Do you know anything about Rainbow's mother?"

"No."

"Cedar's mother? Shoshanna? Sharon Woods. Did she ever look you up? I know she was in Australia at one point."

"No. No one has ever looked me up except for Duffy. About ten years ago."

"What was he doing in Australia?"

"Some unlawful venture, I presume. He had something going in the Philippines. Importing nannies and domestics to Canada. Perfectly legal, he assured me. But me thoughts he protest-th too much. He dropped phrases like *transnational trade* and *Pacific Rim possibilities*. Excited at the opportunities Australia offered. Tried to impress me with a limousine and an expensive dinner."

"What did he want?"

"To make me president of his newest company. Nothing concrete, no business plan. To be discussed at a later date."

"He wanted you to front for him."

"He had approached me previously, in Vancouver. Barbara was still in high school. He offered to double my money. A sly one, that Duffy. Both times I told him I am an academic, not a business man. I was not interested."

Mike asked a few more questions, but the professor soon came to the end of coherent conversation, and, without stopping for breath, forged ahead into wine-fuelled jabber.

Mike said good bye before the jabber had time to turn into blubbering.

THIRTY-FOUR

At ten o'clock, after five hours sleep, Mike's eyes popped open and he was up and at the phone before he even made coffee. He spoke to a nurse on Rainie's floor. Doing well, probably be released in the afternoon, she'd relay the message that he'd called.

He made coffee and had a couple of tokes. Just enough to keep the party going. He dropped the long roach in the baggie, folded it small, and stuck it down in his jeans pocket.

It gave him the energy to chop wood, carry water, starting on the empties in the living room, doing the dishes, putting the photo albums back in his room. He balled up Rainie's bloody bedding. Even the blankets were stained.

That reminded him of his dirty jean jacket. Laundry time. He stuffed his duffel bag and carried it down to the laundry room on the lobby floor. On the way back he stopped to talk to the day clerk, be friendly, squash rumours and order replacement bedding.

He'd been emptying his pockets into the night table drawer. He opened it and took out Constance's papers. He brought them to the kitchen and sat down with a fresh coffee. He read through two pages of single spaced detail of Duffy's holdings and on to the pages titled Interlocking Directorships. He only had the vaguest idea of what it meant. She'd listed the directors of each company. A dotted line connected Duffy or the others to positions elsewhere.

He read the names and *knew* what they were, white men living behind Big Doors. Just another piece of shit. The next page looked the same but close to the bottom he read Prairie Dancer Resources, Calgary, *Arthur Kubek*, and crushing the papers in his hand raced for the toilet and puked up the coffee.

He rinsed out his mouth but the acid taste remained. He shook his head at the unshaven asshole in the mirror. He should've suspected. He should've made the connection. But he didn't and now he felt really stupid.

He checked the clock. Lunch time in Calgary. He knew their routine. He showered and shaved while he waited for their housekeeper to clear the table.

He needed the time to cool off. Work out what he wanted to say, phrase it unemotionally, not piss off Grandfather and have him turn to stone. But when he got him on the line and heard his voice, he said the first thing that popped into his mouth, "Prairie Dancer Resources."

"He wasn't going to tell you."

"He didn't. You got me out to Calgary and because of that I wasn't blown away. Why should I complain?"

"I'm relieved you feel that way. How did you find out?"

"My best friend was murdered. Did you think I wouldn't look into it? The cops busted Kaslo."

"Who?"

Mike cleared his throat loudly and waited.

"Was he the one? Have they arrested Portensky yet?"

Mike screwed up his eyes. The only Portensky he knew of was a nasty Russian gangster named Ivan Portensky. He played it cool and said "Not yet."

"What about Duffy?"

"You been out to Sea Spray recently?"

"You know about that too?"

"I own it now."

"Well, well. You have been a busy boy."

"Why don't you tell me how you first met Duffy?"

"Let me see, that was back in the early seventies. Just a minute while I pour myself a drink."

Grandfather came back on the line with a clink of ice cubes. "He made an appointment to see me in my office. He had a business proposition. If I invested five thousand dollars he guaranteed to double it within a month. Here was this long haired young man in a well cut silk suit. Eager, energetic, I admired his nerve. He said I wouldn't be risking anything. He had collateral. He opened his briefcase and showed me ten thousand dollars. I was to hold it until the deal was done."

"What was the deal?"

"That was the string attached. He refused to say. But I counted the money and it was all there. All perfectly good Canadian hundreds, not counterfeit. I asked what would happen if I didn't give it back when the deal was done. He said I'd meet his partner. And I wouldn't want to do that."

"Snake?"

"Yes. From his tattoo."

"The deal went through and you doubled your money?"

"Yes."

"And there were other deals, the same kind? Where you were protected by ignorance?"

"Not many. He went on to bigger and better things."

"Like Prairie Dancer?"

"Oil and gas exploration. Hasn't been active recently."

"All it'd take is a press release of some good drilling results. Plus your fine reputation in the industry. Isn't that how it works? The shares shoot up and you pocket a bundle. The free enterprise spirit, there's nothing like it. Did he speak about my mother and me?"

"Only when he introduced himself. He explained how he knew of me, from meeting my daughter on the commune. He called it his hippie phase. He said hippies were passé. They had gone backwards when the rest of the world had gone ahead. I couldn't have agreed with him more. But he still had the hair. He said it was helpful in establishing rapporteur with certain people. I said nothing more. You owe him your life, I hope you realize that."

"Actually, I've been having a hard time with that concept."

"Don't be silly. He knew Portensky was up to no good. He's not Ukrainian. He's Russian. You can't trust those people."

"What exactly did he say?"

"Gang warfare. Like the Mafia. Only between Russian and Canadian instead of Sicilian. He said he'd deal with it. But he knew you were due to be released and told me to keep you out of harm's way."

"Why me? What did I have to do with it?"

"He didn't elaborate further. But he gave the impression you'd been mixed up with that Russian before."

"I knew him, that's all. He isn't someone I would've looked up when I got out. He's shit. No pretences to legitimate business like Uncle Duffy. What are they fighting over? Control of what?"

"He didn't say."

"This isn't the time for secrets."

"He never talked about his *other* dealings." He clicked the ice cubes and burped softly. "I called him when you said you were leaving here. He wasn't happy about that. He said the Russian was on a rampage. Killed a friend of yours. And, out of pure viciousness, picked off one of his employees at random. Sent Snake out to deal with him once and for all. But couldn't find him. Duffy couldn't very well go to the police with what he knew. That's why he put up that reward."

"And you just sit there in Calgary, no curiosity whatsoever?"

"It's none of my business."

"Like your earlier deals? Protected by ignorance?"

"He called me when he thought I might be affected."

"Must've been a shock. Coming like that out of the blue."

"It certainly was unexpected. But I did know you were in jail. He'd told me that before. I'd have preferred if he told me you'd married and settled down, but that was not the case. Have you found a job yet?"

"Oh sure. With Facetious Construction." He'd used that line with Essery once and got a punch in his wiseass mouth. But Grandfather didn't get it and said he was on the right track. Granny'll be proud. Mike should call her. He'd promised he would and she'd been waiting. She was napping at the moment though. He'd have to call again. It sounded to Mike like Grandfather was trying to wind the conversation down. But he still had questions.

"When was the last time you were on Sea Spray Island?"

"Last summer. I caught a twenty pound salmon."

"Congratulations. It's a fishing lodge?"

"I thought you said you bought it?"

"No. I said I own it now. I've never been there. Just saw aerial photos. Tell me about it."

"No. First tell me how you wrestled it from Duffy. The island is his pride and joy."

"He had someone front for his purchase. In her name. She died and willed all her chattels to me."

"Does he know?"

"Not yet. When was the last time you heard from him?"

"The call I told you about. When you were leaving here."

"He got scared and skipped town. Would he go to Sea Spray?"

"Without a doubt. It's paradise. Everything a man could want. He could live there contentedly and die a happy old man without ever setting foot in civilization again. They produce their own power, grow all their own fruit and vegetables. Grape vines for wine. And a still. It's a fishing lodge only in the sense that he entertains his more important business associates there. But it's his private refuge and I warn you not to drop in unannounced, no matter what you may have in your head about ownership."

"I wouldn't dream of barging in. Who lives there?"

"There's a Filipino couple in charge. Been there for years. They oversee the labourers. I'm not sure how many. Five or six. Maybe more. The girls change. Take jobs in the city. All Filipinos."

"You said everything a man could want. The girls do more than labour in the gardens?"

"You won't tell your granny, will you? She wouldn't understand."

"Man to man."

"He always keeps the most beautiful girls there. Young and lovely and always cheerful."

"Sounds like paradise, all right. Anyone else live there?"

"Not full time."

"What about Snake?"

"He's a frequent visitor but he doesn't live there. And no one calls him that anymore. He's Rick Howard."

"You know where he lives?"

"Vancouver, I think. But he has the run of the island. The only one Duffy allows access when he's not in residence."

"The snake in paradise. I think I've beard this story before."

THIRTY-FIVE

Rainie didn't mind being in the hospital as much as she would've thought. It was so strange and outside of normal experience that it seemed a great adventure. The nurses checked her often but she knew as well as they did there was nothing wrong except a cut and bump. Not like the other people she saw, truly sick or racked up badly with injuries. She didn't want to think about her hair.

She felt bloated and looked for menstrual stains when she went to the washroom. None yet and she wondered, but life was a lot easier without it. She walked down the hall and chatted with a few other patients in the lounge. It was a little odd talking to strangers while wearing the hospital gown and robe, but everyone was the same and that made it okay.

She retreated to her bed, waiting for the doctor to approve her release, and thought about the mothers. They were all dead or disappeared. She wondered what that meant. The lunch tray arrived and she wondered why the food was so terrible. It seemed to be a day for wondering.

She had just finished dessert, a uniquely tasteless version of rice pudding, when Ron Essery arrived. He eyed her bandage, closed the curtains for privacy, pushed the swivel table out of the way and sat at the foot of the bed. "They told me in the hotel you were here. How you feeling?"

"Tired and lumpy. I didn't get much sleep."

"You wanna tell me what happened?"

"I had a vivid dream and ran out of bed. Hit my head."

"On what?"

"Door, wall, I don't know, it was dark. I cut it on the edge of the dresser."

He leaned forward, speaking softly, "What was it? Mike tried to get into bed with you?" His jacket fell open and she could see the gun in the holster under his arm. She went cold all over, wondering how she could trust a man who carried a gun. He saw her looking and straightened up, buttoning the jacket, shrugging, "It's the job."

"You ever shoot anyone?"

"Not since Vietnam."

"You were in the American army?"

"Yes. Joined up after high school."

"You came out and became a cop?"

"First job I applied for."

"You were never a hippie?"

"I was on the other side. The reactionary right."

"Why?"

"Why?" He quirked his eyebrows. "Same reason I joined the army. I come from a long line of red-necks. I was raised with a Bible in one hand and a hunting rifle in the other. I fought Commies in Southeast Asia and came home to Vancouver and found them stoned on the street. I've mellowed since then."

"Why?"

"You're full of difficult questions today. I think I understand people better now... because I know I'll never understand. Human behaviour is too complex. I'm continually surprised. But still, when you get down to it, it's usually the simplest motivation. The contradiction between complexity and simplicity interests me and I've done a lot of reading. Or maybe I'm just getting old and tired and lost the passion for law and order."

"You do look tired."

"And you look like you were assaulted by your roommate."

"No. It's *simply* the way I told you. No *complexity* to the motive at all."

"You're a beautiful woman, and he was wired and just out of prison."

"Get your mind out of the gutter!" She touched the bump on her forehead, "You're giving me a headache. And he's been with women since he got out. Two that he told me about. One was in Banff. It's nice of you to drop in and all that, but do you have any real news?"

"There's been a few developments but not much I can pass on."

An aide came for the lunch tray and then a nurse, checking her again, asking about nausea, glaring at Ron, saying it wasn't visiting hours. He showed his ID and smiled. The nurse went away.

Ron perched on the bed again. "I want to be sure you're safe."

"Been fine so far."

"Except that you're sitting in a hospital bed."

"Self-inflicted accident."

"I want to move you to a safe house."

"I have one already."

"One of ours. No charge to you."

The nurse slid back the curtain for the doctor, a tall, angular woman with spiky grey hair and a long, white coat. She read the chart, looked in Rainie's eyes, asked a couple of questions and bestowed her blessing on the release.

Ron returned to stand beside the bed, "Good. You can go. I'll take you there now. It's a nice place. You'll like it."

"What's the rush?"

"I don't want to scare you, Rainie. Just trust me."

"I have to call Mike."

"He's not in the hotel. I just came from there. Know where he is?"

"No. But the nurse told me he called this morning to see how I am."

"He spends a lot of time away, doesn't he?"

"I guess so."

"You don't really know where he goes, do you?"

"He tells me."

"But maybe not everything."

"What are you getting at?"

"I've been taking a lot of heat since Duffy disappeared. And there's other things I'm not free to discuss. Makes me think Mike's been playing games with me. I've never been one of his favourite people."

"But he *told* you."

"He knows more than he's telling. I only have his word to go on."

"And his word isn't good enough?"

"He could be lying to you, too. You seem to think he's a saint. Believe me, he isn't."

"This is all because I hit my head?"

"No. You said it was an accident. Okay, that's what it was. But I'll bet if he hadn't brought dope back to the hotel, there wouldn't have been an accident. I don't want to worry about you. I want you to be safe."

She shook her head. "Thanks anyway."

"Maybe I *should* scare you. Maybe you should think about this, Mike being out so much, driving in his truck, think about him being followed back to your hotel. Snake following him back. Back to you. *Snake.*"

He wasn't stupid. He knew which button to press. But there was another button and he'd hit that one hard too. Trust me. Believe me. She wasn't allowed to know anything but it was for her own good. Move. To another foster home, another psychologist, another set of lies.

He took her silence for yes and touched her hand. "It'll be okay, Rainie. You'll be fine. Get dressed."

"You're trying to rush me out before Mike gets here. You don't want me to be with him anymore, do you?"

"No. It's for your own good."

She nodded and pretended to think about it. She didn't throw herself into a screaming fit like she did when she was a kid. She didn't think it'd work and it'd disturb the other patients. "I have a better idea. I don't feel right living on the tax payer's money. Why don't I get out of Vancouver entirely? I can go to Leo's aunt in Nanaimo. There's a bus that goes across on the ferry. She can pick me up on the other side."

He hemmed and hawed. Whatever he wasn't telling made him shake his head. "What if you have a panic attack all alone on the ferry? They don't let you sit on the bus during the trip, you know. They lock it up and you have to go upstairs with the crowd. And with your injuries people will stare at you. And remember you. It's better if you stay in town. We can keep an eye on you, and I'll be able to visit. Maybe I can get someone in to talk to you about the agoraphobia." He looked at his watch. "I'm on a tight schedule. Get dressed and I'll drive you over."

"You going to stand here and watch?"

He smiled. "There's an outside terrace on this floor. I'll go and have a smoke."

She slipped off the bed. Her clothes were in a locker at the other side of the night stand. Her hands shook as she put on her bra and panties. The jeans had blood stains but they were far enough from her face that she could stomach them. Not the blouse, too gross and disgusting, stiff with dried blood. She put the green hospital gown on again, overlapping the opening in front, rolling up the bottom, tying it and tucking it into her jeans. Hospital chic. About as chic as their food.

She went out to the hall but didn't see him, lots of other people around—nurses and patients walking or in wheelchairs, aides pushing tall lunch tray carts. Two doctors waited for the elevator. The terrace was at the end of a short corridor to the left.

She could sneak out by the staircase. Lose herself on another floor. Go out. *Go out.* She could do that now. She could. But Mike had taken her wallet back with him and she didn't even have bus fare. He only left her with two quarters for the telephone. They were still in her pocket.

But Ron said Mike wasn't in the hotel. She had no one else to call. No one. There was only a man with a gun who said *trust me* and a man who called her Little Sister.

She wasn't a criminal and she wasn't a minor. He couldn't take her where she didn't want to go. This wasn't Zem-Zem and she wasn't six years old.

Mike walked out of the elevator carrying a plastic shopping bag. He didn't look in her direction. He walked to the nursing station. He spoke to the red-haired nurse, then turned and saw her. His face lit up. He held up the plastic bag.

Rainie shook her head vigorously, motioning him back. He looked puzzled. She shook her head and mouthed the one word she knew he'd understand, *cops*. He scooted behind a lunch tray cart.

Ron walked down the short corridor. When he came close enough he said, "Ready?" He looked at her shirt, "What are you wearing?"

"My blouse is all covered with dried blood and it's too gross to wear."

"What you have on is okay."

"No, I can't go out in it. I look ridiculous."

"You look fine."

"And I'm not going to steal hospital property. I need a tee shirt or something."

"I'm sure it's okay."

"You're telling me it's okay to *steal*?"

He sighed and checked his watch, "Look, there's a gift shop downstairs. I think they have tee shirts. But if not, I'll take the heat, okay? Wait in your room. I'll be right back." He walked to the elevator.

An aide grabbed hold of the lunch tray cart and pushed it away. Rainie nearly had a heart attack right there. But Mike had disappeared. She let out her breath.

She turned and started down the hall so Ron would think she was actually following his orders. When he'd entered the elevator and the doors slid closed, she hurried back, looking left and right. Mike was hiding in a linen closet.

"Let's get out of here." She pulled him by the shirt, saw an EXIT sign and raced down the stairs ahead of him. "Do you know where the gift shop is?" She called over her shoulder.

"Yeah, I saw it on the way in."

"We have to avoid it. Find another way out."

"What's going on?"

But she was running too fast to explain.

THIRTY-SIX

Mike parked the truck on a residential street far, far from the hospital. Rainie waved her hands angrily, touching her head, repeating what Essery said, remembering something, going back, saying fuck *this* fuck *that*.

"Now you know why I don't like cops."

"Was there any truth in what he said?" Her blue eyes challenged him. "Were you playing games?"

"No. Sounds like he's describing himself."

"That's what I thought."

"How're you feeling?"

"Pissed off."

"I can see that. I mean physically."

"I feel like I got hit on the head. And I'm getting my period soon." Her eyes shot with defiance, "Does that embarrass you?"

"No. It's one of the things that make women special." He started to laugh.

"Is that funny?"

"No. It's better for you to be bitchy with PMS than frozen with fear."

"Damn right it is. I'm finished with fear. I'm sick of fear."

"What you do want to do now? Find another hotel?"

"I'm sick of hotels. Sick of everything."

"Me too. But we can't go to your place. Kevin's house is out. So's the Royal Arms, might as well call it Pig Arms."

"I don't want to go anywhere. How do I look?" She touched both hands to her head.

"You could wear a paper bag over your head for a few days. There's a mirror under the visor if you wanna see."

"No, I'll take your word for it. Ron wouldn't. He'd insist on reading the medical report. Are you mad about that?"

"No. More depressed than anything. I tried, Rainie, I really did. Look what I got today. It's really cool." He took a small cellular phone from his jacket pocket. "I got it before I went to the hospital."

She held it in her hand, flipped it open, pulled up the antenna. "That's neat. And it'll come in handy now that we're homeless."

"Yeah." He closed it up and put it back in his pocket. "I called the number Duffy gave me. Left a message on the machine. Day or night," he tapped the pocket, "I'll be waiting to hear from him."

"You really think he'll call?"

"If he's far enough away and feels safe enough he might. He likes to brag."

"You were going to tell Ron, weren't you?" She shook her head angrily, "You're doing your share. I don't know what his problem is."

"I'm a handy scapegoat if he's taking heat. I talked to Duffy. Duffy skipped. Must be my fault. Only thing is that now there's been a twist. And I'm not sure if I should continue to share. Even without this bullshit." He told her about the call to his grandfather. "I don't like him on a personal level. And as a family patriarch he's less helpful than shit..."

"But he's still family?"

"Yeah. Goes against the grain to snitch on him. But it seems important. Duffy knew something was going to go down. Wanted me out of the way. Didn't sound like Duffy told him what it was... But it'd be the kind of thing I'd tell Essery. If there wasn't this conflict." He put the key in the ignition, "Think I'll move the truck a few blocks. Better if we don't stay in one place too long."

She looked in the shopping bag he'd carried to the hospital. "You bought new things."

"A tee shirt and a sweatshirt. There was a store next door to where I got the phone."

"You're really nice, know that?" The navy blue sweatshirt was more of a jacket, with a long zipper and cozy hood. "Thanks." He'd taken off the price tag. She snuggled in.

"Not that nice," he smiled. "Wasn't until I saw the store window that I realized you'd need something fresh. Hope you like it."

"It's great. Thanks."

He parked the truck in front of a pink stucco house with a California tile roof. The For Sale sign said Delta Realty.

"What's going to happen to Duffy's business?"

"I don't know, Rainie. Out of my league." He told her about his conversation with Marion's ex-husband.

"He and Duffy both sent her a thousand before Christmas."

"Yes."

"What did she do with it? How did she end up in squalor? In January she was on welfare under her maiden name."

"Gifts for the grandchildren. Moving expenses. But she didn't move her furniture. That dumpy crap came with the trailer. Wouldn't have cost that much. Rent a truck maybe, to move what she had. Unless she blew what was left..."

"But on what? New clothes? Old bills?"

"Not on bills. She stiffed hydro and the phone company when she left Nanaimo. And she was never much into fashion. No, something happened after she got the money to scare her into dropping everything and taking off."

"We know what scares us. *Snake*."

"What was the weather like last December?"

"I don't know. I wasn't going out."

"I was stuck inside too. But I kinda remember it wasn't too bad. Didn't snow. At least where I was."

"What does the weather have to do with Marion?"

"She was still talking about the reunion. Maybe she got it into her head that Sea Spray Island would be the perfect place. Her name was on the papers, maybe she thought she had the right to go and have a look. I can see her getting all excited about the trip. Going down to the Nanaimo wharf and making arrangements for a boat. Don't think she'd know how to pilot it. She'd need a captain."

"Those pictures in that *Snapack* folder showed a rough cabin. If that's the way she still thought it was, she'd want warm clothes and a sleeping bag."

"She wouldn't scrimp. Not if she had money in her pocket."

Rainie carefully draped the sweatshirt hood over her bump and bandage, "Think I'll hide while I imagine it. The boat docks. She's Happy again, with a capital H. She follows the trail. There must be a trail from the dock to the houses. Just delighted when she sees them."

"Perfect for the reunion."

"Then she sees all the people."

"Filipinos toiling in the fields. It was winter, toiling in the greenhouse, doing whatever they did."

"They tell her it's private property."

"She goes into her rap. Then the man with a snake tattoo and missing pinkie finger plants himself in front of her and next thing she's back on the boat."

"Hey, the captain would remember her."

"Yeah, but that's a Mountie job, asking around, finding him."

"It's only a theory."

"But it makes sense. Snake scared her enough to move, and Duffy knew her address in Nanaimo. The trailer in Courtenay was shitty, but it had one thing going for it, it was out of the way, off the beaten track."

Rainie pulled the hood back off her head. "You could be right. Maybe Snake's on the island now."

"Which would've made it really interesting if I'd done what Ferrier wanted, and gone exploring."

"I don't think I'd use the word *interesting*. What were you going to do today?"

"Bring you back to the hotel. Make sure you were comfortable and try to figure out who I could talk to about Ivan Portensky."

"You might as well do your figuring from the truck."

"Yeah."

"You said you know him."

"I've been around. He's been around. You get to know people. He's nasty like Snake. If I wanted to turn over jewellery or something he'd be the last one I'd see. Not even the last one. I wouldn't deal with him at all. Not worth the hassle putting up with an asshole like him, worrying if I'd get ripped off."

"So he was into stolen goods?"

"And drugs and prostitution."

"Duffy's girls on the island."

"And Duffy's company that brings so-called nannies and housekeepers from the Philippines. That must be what they're fighting over. Along with whatever other shit Duffy's into."

"Who can you ask?"

"I'll think of someone. One of the few good things about being inside, from juvie on up through the system, is all the friends I made over the years. Some are sinful degenerates and others are scofflaws of a more philosophical bent. I've pretty much always been able to get what I want. Either information or materials. But finding someone after three years might be a problem." He drummed on the steering wheel. "Nick Drake. He likes to know what's going on." He started the engine. "And they'd let us stay at their house—if they're still alive. He and his wife are pretty old."

Mike kept to secondary streets to avoid cops in case he was wanted. Although he didn't know why that would happen, but with Essery anything was possible. He stopped at a red light to cross Main Street, but he didn't see any cop cars. "Look at the gorgeous clothes," Rainie said, admiring the Punjabi women out shopping, glowing in their brilliant saris.

"Nick said he was glad they'd moved in, that they added a little colour to the neighbourhood. But it's the same as any other wave of immigrants, like the Ukrainians my grandfather's so proud of, give it a generation and the traditional duds became a costume for dress-up at weddings and multi-cultural festivals."

"I'd love to have a scarf from some of that fabric. To cover my wounds."

"Yeah? Lots of fabric stores around here." The light turned to green, he made it safely across Main. "Want me to get you some?"

"Be a lot more chic than a sweatshirt hood. And it's sunny. A lot less obvious."

He found a parking spot in front of a small apartment block. Rainie said she'd wait. She looked at the tee shirt he'd bought for her. Apricot colour, with a v-neck, it'd be easy to pull over her damaged head. He'd taken the price tag off that too. But it was good quality, so was the sweatshirt, and she guessed they weren't cheap.

He didn't take long. He slid in behind the wheel and handed her a bag. "There was too much to pick from. So I got three different kinds. One solid blue, one red and blue. They're the subtle ones. But try the other one first."

It was a kind of brocade pattern of electric blue shimmering with gold threads. "Wow. It's gorgeous."

"Thought you'd like it."

She tied it around her head and chanced a look in the mirror. The colours set off her eyes, making them appear bluer and more striking. She pulled it further down her forehead, tucked her hair up and retied it. "I don't look wounded now," she smiled. "Thanks."

The modest bungalow looked the same as he remembered, with a patch of lawn and neatly clipped evergreen hedges. Nick always said keep it simple, be a good neighbour and don't call attention to yourself.

"You want me to wait here?" Rainie asked, "While you see if they're home?"

"Yeah, sure."

"Who are these people?"

"Nick's an old crook of the philosophical type. He used to repair clocks and watches before he started having trouble with his eyes. He was a fence, and kind of a broker, put you in touch with whatever you might want. Last time I saw them, Silvana was sewing stripper costumes and fantasy outfits for hookers."

"It'll be nice to meet some of your old friends," she laughed. "Go see if they're home."

THIRTY-SEVEN

Silvana opened the door and recognized Mike right away. She bubbled with laughter and gave him a hug before she dragged him inside. She moved slowly with age, but still gracefully. Her white hair was pinned up in a loose bun. She wore elaborate gold earrings, probably from one of the East Indian shops back on Main.

The living room had a wall of books and the same maple colonial furniture they bought in the early fifties after one of Nick's major scores. Mike looked around and raised an eyebrow.

Silvana shrugged. "He cashed in his chips last year."

"Shit. I'm sorry."

"He didn't suffer. Had a good run for his money. Eighty-four years old, collapsed with a heart attack in his favourite second hand bookstore. Cop came to the door, I thought, uh-oh, what's the geezer got himself into this time. But he went quick. They said it was just like turning off a light bulb."

He put an arm around her shoulders, "How you holding up?"

"Not too bad, all things considered. Still healthy. I get lonely sometimes. Had him around for fifty-two years. Hard habit to break cold turkey. You're looking good. In spite of everything. I heard about Kevin."

"Yeah. Lost a brother and gained a sister. I think I told you that when we were taken from the commune they grabbed a little sister too."

"You found her? That's great!"

"Yeah, she's out in the truck. But the reason I found her isn't so great. Long story. Is there room for me to park in the back? We need to keep out of sight."

"Drive around and I'll unlock the garage. I sold Nick's old beater so there's room in there now."

He parked beside her Escort and locked the garage door.

Silvana stood to the side and beamed at Rainie. "So you're Mike's little sister. He's talked about you."

"You have?" She looked at him.

"Told you I always wondered what happened to you."

He made the introductions and they followed Silvana through the connecting door to a narrow room hung with oil paintings. "I built this," he said proudly, rapping his knuckles on the wall. "Rebuilt the garage and added the room to the back of the house." They wiped their feet on the sisal mat and walked into the compact kitchen.

"Sit down," Silvana said. "What can I get you? Had lunch yet?"

"I did," Rainie said.

"I didn't." Mike pulled out a chair. "But I'm not hungry. Coffee would be good." They sat at the oak table in the corner while Silvana got the coffee maker going.

"I don't have any cookies or anything."

"Shit, no cookies? Let's get the hell out of here, Rainie. There's no cookies!"

Silvana's delicate face crinkled into a smile, "I missed you, Mike."

"My following is small but loyal."

"Did Gloria stick around?"

"No."

"Shit happens."

He smiled and bobbed his head.

"Speaking of shit, what happened to Kevin?"

"Blown away with a .45. Then they arranged roaches and scales and coke so it'd look like he was into dealing again. But he wasn't. Not for years. Straight as a prairie highway. You still keep in touch?"

"Not as much as Nick did, but I hear things."

"Ivan Portensky."

"Computers and office equipment. There's a hungry market in Eastern Europe. He's supposed to be connected to a Russian Mafia type family. Keeps a dangle of ring-a-dings dizzy."

"He get busted last year?"

"Trafficking. With four others. I think it was ten pounds of coke. But he got off on a technicality."

"Has he been throwing his weight around recently?"

"More than usual? Not that I've heard. But I don't hear as much as Nick did." She stood up and brought mugs from the cupboard.

"Can I help?" Rainie asked.

"No dear, you just sit. This kitchen has always been too small for two people." She set out spoons, cream and sugar but the coffee wasn't ready yet and she sat down.

Rainie tugged on Mike's sleeve, "What are ring-a-dings?"

"Kids who steal for him. Pays them in drugs and pocket money. Like Raymond Kaslo."

"I've never heard of him," Silvana said.

"He either killed Kevin, or was around at the time it happened."

Rainie leaned closer. "Did Kevin sell computers in his store?"

"No. TV's, VCR'S, stereos. But I see where you're going. Ivan'd be into those, too. But Kevin wouldn't have gone for it."

"But what if he was approached to sell stolen goods? And then he threatened to go to the police?"

"Doesn't sound like Kevin. He'd just tell them to fuck off. What do you think, Silvana?"

"Wouldn't put it past Ivan to muscle his goods. The paper said Kevin managed Quality Systems?"

"That's right. High end market."

"Ivan'd like that. And if he knew Kevin'd done time but his employers didn't, maybe he'd push him with that."

Rainie turned sideways in the chair, adjusted the scarf and rested the back of her head against the wall. "*That's* what Leo must've seen when he was working in the warehouse. Computers going to Russia or stereos going somewhere. And Leo *would* go to the police. Duffy Dell's warehouse, doing dirty business with this Ivan Portensky, using Snake as a hit man. Leo was my husband." She looked at Silvana, "And Snake killed him."

Rainie shook her head at the ceiling, "What more do we need, Mike? What question? What answer? We know who and we know why. And none of this other crap matters. Can't we just find Snake and kill him? I'll kill him. Then I'll turn myself in. How bad could jail be? You just got out Mike, tell me, is it any worse than the rest of my life?"

"Not by much." He grinned at her until she had to smile. He could see the coffee was ready and he brought the pot around and filled their mugs. Silvana was an old lady, no reason for her to jump up every five minutes. He felt bad about Nick, but he half expected it, and at least it wasn't suicide or murder.

He went to the washroom, mostly because he wanted to be alone for a few minutes. Alone, because that was how his spirit felt. And if he could balance the inner and outer, he'd be an Enlightened Being, with answers before he even thought of the questions.

He wanted his mother. He wanted Mum. He wanted her to hug him and make him laugh and say everything would work out. He wanted tea and toast, the two of them sitting at a kitchen table. There'd been a lot of kitchens. He'd lost count, sitting and talking and catching up. He wanted to be a little kid again and be taken care of; he wanted his mommy.

He went back to his coffee. Rainie was looking pretty haggard. Blotchy, with bags under her eyes, glazed over. Shaky hands stirring sugar into a refill. She nodded at him as he took his seat. "We were talking about hookers. Silvana knows more about that than the other stuff. Duffy and Ivan are corrupt in different classes of society. Duffy calls his a private club and Ivan probably just says whorehouse, but they both have woman here illegally, selling their bodies. And when Duffy has them on the island they have to work the farm too. His are from the Philippines, Ivan's from Romania and Russia. I hate to think about what life must be like for them." She shook her head slowly. "So maybe this will be good for them. Even if Immigration sends them back. But the big thing is that Silvana's heard of a man called *Rick*, who muscles, as she put it, for Duffy's club. Snake flies in and out of the island on the helicopter with the women. I don't want to think about that, I don't want to visualize it because that's the closest thing I've ever heard to the bottomless pit of hell." She stared into the bottom of her mug. "Guess you should tell Silvana what it's all about. She still doesn't know."

"Yeah. And we haven't said anything yet about Barbara. Barbara Fleming? Duffy put up that big reward for her killer?"

"Knew this had to be about the reward." Silvana nodded. "Thought I'd wait for you to get around to the subject yourself."

"It's not. I haven't thought about it and I don't take it seriously. Especially since Duffy's disappeared." His coffee was cold but he needed the caffeine. He gulped it down. "Barbara was on the commune with us. Two days before we got yanked from there, Rainie, Kevin, Barbara Fleming and me, saw Snake kill a man."

"And my mother," Rainie said, "My mother saw too."

"Yeah, they were fighting over Rainie's mother. She hasn't seen her since that day. He threatened he'd kill us if we told. Now, Kevin and Barbara are dead. Leo was killed last fall, but it was a drive-by with Rainie standing right beside him."

"Missed me. You probably heard about it if you watch the news. He hit a few other people."

"I'm sorry, dear. But it occurs to me, and this is something I'd never say lightly, that you should go to the police with this."

He smiled tightly. "I did. You remember Essery? The one who thought he'd been appointed by On High to set me straight? He's a detective now. Working on Kevin and Leo's cases. I told him everything. Any little scrap I picked up. I went to see Duffy and repeated the conversation back to him word for word. Duffy wasn't a witness, but he helped dispose of the body. Duffy's skipped and suddenly it's all my fault. I was playing games, holding back, a real bad-ass. We've been staying in a hotel. Make it hard for Snake to look either of us up. Now he wants to move Rainie to his own safe house. No idea what he wants to do with me."

"I could ask him," Rainie said. "I should call, since I ran out on him. If we can work out a good story."

"Tell him you're staying with an old friend. I *am* old," Silvana smiled. "And you're welcome to the spare room."

"Thank you. I can put his mind at ease, tell him I ditched Mike."

"Leave a message for me at the hotel first," he said, "to make it look good. Here," he pulled the phone from his pocket, "I'll let you use my new toy."

Silvana looked up the number of the Royal Arms in the telephone book and Rainie made her first ever call on a cellular phone. She asked for the room, let it ring until the clerk got back on the line, and left a message.

Mike brought the coffee pot around for refills. Rainie wrapped her hands around the warm mug and closed her eyes.

"Tired?"

"No. Yes. But I was thinking about what your grandfather said."

"Grandfather?" Silvana asked, "Is this someone else from the commune?"

"No. My real one. My mother's father. We'll have to stay up pretty late for me to explain everything."

Mike and Rainie looked at each other. "It's a two person story, isn't it," she said, "I mean it'll take two people to tell it." She turned to Silvana, "Mike simplified it to the bare bones. We witnessed. We were threatened. And now we're dying. But he did leave a lot out."

"Duffy and my grandfather are business associates. That's something I've haven't told Essery. And I only heard about it this morning."

"According to Mike's grandfather, Duffy and Ivan Portensky are feuding. Ivan couldn't get to Duffy because of all his bodyguards and security. But he wants to show how nasty he is, so he has some people killed."

"He didn't actually say that, but that's how it sounded. He said Ivan was on a rampage and killed Kevin. No reason given."

"But he also said Ivan picked one of his employees at random. *Barbara.* But that's not really random. Or we go back to coincidence and we've already decided that's impossible."

"My grandfather doesn't know the background. But we do and so does Snake. He said Duffy sent Snake out to deal with Ivan but couldn't find him? The reason seems completely reasonable and logical to me. *Snake was siding with Ivan.* You want to scare Duffy? Show him no one's safe? I'll take care of it. I'll kill a couple of people for you. Perfect occasion to deal with old issues. If Marion went over to Sea Spray like we think, then he heard about the Zem-Zem reunion. Maybe about her photo album too. The question we haven't asked yet, what's the connection between Snake and Ivan? And it isn't even our question. It's Ron Essery's. So there you go. All figured out. The mystery's solved. Don't we all feel better? Go home and get a good night's sleep? But we can't, can we?"

"No," Rainie shook her head, "Not with Snake still out there."

THIRTY-EIGHT

Ron Essery wasn't available to take her call; Rainie left her message with another cop. She said she'd be staying with an old friend, declined to give the number or address, but she'd watch the news and call after she heard Snake had been captured.

Rainie handed the phone back to Mike and leaned against the wall, closing her eyes, relieved she didn't have to talk to Ron. Lack of sleep stiffened her neck and weighed her sore head but her mind still whirled and analyzed. "Mike," she said, opening her eyes, "Have you talked to Barbara's husband?"

"Only that one time. When I called him after I found Marion."

"Do you think Snake would go there? See if Barbara had any Zem-Zem pictures saved? Or just to harass him?"

"I don't know what Snake would do."

"Because I want to see her husband. We have something in common, Snake killed both our spouses. And I want to see her kids too. How old are they? The ages we were in Zem-Zem?"

"Around that, I guess. You want to see him now?"

"No. Later. Tomorrow. Next week. Don't think I can move right now. It's nice here. Quiet and peaceful."

"Looks like it's bedtime."

"Yeah. If I can get up." She struggled to her feet. Silvana took charge with a gentle hand on her arm and led her down a hallway, pointing out the bathroom and opening the door to a small bedroom. "You'll be comfortable here, dear."

"Yes. Thank you. Wake me up when it's over." She began to untie the scarf. "I hit my head last night." She showed her the wounds and explained how it happened. They talked about make-up and hairdressers.

Silvana slid open a drawer of the old bow-front bureau and brought out a long flannelette nightgown. "This one's seen many a cozy night." She laid it on the pink flowered bedspread. "Anything else you need, just help yourself."

"Thanks. It's very kind of you to do this."

"You're doing *me* a favour. I appreciate the company. It's been hard being alone so much since my husband died. But you'd know about that, wouldn't you?"

"I sure do."

"You have any children?"

"No."

"You're young. You have time. Before I met Nick I had one of those back street abortions. Left me sterile." She shrugged. "That was that."

"I had an abortion too. But it was a regular doctor and I'm okay. I didn't tell Mike about it. Guess he thinks I'm Snow White."

"We all have our little secrets, dear."

"Talking about this reminds me that my period's a couple of days late. Left the napkins back in the hotel so I hope I don't bleed all over your sheets."

"There's a box of Tampax in the bathroom vanity. One of the girls left it a couple of years ago but I don't think they go bad. And if it turns out you don't need any, well, I think Mike would make a very good father."

"Oh no, I'm not pregnant. It's stress or something. We don't sleep together. We're brother and sister. We had separate bedrooms in the hotel. One of those furnished apartment hotels."

"I see."

"You think it's strange?"

"Unexpected, that's all." She wiggled her nose, "Ah, the pungent aroma of mara-hoochie. I'd better get in there before Mike smokes it all himself. You have a good sleep and we'll talk again later." She walked out to the hall.

Rainie had a question and called her back. "Silvana? Are there any rules?"

"Rules? This isn't a college dormitory. Just make yourself at home."

"No. I mean, I don't know how to say this, you're a senior, but you smoke pot. You know about hookers and thieves. And there was your husband. And Mike just got out of jail. I think he used the word *scofflaws*. But you're all really nice people. I'm sorry, guess I must be tired."

"We know who our friends are." Silvana's smile reached to the wrinkles surrounding her pale blue eyes. "We don't rat on them. We stand by them."

Merlee had cookies and stuff ready when they came back from school. After they ate Amy and Billy went out to play with their friends. Merlee said it was a sunny day outside and she should get fresh air too but Charlie didn't want to and stayed in the kitchen watching her make supper.

After a while the door bell rang and Merlee went to get it. It was Detective Ferrier and another one, a lady in a uniform. They talked at the door and he said something about papers. They went down to the basement to Merlee's room.

Charlie didn't understand because they didn't buy the newspaper so she went and sat on the stairs and listened. Merlee gave him ID and stuff and he talked and said she didn't have the right things. She started to cry. Charlie got scared and ran up the stairs.

The police came up with Merlee. She had her purse. He said Merlee was going with him because he had to talk to her in the office. He didn't know when she'd come back. Charlie started to cry. Merlee was crying too but she said they were the police and she had to go with them.

He asked if Charlie was alone and she said yes. Daddy was at work but he'd come home for supper. Merlee said what time and that the other kids would be back then too. She told the lady cop that she was cooking and if she could turn the heat down. The lady said yes and went to the kitchen with her.

Detective Ferrier said if there was a neighbour she could go to until Daddy came home because he couldn't leave her alone. She said she could go to Nancy's house and he walked down the block with her. Then he wasn't sure he would let her because the granny didn't know English but Nancy's older brother talked Chinese to her and she said yes, yes, because that was all she knew how to say and she gave Charlie a hug. And Nancy was there too and Charlie said she played there a lot. So he said it was okay.

Charlie didn't want to play or eat or anything. She was crying. She stayed by the front window and waited for Daddy to come home. She saw the police car go away and Merlee was in the back seat and she cried harder.

Nancy's brother asked her questions but she didn't know anything. The granny brought her tissues to blow her nose. All Charlie wanted to do was stay at the window and wait for Daddy's car. Nancy waited with her. She sat in a chair and looked at a book.

After a long time Charlie saw Daddy's car. She ran out. Amy and Billy were already home. Everyone was wondering where Charlie and Merlee were. She told them what happened. Daddy got mad at Uncle Duffy. He said bad words too. He said he trusted him and might get in trouble even though he didn't know. He told them what papers meant but he was really mad and started yelling about Uncle Duffy making it worse for his children.

Daddy took off his jacket and necktie and went to the kitchen. There was meat in the oven and cut up vegetables in the refrigerator. Daddy put salad dressing on the vegetables but no one ate it much. He cut up the meat but it was all bloody inside and everyone said it was yucky so he put it back in the oven. He called up for pizza and said it was back to square one.

Billy asked if Merlee was coming back but Daddy didn't know. He said he was going to be smart this time and call his lawyer first and have him talk to the police. But if she couldn't come back they'd get another housekeeper but the right way so the police wouldn't take her away.

Charlie didn't know what the right way was but she wanted Merlee back, not anyone else and she started to cry again. Daddy told her not to cry. It would be okay. He went to the den to make phone calls until the pizza came.

Mike had two tokes from the joint he'd been working on all day and propped the remainder on the handle of a teaspoon, too lazy to look for an ashtray. When Silvana returned to the kitchen she thanked him for leaving her the roach.

"It's the kind of dope the cops advertise as being ten times more potent than the shit from the sixties. If you don't want to go comatose, one toke's enough."

"Groovy," she laughed, "But I think using an ashtray would be far more civilized, no matter what the potency." She disappeared to the living room and brought back a ceramic boomerang shape in bright turquoise. She lit up, sucked in her creases and folds, and held them. Mike rubbed his eyes, scratched his scalp and wished he had a cigarette. He heard the toilet flush down the hall. He thanked Silvana for the hospitality.

She nodded, and when her breath returned to normal, said he could repay her by telling the whole, long story from the very beginning.

He did. He had it down pat and polished now, without sweating, without the churning stomach. Halfway through he asked if she had any cigarettes kicking around but she shook her head no. He continued, trying to keep his voice level, pouring it out, trying to stay cool, the weed taking the edge off the anxiety. When he finished he spread his hands, palms out, wordlessly asking for her help.

She tapped her lips with an index finger, said she'd make some calls, and left him alone in the kitchen.

He made a call on his own phone, to the hotel, and received Rainie's message. She'd be okay and safe. He didn't have to worry about her now. But his family of ashes was still back in the hotel and it wasn't right to abandon them.

He went to the living room and looked around for an urn of Nick's ashes but didn't see one. He went to the den, the small room he'd built between kitchen and garage. No urn there. Before he went inside she'd used the room for her sewing. She must've retired because the sewing machine cabinet supported a heavy nineteenth century pendulum clock. The paintings on the walls: typical B.C. stuff, crashing waves, the smell of cedar, mountains reduced to canvas size, paradise Sea Spray reduced to a brothel work camp, trees and ocean, no way out. Grandfather, *stay with your own people Mike* fucking *Beautiful and always cheerful* Filipino women. *They let too many in. They take jobs from Canadians* Snake taking turns, Snake sitting on the deck drinking. Snake his enemy with the tattoo curling down the arm, eating fingers, hands, lives, souls.

Silvana tracked him down. "I can see how Essery'd get his bowels in an uproar. Ivan Portensky got blown away early this morning."

He snapped into focus. "And all the angels sang. But what time? Hope I have an alibi."

"Around four."

"I'm okay. I was talking to Australia on the hotel's line. I'm okay. How'd it happen?"

"The shooter climbed in through an upstairs window. Shot him in the head while he was sleeping. There was a girl asleep next to him, but he let her be. No one else was in the house. She didn't see anything. Too dark. Too much of a shock. What a way to wake up, eh? It was on the news. They're calling it an underworld execution."

"Snake's getting real adept. His drive-by, blasting his way down the block, is downright crude in comparison."

"It wasn't Snake," she shook her head, "He would've wasted the girl too. No, that was a real pro. I'd lay odds Duffy's behind it." She sunk into the armchair beside the antique clock. "You're right about the pot. Don't think I should have any more until after I make supper." She rubbed her knees, "And it makes my legs ache. Don't have the tolerance I used to. Would you get me one of the painkillers from on top of the refrigerator, please? It's a bitch getting old."

He shook out a tablet, filled a glass with water and waited while she got the pill down. She gave him back the glass and rubbed her pale hands together. "Turn on the baseboard heater. It gets cold this side of the house."

"I'll put in a skylight when this is over."

"For now just turn up the heat. Put that glass in the kitchen and come sit down. I have other things to tell you."

He did as he was told and came back to sit on the loveseat.

"Duffy put out a contract on Rick the Snake. That's what that reward really is. A quarter million dollar contract, announced in a televised press conference."

"He didn't tell me that when I talked to him."

"Everyone on the street knows that's what it is. There were four girls on that little island the day the police helicopter took pictures. Just the girls and the couple who caretake. Gardening, working in the greenhouse. They all hid until it was gone. A few days after that, Duffy sent his own helicopter and brought everyone back to the city. He closed his club, handed out severance pay and airline tickets home."

"One step ahead of the pigs."

"They were starting to ask the right questions. Both his helicopter and yacht are gone. Rumour puts him in the Philippines, sailing to South America, or dead."

"I'll ask him if he gets back to me. What about Snake?"

"Rick's running scared. Armed and dangerous and desperate. He got out to that little island because he had money stashed there. Girls gone, caretakers gone, his stash gone."

"And weeds in the garden."

"The last anyone's heard of him was the night of that big storm. Ivan was partying with some Russians and three girls. I talked to one of the girls. He got a beep on his pager. He called back and it was Rick. Demanding money. Ivan laughed and hung up. Just then the power went out. The Russians pulled out guns and the girls hid under the beds. Until they realized it was just the storm, and that Rick couldn't know where they were. But someone did, because that's the house where he got whacked."

Interesting, but it didn't tell him where to find Snake. Silvana massaged her knees and yawned. She probably got off on the excitement, reminded her of old times, but she'd need a nap pretty soon. He stood up and stretched. "Don't worry about supper."

"And don't worry about Rainie. She'll be fine. Listen, Nick left me a few pieces. You can have your pick."

"After I talk to Essery." He pulled the baggie of pot and the rolling papers from his pocket. "Better leave this here too. One less reason to get hauled in."

She tried to stand up but missed the first time around. He gently lifted her to her feet and helped her out of the room.

THIRTY-NINE

Stoned and on the move, without Rainie to worry about, with the sun smiling and shining, jingle in his pocket and a full tank of gas. Mike stopped at a red light beside a cherry '65 Mustang convertible: Perfect day to have the top down. The driver was a tiny woman with long black hair, singing along to Tom Petty's *Don't Back Down*. She noticed Mike smiling at her, smiled back, and gave him the power salute. The light turned green, she made a left, and Mike continued on his way to the Royal Arms.

He asked at the desk for messages. Nothing new, but the interested and slightly nervous clerk made him suspect the cops would be called as soon as he stepped in the elevator.

There wasn't much he wanted. The prison letters, various papers. He stuck those in his tee shirt. He tucked Kevin's urn in one arm, Marion's raku vase in the other, and carried his mother's mason jar in his hand.

He crossed the lobby, ignored the clerk, and took the stairs down to the garage. With his arms full he couldn't get at his keys. He carefully lowered Kevin to the ground and dug them out. With the clock ticking, imagined sirens screaming down the street, he took off his jean jacket and made a padded nest on the floor of the passenger side.

He drove up to the street cautiously, expecting a blockade and drawn revolvers. But the cops hadn't arrived yet and he made a quick getaway, avoiding the main drag, sticking to residential streets.

But he had nowhere to go. And nothing to do. Except call Essery. He pulled behind an apartment block and parked in a visitor's spot.

He loved his little cell phone. He flipped it open and punched in Essery's number. He hoped he'd be *available*, and waited, phone to his ear, lounging against the passenger door, fingertips tracing the contours of his family vessels.

He still wasn't in. But Mike liked the female voice on the line so much he gave her his alibi for the time of Ivan's murder. He sent his love to Essery and told her to have a nice day.

Having exhausted his entire To Do list, he flipped the phone closed and turned on the radio. He heard that the police had released the name of the gangland execution victim, but not what he wanted to hear, nothing about Snake. He wondered how long he could stay there out of sight, it felt safer than driving around the street. He saw a Blue Box beside the garbage dumpster, went out for a look and brought back a stack of the *Vancouver Sun* and *Province*.

As far as he could tell, skimming the pages of the last few days, Raymond Kaslo, the UFO reject, had not been charged with Kevin's murder. Nobody he knew had been charged with anything. He settled in for a good long read.

He was deep into an analysis of the G-7 conference, (shit, he'd missed it,) when his mind drifted back to Snake. Mean, nasty and desperate. Where would he go? What would he do? Mike didn't know enough about him. What would he want, was a better question. What would he need to regain his personal balance?

If Snake was a sociopath, and he probably was, the wants, needs, and the balance itself, followed an internal logic. And he wasn't stupid either. He'd stayed clear of the cops for years, except for one drunk driving offence.

Mike could only think of one thing. If killing the witnesses to Raven's murder held importance, then closing the circle of dysfunction, killing them all, would satisfy the demands of balance.

Mike could be the bait to flush him out. With the cops there, clicking on handcuffs, Mike looking him in the eye, saying, *Snake, I told.*

Daddy's lawyer, Mr. Morgan, came to the house and asked Charlie lots of questions about Detective Ferrier and Merlee. He said it was against the law for the police to leave her at Nancy's house. Charlie said it was okay because she played there a lot and the granny let her. He said they didn't know English. She said it was okay because they were nice.

Daddy said they weren't allowed to leave her with any one but him. Mr. Morgan was going to go to the police and complain. When he was there he'd see why they took Merlee away. And try to get her back.

Charlie liked that. She wanted Merlee to come back. Mr. Morgan said he would try very hard. Daddy told her to go and play. She went to the backyard and sat on the swings and wiggled her front tooth. It was very, very loose. She could taste blood and it hurt a little bit so she stopped.

Amy came out and gave her a push. She went high. But Amy went really high. She didn't tell her about her tooth. She wanted to do an experiment.

One time her friend Megan lost her tooth at school. It fell on the floor and she couldn't find it. She was crawling under the table looking for it and crying because the Tooth Fairy wouldn't come if she didn't have it. Some of the kids laughed at her. They said there was no Tooth Fairy. That it was just your parents. Charlie sort of knew that. But she wanted to do an experiment and find out.

She played in her room and then Daddy came in and talked to her but she tried not to wiggle the tooth so it wouldn't come out yet. But then she couldn't help it and it came out when she was in the bathtub.

She didn't tell Daddy. She didn't tell anyone except Mommy up in the sky. She put on her nightgown and got into bed and put the tooth under the pillow right next to Mommy's picture.

When Daddy came up to tuck her in she made believe she was asleep. He kissed her head and pulled up the covers and went out.

Mike had a cop on his tail for a few blocks as he drove around looking for a hardware store. When the cop turned off, and Mike's heart rate slowed, he saw the store he wanted and went in to look for a heavy duty plastic bin. He had his choice of see-through or slate blue. He bought the blue.

He opened the passenger door of the pick-up and put the bin on the seat. He tore off the price tag and the label. He put the real estate sections of the newspapers on the bottom.

He wrapped Kevin in Entertainment, Mum in Cooking, and Happy Marion in Books. He snapped the lid down tightly. The bin wouldn't fit on the floor. He pulled the seat belt as far as it would go and belted his family in.

He got behind the wheel and patted the top of the bin. He tried Essery again. This time he was in.

Mike had to wade through major shit over Rainie. Then it was Essery's half baked theory of collusion, games, fuck the pigs, how come Duffy knew to clear everyone off Sea Spray Island when Mike was the only one who knew? The Horsemen dropped a squad in and there was plenty evidence of recent habitation, but not a soul. And did Mike know how hard it was to keep his C.I.'s name confidential when he sat in a conference, like he did that afternoon, liaise with the Horsemen, worry about how Mike may or may not have screwed him over royally?

Mike lost patience. "You think Snake's still in town?"

"There's been sightings."

"What's he driving?"

"Anything he wants. He's been boosting cars. Fills the ashtrays with Player's Light. Litters the interior with fast food bags."

"What's he sticking around for?"

"Money. He was trying to play both Duffy Dell and Ivan Portensky. Now the Russian's dead and Dell's split. He got ripped off from both ends."

"Besides staking out every drive-through, you have any plan to catch him?"

"We're working on it."

"I have an idea."

"Oh?" He blew smoke across the receiver. "Another idea of how to get me in shit?"

"I want to put the word out that I'm looking for him. He killed my brother and I want a showdown. Because I think he wants me. It's a dare he won't refuse. I'll wear a wire this time. A bullet proof vest would be cool too. You guys tail me. You and the whole damn Emergency Response Team. But you'll have to tell me where to start looking. Who to bully. What parts of town he hangs in. I don't have a clue."

Essery didn't say a word. Mike could hear him smoking.

"Are you serious, Mike?"

"It's the only thing I can think of. I won't have any peace until he's caged up. There hasn't been any normalcy in my life since I got out. I don't care about confidentiality anymore. Whatever it takes. I just want it over."

FORTY

Charlie woke up and the first thing she did was look under the pillow. The tooth was still there and so was Mommy's picture. She went to the bathroom and got dressed and went downstairs to the kitchen. Daddy was there drinking coffee.

He said she was up early. Then he said he had a headache and didn't feel good. She did the second part of the experiment. She showed him her mouth and the tooth. Daddy smiled and everything. He said his baby was growing up. He said she had to put the tooth under her pillow that night for the Tooth Fairy. She didn't tell about the experiment.

Daddy drank his coffee and then went to wake up Amy and Billy. He made eggs for breakfast. He drove them to school. Charlie kept sticking her tongue in the place where her tooth fell out.

Mike awoke from a hard night in a cheap motel in Surrey, with the smell of mildew, a sagging mattress and the constant roar of traffic. He was supposed to meet Essery at the same greasy spoon they'd been to before, but was running late. He had a quick shower to clear his head. No fresh clothes, no razor, no toothbrush.

He hit the morning rush on the Fraser Highway, followed the pack of worker bees onto King George and over the Pattullo Bridge, listening to the radio, hoping for good news.

Traffic moved swiftly but it was still half an hour before he got to the coffee shop. Essery was seated in a booth in the back corner with coffee, cigarette and the remains of bacon and eggs.

"You're late. Thought you changed your mind."

"I don't have an alarm clock."

"You look like shit."

"Better than I feel." He turned the empty coffee cup upright and motioned to the waitress.

"Go on a bender last night?"

"No."

"How's Rainie?"

"Fine, I guess. Didn't hear anything bad on the news."

"Yeah." Essery grunted and blew smoke straight at his face.

Mike lit one of Essery's cigarettes and blew smoke straight back. The waitress interrupted what may have escalated into nuclear war by bringing the coffee pot around. Mike ordered eggs over easy.

"You given up pinning the blame on me for everything?"

Essery shrugged. "The jury's still out but it looks like acquittal."

"What's the verdict on my voluntary victimization?"

"You have a will?"

"Yeah. Made one before I went inside. I'll have to rewrite it. My mother and Kevin were the beneficiaries." He drank the coffee and smoked the cigarette. Good combination. And Player's Light, too. Same brand as Snake. "When do we set this thing in motion?"

"Tonight. And it's an *operation*. Operation Reptile."

"That's clever."

"There's a lot riding on you. Don't go on an ego trip."

"That's not the purpose."

"No, it's not. This operation screws up and I'm in deep shit."

"Sounds like you're the one on an ego trip. What is it? You been a bad boy from time to time? Called on the carpet?"

"That's neither here nor there."

"I'm right." Mike laughed and stubbed out the cigarette.

"We have a meeting at ten o'clock. You'll meet my boss. And the squad who'll be working with you. Do me a favour, don't embarrass me."

"Would I do that?"

"You'd love to."

"Probably. But I'll save it for another time."

"One thing I'll say for you, you have a pretty clean mouth. Considering where you spent the last three years."

"Thank you. I've made a concerted effort. Got tired of the five word vocabulary: Fuck, shit, asshole, motherfucker and *cock*sucker."

Mike's breakfast arrived. Eggs, hash browns, toast, a curl of orange and fringe of kale. "I can't believe it. That's kale. How come I got kale? You have parsley."

"They must've run out. No one eats it anyway."

"I do."

"You were always a non-conformist."

The waitress brought separate cheques but Essery reached for both. "It's on the taxpayer."

"Not necessary," Mike said with a mouthful of toast.

"Yes it is. You're mine from now on. Short leash, Mike. With a receipt for every fart and whistle. It's you and me, kid. We're married now."

Rainie couldn't believe how long she'd slept. She went to the washroom but couldn't face the mirror. Her period hadn't come yet. She felt icky and sticky and needed a shower but Silvana wasn't up yet and she didn't want to disturb her.

She tied the scarf around her head and padded barefoot to the kitchen to start a pot of coffee dripping. She opened the bottom half of the café curtains and looked out at an amazingly beautiful spring day. It was a shame to waste it. She wanted to go out. Do something. Most of all she wanted to go home.

Mike wasn't around. She didn't know if he'd slept there or not. She turned on the radio on top of the fridge beside a bottle of extra-strength arthritis medicine and listened for the news.

Rainie was halfway to perky by the time Silvana woke up. But one look at the old woman told her she wasn't a morning person. Rainie had a shower and kept out of her way. It took two hours of coffee and mild movement before Silvana joined the human race.

She said Rainie should wash her dirty jeans and gave her a pair of fleece jogging pants to wear while the washer and drier worked. She brought her to the dressing table in her bedroom, sat beside her, and gave instructions on make up application as Rainie transformed herself from hag to the appearance of health.

When she had again dressed in her own jeans, clean now, no longer blood spattered, they took the car and drove to a supermarket for groceries.

Silvana pushed the buggy, moving snail-like down the aisles. Rainie had to constantly remind herself to slow her pace. They were at the check-out before she realized she wasn't bothered by fears.

They had a sandwich lunch in a little tea shop. Silvana told her a bit about herself. She came from Ontario, from a German family, and spoke the language fluently. She'd been a spy in Nazi-occupied Paris. Recruited because of her talent as an exotic dancer. From what she didn't say, Rainie understood she'd been a prostitute too.

Silvana checked her watch and they had to rush back for *Coronation Street*. Rainie had never watched any soaps and Silvana filled her in during the commercials. She found it a little strange that she talked as if the characters were real people with real problems.

Rainie began to worry about Mike. She didn't have the number of his cellular phone. She remembered what she'd thought of the day before, when she was so tired and disgusted. She'd still like to talk to Barbara's husband. Maybe Silvana would loan her the car. She smiled to herself. That knock on the head must've shook some healing loose.

Mike wore a microphone taped underneath his tee shirt. A bullet proof vest had been vetoed as out of character but he was allowed to wear his jean jacket. A surveillance van followed. Essery and a young, wiry cop named Fields rode in a ghost car. No one expected him to stumble on Snake. The plan was for him to stir up the muddy water.

The mud he was to stir first belonged to a stripper named Cheryl, living in a quiet low-rise near English Bay. He gained access to the building by simply pressing the downstairs' bell to her apartment. When she asked who it was, he said *Mike*, and she buzzed him in.

Cheryl was tall, with a huge mane of blonde hair, wearing walking shorts that showed off her fine dancer's legs. She wrinkled her forehead in puzzlement; he wasn't the Mike she knew.

"I'm looking for Rick."

Her eyes widened and fear flickered across her fascinating face. "I don't know any Rick."

He shouldered his way in, laying it on thick; he wasn't a natural asshole. Speedily looking through the rooms, the smell of pork chops frying, Cheryl frightened, her breathing shallow and rapid.

He'd been supplied with pen and paper. He scrawled his cell number and slapped it down on the nearest horizontal surface. "Tell him Moonbeam is looking for Snake."

Daddy was home when Charlie got back from school. He was in bed coughing and sneezing and sick. He asked her to get the cough syrup and cold medicine. She didn't know which box. Amy found the right stuff and gave it to him. He was drinking too and he had the bottle and a picture of him and Mommy in bed there with him.

Merlee wasn't back yet. They had cookies she made that were still in the cookie jar. Amy and Billy went to play with their friends. Charlie stayed home and watched cartoons.

When Amy came back she said she'd make supper. She said she knew how to cook. She got out different pots and took hamburger from the freezer. She got really bossy and Charlie went out and sat on the swings. She felt bad. After a while she went up to her room and put her tooth under her pillow.

Amy made spaghetti and sauce. That was okay. But the meat was burnt in some parts and frozen in the middle. And she put other stuff in there with it and it was yucky. Charlie went to tell Daddy but he was asleep. She tried to wake him up. He picked up his arm and opened his eyes and said something that sounded like words but didn't. Then he turned over and wouldn't get up. She tried and tried and then she went down and told Amy.

After they had the spaghetti Amy said that she cooked supper so Billy and Charlie had to clean up. She went out. Billy said Charlie should do it and he went out too. Charlie didn't feel like cleaning up and went to her room.

The doorbell rang. Charlie ran down and knew it was Merlee coming back but when she opened the door it wasn't. It was a lady she didn't know. She wore a pretty scarf on her head. She wanted to talk to Daddy. Charlie said he was sick and in bed. Then the lady asked if she was Barbara's daughter and Charlie said yes. The lady said she knew Mommy when she was her age and was very sorry about what happened. Charlie said thank you because that's what Daddy said to say when people said that stuff.

Then a man with a beard and glasses came in the front yard and walked up the stairs and looked at the lady and grabbed her arm and said Lotus. She didn't say anything and her face got all red.

Charlie got scared and wanted to close the door because the man looked mean. She started to but the man pushed it open and didn't let go of the lady and pushed her in and pushed Charlie too. He closed the door and Charlie saw his hand looked funny and that scared her too. He kept holding the lady and looking at her and they walked and went to the kitchen. He made the lady sit at the table and told Charlie to sit down too.

He said to get Daddy but Charlie was too scared to move. Then the lady talked. She said her name was Rainbow and she was Lotus' daughter. He said swear words and the f-word and said he didn't get a good look at her before but she looked just like her mother. He talked a lot. He said Barbara and Duffy and other names Charlie didn't know. He said Duffy went away and did the lady know where he was. Charlie tried to listen hard and pay attention because she knew it was important but she didn't understand it all.

He thought Daddy wasn't home because he couldn't see him. He knew about Merlee working there and yelled her name. Charlie didn't know what to say. He thought she was out shopping and said about a babysitter and Charlie shook her head.

Then the man said not to be scared he wasn't going to hurt anyone. He wanted to talk to Rainbow. He said she should get something to eat and relax. He said have Fruit Loops or something. He said kids always liked cereal. And when he said CEREAL she knew he was the CEREAL KILLER and the one who killed Mommy. Daddy was asleep. Nobody was there. Only the lady she didn't know.

He had aged, grown a beard and put on glasses but he couldn't disguise his cold brown eyes. Crazy, dilated eyes staring straight through her. Rainie saw that hand again, the scars where the pinkie finger should have been, scars up the side of the hand to the snake hidden, waiting, beneath a jacket sleeve.

They sat at a round table in a windowed alcove off the kitchen. A breakfast nook. Beyond his head she saw long clusters of yellow flowers dripping from the slender branches of a golden chain tree in the backyard.

The child had gone pale. She was trembling. And wiggling in a way Rainie recognized. She asked if she had to go to the bathroom.

He said where was it and Charlie pointed down the hall. It wasn't near the door and he said it was okay but she shouldn't try to run away. He put his hands on the lady's neck and said he'd kill her if she tried to get away.

This was the man who killed her husband and took her mother. He was looking over towards the washroom, watching for the little girl, talking again, talking crazy, spinning fantasies, who crossed him, who owed him, she owed him, turning to her with the crazy eyes, because she stole his money, turning back towards the hall.

Charlie was very scared. First the man said he wouldn't hurt anyone then he said he'd kill the lady. She went to the bathroom and locked the door. Daddy's portable phone was on the back of the toilet where he always forgot it. She peed because she had to real bad. When she got up she looked at the phone again. When they talked about touching they said you had to tell. Charlie picked up the phone and pressed 911.

He wanted his money back, flaring his nostrils, puffing, vile breathe, working up anger and madness, she stole his money, she hadn't changed in all the years, cheap cunt, running out on him, she wouldn't run out this time, she stole his money from the island this time he'd get it back this time she wouldn't get away. He turned to her with yellow teeth, with a caricature of a smile, the scarred hand reaching inside his pants.

Rainie lunged across the room and grabbed the first thing she could get her hands on, hefting it like a baseball bat, swinging with her whole body and spirit and all the years of fright and tears and anger. She heard *the crack*, the same crack she heard when Raven died.

Charlie unlocked the bathroom door and tried to be very quiet. Then she saw the lady standing in the kitchen. But she didn't see the man. She tip toed and then she saw he was on the floor and all bloody. She told the lady that she called the police.

"Good. That's good." Rainie took a step closer and looked at him. He appeared to still be alive. His arms and legs were moving a little and there were strange gurgling sounds. There was a lot of blood. She'd connected with his nose, glasses and cheekbone and he'd fallen backwards against the wall. She looked at what she was holding in her hands and discovered her weapon had been a cast iron skillet.

Rainie looked at the little girl. "Maybe you shouldn't be seeing this. It's pretty gross."

"It's okay. He killed my mother."

"He killed my husband, too."

"Is he dead?"

He'd stopped moving. He'd stopped gurgling. "I don't know."

"Should we tie him up?"

"I don't think we need to." She put the skillet down on the counter and wiped the sweat from her hands. "And I don't want to touch him."

"He had a gun." The child pointed at the handle sticking out of his waist band.

"I guess that's what he was reaching for. I thought it was something else when I hit him. What's your name?"

"Charlie. It's really Charlotte but everyone calls me Charlie."

"Mine's really Rainbow but everyone calls me Rainie." She took her hand, "Let's go outside and wait for the police."

Mike walked out of an auto body shop, totally pissed off at the whole deal of walking in Snake's footsteps, stirring up the people he'd recently terrorized, or, worse, seeing the low-lifes he called buddy.

The ghost car was parked right out front, Essery honking the horn and waving his arm out the window, grinning from ear to ear, shouting, "You're not going to believe this!"

"What? You caught him?"

"Rainie did. Knocked him out cold." Essery gave another honk on the horn.

FORTY-ONE

The police woke Daddy up and he was sick and sleepy. He didn't understand at first but then he did and hugged Charlie real hard. He got dressed and came downstairs.

There were lots of police there and ambulance people and they took the man away. They said he might not make it and Rainie said they shouldn't work too hard at it.

Billy saw all the police cars and the ambulance and he and his friends ran down the block to see. He was mad that he missed it because he wanted to be the one who caught him. Then Amy came back and all the time Charlie was telling what happened.

More police came and Detective Ferrier and she asked him about Merlee. Daddy said he had the flu and really needed her to look after the children. Detective Ferrier said he'd bring her back and she helped him a lot because she worked for Duffy before and told him stuff but Charlie didn't understand.

Then Detective Ron came with a different man and the man hugged Rainie and she told him what happened. He shook Daddy's hand and said hello to Charlie. She looked out the window and there were people with TV cameras outside. They wanted to take pictures and talk to Charlie but Daddy said no.

All the police and everybody left. Charlie went to the kitchen and looked at the blood on the floor. Amy said it was worse than yucky and Daddy said not to go near it because it might have germs. But Charlie looked at it and thought about Mommy.

Then she heard people in the backyard and they had cameras and were taking pictures through the window. She ran and told Daddy and he yelled at them to go away it was private property.

They sat in the family room and Amy got a blanket for Daddy because he was cold. He felt bad because he'd been asleep when the man came and was saying all the bad things that almost happened. He started to cry and so did Charlie and everyone was crying when the doorbell rang. Daddy said not to answer it because it was just reporters but Billy looked and it was Detective Ferrier with Merlee. Everyone got excited and she came in and hugged Charlie and said she was a very brave girl. She got rubber gloves and the bucket and said she was happy to clean the blood because it was Rick's blood and she knew him and he was a very bad man.

After she cleaned the kitchen she made them stuff to eat. Daddy went back to bed. Charlie had a bath and got into her nightgown. She knew Daddy couldn't tuck her in because he was sick so she went and tucked him in and said good night. He said she should get Amy and Billy too. When they came in he gave Amy the bottle and said she was the oldest so she should pour it out in the sink and throw away the bottle. He promised that he wouldn't drink anymore.

When Charlie got up in the morning she almost forgot about her tooth but she looked under the pillow and there was a five dollar bill next to Mommy's picture.

She went to school and Ms Lundel showed the newspaper. It said *CLOBBERED* and had a picture of Rainie holding a frying pan. Charlie told what happened and everyone asked questions. Then they drew pictures about it and everyone wanted to see what Charlie made. She drew the man on the floor with the gun sticking out and the broken glasses and the blood but it didn't look the way it did in her head. Charlie thought that when she grew up she'd be an artist so she could make the pictures come out right.

Rainie called her in-laws before they had a chance to be shocked by the news reports. They were overjoyed to hear from her again after so long. She gave them her unlisted phone number and promised to write.

An unlisted number proved no barrier against the media hordes; Mr. Marshall did his best to keep them at bay outside the apartment building but it didn't take long for Rainie to be jolted by a bright and shiny awareness.

She had nothing to fear. Nothing. She'd confronted her worst nightmare. And clobbered him into a coma. She changed into her blue suit, washed and dried a cast iron skillet approximating her weapon, and called down to the manager to open the flood gates.

Mike refused to participate in the circus but they kept in touch by phone. Several TV producers contacted her for movie rights to her story and with offers to appear on talk shows. Her father-in-law called to say he was taping everything off the TV and keeping a scrap book of articles.

Her clients understood why she'd been in hiding. She said it would take a few days to get back into a work routine. Neighbours knocked on her door to talk. A set of foster parents she had when she was fourteen looked her up. She took Silvana out to dinner at an Italian restaurant and the owner recognized her and wouldn't take her money. She received fan mail care/of a local TV station.

The whole world wanted to know about Uncle Duffy, too. The self-made millionaire, who, allegedly, hired a hit man to kill his arch rival and then absconded with as much lucre as humanly possible, leaving several hundred people jobless and angry, and umpteen creditors holding an empty bag.

But he was serious about the reward. A courier arrived at Rainie's door with a lawyer's letter. The media went through another round of frenzy when she was presented with a certified cheque for $250,000.

She gave one third to Mike, and put one third in trust for the education of Barbara's children. She had no idea what to do with her share, but she bought the newspaper and looked at ads for condominiums.

The bruise on her forehead faded, the gash over her ear began to heal. She went to a salon and had her hair cut short and snappy. She cleared away her backlog of work. She got her period. She wrote letters and met old friends for coffee. She gave Kari a hundred dollars and said she wouldn't be needing her to run errands any longer. Kari took an after-school job in a bakery.

Her birthday rolled around. She thought of Leo and the helicopter picnic. Mike called. She received a few cards. One came in an envelop with Brazilian stamps but no return address. She couldn't read the Portuguese greetings, only the English, Dear Rainbow, and underneath,

I never forgot you.

Love,

Your Mom.

Mike hired a water taxi on the mainland to drop him off at the dock at Sea Spray Island, intending to have a look around and spend a couple of days of solitude. July First and he was still there, celebrating Canada's birthday with a bottle of blackberry wine from the wine cellar.

He wasn't alone, a gaunt chocolate point Siamese had come yowling from under one of the smaller houses that first day. He named her Zooie and she followed him everywhere. The island lacked a satellite dish, but it had a decent radio with an antenna strung up a tree and a sound system with a large and diverse music collection. He hadn't made a dent in the food supply yet. Rice, coffee, cooking oil and other non-perishables were stockpiled beside home canned produce in a walk-in pantry off the kitchen of the main house. And he'd found a few marijuana plants the Mounties missed because they grew out in the bush away from the houses. He figured out the wind generated electrical system. He filled the outboard on the runabout from the fuel barrels in a metal shed and went fishing. He always brought one fish down to a cove on the southwest side of the island and left it as a gift for the eagles. He dug clams and picked oysters off the beach. He cleaned up the debris left by the big storm and worked in the greenhouse and gardens.

The house Zooie favoured was the women's house. They'd packed in a hurry and left clothes and bathroom articles. The smallest house still smelled of incense. It had one bedroom with mirrored walls and one without, both with VCR, TV and racks of porno movies. He found sex toys and bondage gear. Zooie refused to enter. She stayed outside and yowled.

The caretakers had their own house but he left it as is, in case they returned for their things. So far they hadn't.

The four bedroom main house was the fishing lodge, hombre zone, with framed fish prints and a crib board drilled into a deer antler. He used a bedroom there.

He had his cell phone and spoke to Rainie every few days. She told him about the birthday card from her mother, slightly excited but mostly miffed there'd been no apology. She was still ambivalent about contacting her grandparents.

He tried calling his own granny once, but his grandfather answered and Mike hung up.

The P.O. knew where he was, but not that he had a phone. Essery was the only other person who had his number. He called once in a while with news. Bullets from Snake's gun had killed both Kevin and Barbara. *He remained in coma.* A signed confession by the wheel man in the drive-by, the guy at death's door in the hospital, stated that Snake had killed Leo. *He remained in coma.* DNA fingerprinting matched Snake to the dried saliva on the roaches left at Kevin's house. *He remained in coma.* Raymond Kaslo, the UFO reject, got busted again, for armed robbery; his bail revoked for the unarmed robbery of Kevin's place. *Snake regained consciousness, but would not be charged with any crime.* Richard Howard Nixon, a.k.a. Rick Howard, a.k.a. Snake, was brain damaged, blind in one eye, and paralysed from the neck down.

Mike sat in a rocking chair on the deck of the main house, drinking from the wine bottle, Zooie purring on his lap, watching work boats ply Sabine Channel between Sea Spray and Texada Island, watching the garden grow, flowers bloom, cedar trees swaying in the gentle sea breeze. If he sat there long enough he'd watch the sun go down and the stars appear. In the morning he'd watch the stars fade and the sun come up.

There were still things to be dealt with back in the city, emptying Kevin's house, retrieving his family group of ashes. But when he thought of leaving he remembered what it was like out there in the world, violent and unpredictable and filled with death.

He'd never been to Texada, it was a sizable island and populated, it must have a pub, a post office and a store or two. He could buy some books. There weren't any on Sea Spray. Not a single solitary one. And there'd be a bulletin board too, pin up a Help Wanted notice, hire some people for the summer, because there was too much work to do alone. Maybe he'd run the island as a retreat. Healing workshops. Campfire sing-alongs down on the beach. He knew he could never really own the island, Marion's grandchildren would eventually inherit, but he could caretake until they were ready. He'd have to empty the smallest house first, before he brought anyone over, and figure out a purification ceremony to cleanse the island of evil spirits.

And he had to find a woman to share his west coast paradise. Maybe in the morning. He could try out the 24-footer from the boat house. Take a day trip. Maybe in the morning, after the sun rose, after he fed Zooie fish stew and hoed the peas. No doubt about it, lots to do and endless possibilities.

Other Trade Paperbacks from Electric eBook Publishing:

Suspense:
* Zem-Zem by Jeanie duGal; $13.95 USA / $18.95 Canada
* Lady Blue by Judy Bagshaw(Romantic) ; $13.95 USA / $18.95 Canada
* Strangers Call in Moonlight by George WJ Laidlaw(Romantic) $13.95 USA/$18.95 Canada
* Tour Into Danger by Lea Tassie; $13.95 USA / $18.95 Canada

Romance:
* Rescued Heart by Vanessa Kay (Historical); $13.95 USA / $18.95 Canada
* Morning Joy by Barbara W. Campbell (Inspirational); $13.95 USA / $18.95 Canada
* To Be Three by Phyllis N. Lake; $13.95 USA / $18.95 Canada

Poetry:
* Ms. Magenta by Carla Mobley; $12.95 USA / $17.95 Canada

Nonfiction:
* More Baseball Trivia: A Triple Play by Bob Alley (Sports Trivia); $12.95 USA / $17.95 Canada
* Dangerous Slums by Charles Hinton; $13.95 USA / $18.95 Canada

Action/Adventure:
* Escape by Brian T. Seifrit; $13.95 USA / $18.95 Canada

Thriller:
* Paranoid Schizophrenic by Daniel Martinez; $13.95 USA / $18.95 Canada
* Mr. Hate by Terry Vinson; $14.95 USA / $19.95 Canada

Young Adult:
* There and Back by Pat Riordan
* The Face Behind the Window by Adriana deRoos (Historical); $12.95 USA / $17.95 Canada
* Child of the Wild Wind by Claire Garden; $13.95 USA / $18.95 Canada

Middle Readers:
* The Willow Tree Girl by Joanna M. Weston (Middle Reader); $12.95 USA / $17.95 Canada
* Shannon Holmes, Private Detective by Barbara Saffer (Middle Reader); $12.95 USA / $17.95 Canada

Order Form

	Title	Qty.	Price
Name			
Address			
Phone			
			Order _____
Method of Payment ☐ Check ☐ Money Order			Tax: _____
All prices include shipping; Canadian residents required to pay applicable taxes.			Total: _____

Electric eBook Publishing
PO Box 211
Powell River, BC CANADA V8A 4Z6
Phone: 1-877-483-9614 Fax: 1-877-483-9615
Email: sales@electricebookpublishing.com
Order online at: http://www.electricebookpublishing.com